The Right One For Me

Samanthya Wyatt

Love Endures

The Right One For Me

Copyright © 2014, 2021, 2024 by Samanthya Wyatt

Print ISBN: 978-1963776027

Cover Design by Erin Dameron-Hill

Published in the United States of America

Also by

THE BROTHERS GREYSTOKE
The Daunting Greystoke (Book 1)
Greystoke Heir Apparent (Book 2)

ONE AND ONLY COLLECTION
The Right One For Me (Book 1)
My Angel The True One (Book 2)
The Only One My Love (Book 3)

To my loving husband.
Thanks for pushing me and keeping my spirits up.
You were there for me every step of the way.
We did it!

Contents

Chapter 1

Whetherford Manor, 1825

"Oh, Sir. Thank God, you are home."

Home. After years of absence, Whetherford Manor was still home.

Gone were the days when his family would welcome his presence. Gone were the hugs and embracing love he longed for.

Lightning flashed as Morgan Langston, Earl of Whetherford, closed the solid oak door. Heedless of the drops of water sliding from his rain-soaked cloak, he took a moment for his eyes to adjust to the dim interior. He had not anticipated anyone being up and about. His missive had stated he should arrive within the week. Yet the servant emerged as if he'd been expecting the lord of the manor to appear any second. He settled his gaze on Frederick, a loyal member of his father's staff. Morgan's mouth grew taut as he forced the familiar ache away. He'd lived on the edge for so long he had nearly forgotten the pain that drove him from his home years ago.

"Why the devil aren't you in bed at this hour of the night?"

"Waiting for your return, my lord. We sent a man straight-away to watch for your ship. We had no way of contacting you before you reached the cove."

Morgan shed his soggy overcoat, translucent beads soaking the wood-planked floor, and handed the heavy garment to his servant. Flexing his tired shoulders, he rolled his head side to side, cringing at the ache of every muscle from his stiff neck all the way down to his sore backside.

He stepped past Frederick and headed for the library. As he passed through the double set of doors, a warm glow from the flaming fire greeted him. Wood sizzled, sparks popped, and the smell of burning logs filled him with a sense of family. He closed his eyes. Sentiment threatened. Emotions attacked. After years of forbidding any real feelings, they came crashing in like the hammering thunder outside. His heart increased its tempo.

Shaking off the melancholy, he swallowed the lump in his throat.

The burning blaze cast enough light for him to see an outline of an unlit lamp on a nearby table. He knelt before the hearth and torched a sliver of wood from the fire in the grate. Lifting the glass, he turned the wick to meet the burning flame. A flare of light swathed the room, drawing his attention to the leather-upholstered chair facing the hearth. How many times he'd seen his father in that very spot. With a busy schedule and the responsibilities demanding of an earl, his father had always made time to listen. He had time to deliver a scolding as well—which Morgan and his brother had suitably deserved.

He grimaced, ignoring the slight twinge as the opulent leather came back into focus. He longed to fall into its padded comfort, stretch out his long legs and warm himself by the crackling fire. The thought of a long soak in a steaming hot bath sounded even better. For now, he would settle for a taste of brandy to chase away the sting of the last ten miles he'd ridden in this God-forsaken weather.

He swiped the last drops of moisture from his unshaven face, the stubble scraping the tips of his fingers, and headed to the sideboard, his gaze already spotting the desired decanter. Pouring a generous amount of brandy, nearly filling the glass, he tossed back a hefty swallow. He savored the scalding sensation and waited for the burn of the liquid to warm the chill in his bones.

He leveled his gaze on the figure standing inside the doorway, shifting his weight from one foot to the other. Frederick, his trustworthy servant. Devoted to his father. By the looks of him, he had been up all night. Waiting?

We sent a man straight-away to watch for your ship.

For the first time since Morgan could remember, Frederick seemed as fidgety as a nervous cat. The man had trouble looking Morgan in the eye. "What is so important that could not wait until morning?"

Damn. It was morning.

"She's gone."

Morgan narrowed his eyes. "Who's gone?"

"Miss Eastcote."

Morgan scrunched up his forehead in annoyance. His body ached. Every muscle screamed for sleep. For the past month, he'd been confined to a ship, impatient to return to Whetherford Manor, only to arrive in a raging storm which caused them to dock after midnight. He spent the last hour saddled on the back of a horse, blindly making his way through the downpour. His patience had already taken a beating, and now he struggled to keep a rein on his temper.

"Make sense, man. I am in no mood for riddles."

"Sorry, my lord." Frederick took a deep breath and stepped inside the room. "A gentleman arrived several months ago, claiming kinship. A Lord Eastcote, a distant cousin of your mother. He took over the manor as though it were his right. And that daughter of his . . ." Frederick shivered as though he had been the one out in the storm. Then he straightened as if he'd just received a good kick in the arse. "Miss Juliana is a spoiled child even if she looks like a full-grown woman, fancy as a goose at Christmas."

Ah, yes. He remembered Eastcote, and his daughter. Juliana. A handful. Just as wild as her tempestuous red hair hinted. Impromptu outbursts were a given. A spoiled girl who grew into a desirable woman with the expectation that everyone should indulge her every wish, as her father had. Morgan had been the exception. He enjoyed a woman as well as the next man, but he had no tolerance for bad behavior. Not only was Juliana spoiled, she did not care who she hurt to get her way.

"Lord Eastcote? What the devil is he doing here?" Morgan raised the glass to his lips.

"He is no longer here, sir. He is dead."

Morgan's arm halted midair. "Dead?"

"The doctor said natural causes. Miss Juliana did not seem as broken up about it as a daughter should." Frederick stood stiff, giving the impression he had a rod in the back of his breeches. Chin up, head straight, he stared forward at the opposite wall as if something of import held his attention.

Morgan gave an aggravated sigh. This story proposed to be a long and troublesome one. He pressed the back of his knuckles to his eyes, the warmth soothing his lids. If he wasn't so damned tired . . .

"So, Eastcote inhabited my home? Until his death, I suppose."

"Lord Heyworth would have sent them packing, but he knew the man to be who he claimed. Evidently, Lord Heyworth had met Lord Eastcote shortly after your parents' wedding."

A familiar tightening centered in Morgan's gut. Anguish boiled anew, making old pain as fresh and sharp as when he'd first learned of his family's demise. A ship that took not only his parents, but also his elder brother to a watery grave. Morgan had not wanted the title. It should have gone to his brother. Fleeing his responsibilities had not lessened his sorrow.

Thank the good heavens for the loyalty of his father's friend, Heyworth. The old gentleman had taken it upon himself to function as caretaker during Morgan's absence—or should he say—his withdrawal from society.

That was stating it mildly.

Young and foolish, and full of bitterness, Morgan had accepted any perilous deed he could find. Dangerous missions were better than facing the demons that hovered to choke him. Vehemence and risk replaced torment and anguish. He spent years surviving by sheer force of will. No feelings. Forbidden emotions, vanquishing his agony without a care for his safety. Nothing was too risky, nothing too life-threatening for the dark devil he turned out to be. Putting his life on the line had become a way of perseverance, yet he still had to face his torment, and his duty to Whetherford. If the family line were to continue, he had to do his duty, so he accepted the title he did not want, but continued to risk his life on cagey missions.

He strode to the hearth and stretched his hands toward the sizzling flames. After his fingers warmed, another glass of brandy would be just the thing. "Natural causes, you say?"

"Yes, my Lord."

"And his daughter?"

"Miss Eastcote remained, ordering everyone about as if she were the lady of the manor. Then she left in . . . rather a bit of a hurry."

At least he had his home to himself. Morgan closed his eyes wondering what had prompted Juliana's departure. Impetuous chit. Life too boring in the country, most likely. Not enough disruption to hold her interest. "A hurry, you say. Just like that? She blows in, her father dies, she blows out with the wind?"

"Not exactly." Frederick had mumbled. Frederick never mumbled. Something was clearly afoot.

"Where is she now?"

"No one knows." Frederick cleared his throat. "Uh, my Lord. There is something else."

The distress in his tone triggered a gut feeling. Morgan glanced over his shoulder. Frederick lifted one shaky finger and pulled at the collar of his stiff shirt as though it cut off his air.

Good God. What else?

Morgan turned, putting his back to the grate, and scowled at his servant. "Out with it, man."

Frederick swallowed again. "The safe in your study . . . was open."

Moments ticked by while this bit of news penetrated his brain.

Bloody hell!

Morgan marched through the doorway, shoving Frederick out of the way, not bothering to see if his servant still stood. He stampeded down the corridor, his boots thundering in the silent hallway, each step sounding like a shot in the dead of night. He charged into the study, banging the solid-oak door against the wall. As the sound reverberated through his skull, he came to a sudden halt. Even though forewarned, he was not prepared for the sight that greeted him.

His blood boiled as he stared at the empty safe. *Gone! They were bloody gone!*

A haze of rage blurred his vision. His hands curled into fists while he sucked air over grinding teeth. His gut reflected the hollowness of his vault.

Empty.

She had stolen from *him*? From his *home*? That bit of unscrupulous baggage.

The muscles in his cheeks tightened. His chest pounded as his blood boiled. His temple throbbed as his rage accelerated.

"She could not have done this alone. Find out who helped her and bring them to me."

Juliana Eastcote had provoked the devil.

Now she would have to face him.

───ⅇℓℓ───

Miss Katherine Radbourn had been a willing participant in a great number of escapades. From the time, as a small child, she snuck into the kitchen and stuck her fingers in the cook's baking, her brother had saved her. The time when she ruined her Sunday dress chasing a frog and fell into a mud puddle just before she was to go into the church at her cousin's wedding, her big brother had taken the blame. The time her mother repeatedly shushed her, she jumped up in the middle of the baby's christening and yelled, "I gotta pee," her brother laughed. Still he had saved her from their parents' anger.

At twenty-three, she still had her moments. But they were more along the line of opening her mouth when she should most assuredly keep it shut. Like today. At her best friend's tea. Kat had embarrassed everyone. Well, maybe not her friend so much, but her aunt had nearly fainted when Kat mentioned seeing Lord Haslegrove with that other woman. How was she to know the woman was his mistress? Young women were not even supposed to know about such things.

Stephen had not been here to save her. He had not been home for quite some time. Quite a long time. And it just was not like him. Stephen was her rock. He would never be gone so long without sending a letter.

"I cannot wait any longer." Kat paced back and forth over the woven carpet of her friend's London Town house. Steam rising from the china teapot emitted a pleasant aroma in the floral sitting room. A soothing hot drink would normally soothe her nerves, but she was too wound up to sit.

"Kat? What are you going to do?" Shrewd interest etched Charity's heart-shaped face. The wife of a viscount, she appeared the epitome of grace and sophistication. But, Charity loved life, and she was the one who had taught Kat how to laugh again. After the painful loss of her parents, mischief and daring flowed from her friend's blonde curls down to her uncovered toes.

Kat stopped her pacing. "When did you remove your slippers?"

Charity hid her toes under her gown. "After everyone left. Now, do not change the subject. What are you going to do?"

"I don't know." Kat studied the rose-pattern carpet at her feet. "My uncle plans to leave London the day after tomorrow." The Season was far from over. What made him suddenly decide to return to the country? She paced again—back and forth—her fists clenched in front of her. "If we go to Chelmouth, how will I get word of Stephen? They cannot fool me. My aunt and uncle are as worried as I am."

"Your brother could have a reason for not being here," Charity said.

Kat flung her hair over one shoulder, and fisted her hands on her hips. "What could possibly be reason enough for him to be gone so long and not send word?"

"Maybe he met someone. Stephen is one strapping man. Next to my husband, of course." Charity's eyes twinkled as she gave an all-knowing smile. "A girl can hardly breathe when Stephen is around. Maybe a female finally caught his eye."

"All skirts catch my brother's eye." Over six feet of solid muscle, the man was notably big, and too handsome for his own good. Kat knew her friend was trying to ease her concern. Normally she would enjoy the banter and go off on a tirade about her brother, but she was really worried.

The viscountess tsked and continued. "He could be courting and may not be in any hurry to come back."

"He would never forget about me? This is his home." Kat waved her arms in the air and swung around to pace again.

"The sea is his home, and you are only his sister."

Kat braced one arm on each hip. "True he dumped me on our Aunt's doorstep—for my own good of course," she could not keep the sarcasm from her tone. "And also true, I was bitter when I met you. But, I am older now. I understand why he did it. A girl could not very well live on a ship with men." She knew that now. Of course, at the time she was grieving. She was no longer a child and Stephen had been gone far too long. Her heart grew heavy.

"Stephen was my hero. I worshiped him. I remember running and screaming, and he would scoop me up and hold me high in the air. Maybe it was the difference in our ages. Maybe he felt guilty being gone for months at a time. I don't know why he allowed me to follow him everywhere. I must have been an annoyance, yet he never pushed me away." She swiped the corner of her eye. "Ever since our parents . . . he is committed in coming home regularly. He should have been home long ago. I know something is wrong." Before she started crying, she began pacing again.

"There are many reasons his ship could be late."

Kat stopped midstride and whirled around. "Late? It's been two blasted years."

"He *is* captain of his own ship. There could be any number of things to detain Stephen. He could have set off on a new adventure. His ship could be docked for repairs."

Repairs?

Or his ship could have sunk.

"No, Kat. Don't think that."

"How did you know what— never mind." Her frustration grew.

"Stephen is fine. He will come home when he is ready. Now sit down. You are giving me a stitch in my neck."

Which meant, the conversation was over. Kat plopped in the chair across from her friend.

Charity picked up the teapot and poured the remaining brew into a tiny cup.

"He's all I have left," Kat said, her voice sounding as miserable as she felt.

"You have your uncle and aunt. You have me."

Kat looked at Charity, her dearest friend in the world. She never doubted their deep friendship. A girl of fourteen, overcome with grief, she had learned what it was like to be alone in the world. Not only did she have to deal with her parents' death, but her brother had discarded her.

A ship is no place for a young girl.

Uncle Albert and Aunt Elizabeth had given her love and understanding at a time in her life when she needed it most, but Charity had been her anchor. She had consoled Kat and supported her through her bereavement. Even though Charity was a year younger, she'd been married for three years and had a two-year-old son.

"You are my dearest friend. But, you have a husband."

"You know, Kat, my father made an arrangement with Byron before I ever laid eyes on him. Father believes in the old ways." A wistful expression crossed Charity's features. "Even though I fought him, I will be grateful to Father every day for the rest of my life for choosing Byron."

"He does seem perfect for you." The flame Kat often saw between her friend and her husband gleamed like a lighthouse beacon in the fog. Being in the same room with them became almost embarrassing. They looked at each other with such fire, they forgot she was even there.

That's what I want.

"Believe me, Kat. You will fall in love. And you will know when it happens."

"After twenty-three years, it has not happened yet."

"Oh, you may not recognize love at first." Charity gave a wave with her delicate hand. "In fact, you may not even like him very much. But then everything changes, and you will be drawn to your man like a magnet. So much so, you will not want to be around anyone else." Her face took on a dreamy, faraway look, like a woman remembering a very special moment. "It will be something like you have never felt before. Believe me, Kat. It is a feeling like none other."

Kat grew whimsical as she studied the sappy look on her friend's face. Charity's words not only made her curious, they touched her deepest desire.

"I will not settle for anything less. I want what you and Byron have. The way the two of you eye each other." She drew in a deep breath. "I get so envious sometimes. You have a man who looks at you like . . . I don't know . . . like the world would end if he did not touch you at that moment."

There it was again—the lopsided grin of a woman who held something back. As if she secretly knew something Kat did not. Leaning forward, Charity said, "You need someone to make your blood race and your heart sing."

Kat froze. She had not expected such an intriguing remark. "Is that what you have? Does Byron make your heart sing?"

Charity fanned her cheeks with one hand. Then her face reddened.

"Why are you blushing?"

"He makes my whole body sing."

Kat's hearing sharpened. Charity had her full attention now. Before she could open her mouth, Charity held up a hand as if to hold her off.

"I am not telling you anymore. You will find out for yourself. Trust me. You will meet someone who will take your breath away. Do not settle for anything less. Oh, Kat. This is nothing like the things we experienced when we were young and foolish girls, flirting and thinking we were in love. I did not know what love was."

"And now you do?"

"I do." Charity gave a nod as she answered. "I never dreamed a man could make me feel the way Byron does. When you find a man like that, you snatch him up right away." Her hand reached out and twisted in a gesture to give significance to her words.

Kat laughed. "No one has ever made my blood do anything. How will I know if he will make my body sing?"

Charity's mouth curved in a smile and her gaze held a discerning look.

"I hate it when you do that."

Still smiling, Charity said, "You will know."

Normally, Kat soaked up every tidbit her friend shared about married life. Charity never confided the intimacies of the bedchamber, but Kat wanted to know exactly what put that gleam in her eyes, and just how Byron made her body sing. One day, she hoped to possess such closeness with a man.

Although Byron sometimes wore a look of ravishing his wife, the caring in his eyes far surpassed those Kat had received from admirers upon occasion. The licking of lips from boys fresh out of Eton, nor lecherous sneers from rogues at balls, were not the actions of a man she sought in her dreams. How she longed for someone to look at her the way Byron looked at Charity—as though she were the most wonderful sweetmeat in the world, and he about to devour her.

What would it be like to have a man look at me as though he truly loved me?

"Love?" She waved her hand in the air and shook her head as though the thought were a bother. "I don't know if I will ever find love. I am already on the shelf."

"The dandies are not for you, Kat. You need a strong man who will appreciate your spirit."

"Is that your way of saying I am not married because I'm outspoken and leap before I look?"

"You do speak your mind. But I would never want you to change."

"But I scare men off. Humph." She crossed her arms and rolled her lip out. "At least my family loves me."

A family's love was not the same. She had the love of her brother, but no man had . . .

Stephen!

"Oh, he's in trouble. I just know it."

"You do have a way of changing the subject."

Kat closed her eyes and ground her head into the back of her chair while her brother's image formed in her mind. Her eyes flew open. "Stephen is the subject."

Charity placed her teacup on the filigree saucer. "You are truly worried about him, aren't you?"

"You know how close we are. He would never—do you hear me—never let me worry like this. Not after our parents . . ." Kat choked on the memory. She had survived the darkness and the emptiness, until Charity's friendship and thirst for life gave her a reason to go on.

Charity's worried gaze melded with her own. "I know. Stephen would do everything in his power to keep you from that kind of pain again."

"Exactly. I have got to find out what happened to him."

"But what can you do?" Concern etched Charity's brow.

Kat gripped the arms of her chair as an idea popped into her head. "Captain Danvers."

"What?"

"Captain Danvers." She jumped to her feet and began to pace again. "My uncle mentioned him. I overheard him when he spoke with my aunt. He said Captain Danvers' ship had docked and he'd been inquiring about Stephen at other ports. Maybe he has information." She babbled as thoughts bounced off her tongue. Words rolled out of her mouth, one after another. "All I have to do is find his ship. The *Sea Voyager*."

Charity sprang from her seat. "I am going with you."

Kat laughed. "Byron would not let you anywhere near the docks."

An expression of strong disapproval came over Charity's face. She fisted one hand on each hip. "Neither would your uncle."

Kat resisted the urge that demanded she start pacing again. She chewed on the end of her finger. "Maybe I can find some other way to talk to him. Away from his ship."

"I would hate to think of the establishments he visits when he is not on his ship."

"He must have some principles if my uncle deals with him." Unable to prevent it, Kat spun around and paced in the opposite direction.

"And then again, your uncle is a man. A very important man," Charity reminded her.

Kat came to a halt. Whipping her head around, she fixed her gaze on Charity. "Yes, of course."

Charity sucked in a breath. "What are you thinking?"

"I will tell Captain Danvers who my uncle is and . . ."

Charity cocked her head and pierced Kat with a *you've-lost-your-wits* look. "Do you want him running straight to your uncle?"

Kat scowled at her friend, vexed she had not thought of that. "Drat."

"Have any other bright ideas?"

She dug in her heels and hoped Charity would not talk her out of what she must do.

Because she knew Kat's stubbornness, Charity's face creased with worry. "You are still going to the docks?"

"Yes. I must speak with Captain Danvers."

Chapter 2

Katherine wrapped her arms about herself. The sun had barely risen and the chills racing up her spine had nothing to do with the crisp wind. Wooden buildings lined the London docks, dark passageways between them held little light. Wreckage and debris littered their path. A scarf covering her face, helped to shield the wind, not to mention the stench rising from the mire.

"Oh, mum. This is terrible." The parlor maid she'd dragged along complained every step of the way.

"Quiet, Alice. There's no need to be afraid." Kat was not so sure. Her nerves screamed the opposite. Dirty men and the unruly activity going on around them led her to believe she should have thought her plan through a bit more—or at least brought one of the footmen.

"I want to go back." Alice whined again.

"For the last time. I am not going home until I have talked to Captain Danvers."

"But, mum. Look." The girl shivered and hid her face under her wrap.

Glancing in the direction her maid indicated, she wished she had not. A man had a woman pressed against a wall of a shop, his frame covered most of her body. He tugged at her clothes and his hands squeezed the woman's exposed flesh. When the woman hiked up her skirts and swung her leg up and around the man's middle, Kat gaped. The painful sounds coming from them were conflicting, for they apparently had no desire to stop.

"Mum. Please don't make me go any further." Alice's cry jerked Kat back to awareness.

Seeing tears streaming down the girl's cheeks, Kat relented. "Oh, go then."

Alice grabbed her arm. "You, too. You must come, too."

"I told you. Not until . . . Never mind. Go. Now." Kat gave her maid a slight push. "Go before you call more attention to us."

"Thank you, mum." Alice turned and fled like demons were on her tail.

Kat stayed close to the wooden planks, keeping her back against of the building. Now that she was truly alone, fear threatened to paralyze her. Taking a deep breath, she recounted all the reasons she should not be anywhere near the London docks. But then, not all ships' captains were boorish. After all, her brother captained a ship. She willed the trembling in her body to stop and, for the sake of Stephen, forced her legs to move.

She pulled her cloak tighter to shield her features as she hurried along the street. With her head down, she rounded a corner and slammed into—what felt like—a sizeable mountain.

"Hey now, lovey."

A man's hands caught her shoulders. "What's this fell into our laps?"

The smell of strong ale assaulted her nostrils. *Good Lord. What had she stumbled into?* "Take your hands off me!"

"Well, Augie. We got us a feisty one." That was when she realized there was a second man.

"I don't mind. I like a little bit of spunk now and again."

Blood pounded in her temples as she turned her head from one man to the other.

The taller man jerked her hood free. "Lookie at all that red hair, Augie."

"Wonder if it would burn your fingers." The one called Augie reached out to touch her and Kat smacked his hand away.

"Here now. Don't be treatin' me mate like that. You need to be a mite more friendly, girl."

The hair stood up on her neck as cold dread attacked her spine. "Do not touch me, you blackguard."

"Blackguard, is it? I'll have you know you're speaking to the new man hired to his lordship, Hadderill."

The taller man snickered which made Kat think his cohort lied. "Then you may find yourself terminated in the morning, for I shall tell your employer of your conduct. I doubt any *lord* would tolerate such deportment from one in his employ."

He grabbed her arm with such force, she bit her tongue. "Now listen here, girlie. No harlot is gonna cost me my new position."

"Did ya hear that? No wench is gonna talk to us like that neither," the second man added.

Immediately, she realized her mistake. An angry drunk was unpredictable. A tingling of fear crawled over her skin. If she showed weakness, who knew what they would do to her. A picture of her body—bloody and broken, lying on the ground—flashed in her mind. She shivered and shook the image away. Maybe if she played along, they would lower their guard and she could get away.

"Pardon me, gentlemen. I meant no harm. A woman likes to be treated like a lady. Not so rough."

"You ain't foolin' me, Miss hoity-toity. I seen them women up on the hill in them fancy houses, acting like they was better than anyone else. You and your kind turn up your bloody noses at the likes of us."

The second man chimed in. "You saying we ain't good enough fer ya?"

Kat swallowed the bile in her throat as his face came within a hair's breadth of her nose. The vile man reeked of ale and sweat. He probably had not seen water or a washcloth in a month of Sundays. Panic threatened as they forced her deeper into the shadows. She struggled for her freedom. "Let go of me, you big oafs."

"What's the matter, darlin'? We'll take good care of ya."

Augie rubbed his crotch. "Real good care of ya."

She screamed.

~ele~

Legs braced and arms crossed, Morgan observed the boisterous activity around him. The ship had slipped in to the docks of London just before dawn. He welcomed the early morning chill as he watched men struggle with ropes securing the craft. Winches creaked from lowering cargo nets onto the pier. Stevedores with trunks on their shoulders swarmed up and down the gangway whilst unloading goods and taking on provisions for the next voyage.

Captain Laylock stepped beside him. He scanned the dock below. "Well, my friend. Here we are."

Morgan replied. "Are your men ready?"

"I've already sent Piers and Doc. They fit in anywhere. Doc is a regular and everyone knows him. He's the best at loosening jaws. As for Piers, he knows the right places to start. If there is any information on yer lady friend, they'll find it."

Morgan frowned and gritted his teeth. "Her trail leads here."

"How long has it been since you've seen the woman? She has probably changed."

Her beauty was the kind that only grew more with age. Too bad she had not acquired any admirable merits. The last time he'd seen Juliana, he hoped never to see her again. Funny how life had its own agenda.

"It has been a long time, but she has one feature that sets her apart from the rest. I have never seen that exact shade of red hair on another woman. It is unique. A vibrant, radiant hue of crimson as beautiful as any sunset."

The captain stroked his beard. "Even, so. She may not be easy to find."

Morgan's hands tightened on the rail. "No doubt she is in hiding. But the piece she carries will lead me straight to her."

"The waiting is the hardest." Laylock slapped Morgan on the back. "Come. Let's open a bottle of port."

Morgan studied his comrade, appreciating what he was trying to do. "I have no need to dull my wits with drink. The bottle will not make the waiting any easier."

"I've never known anything to dull your wits, or a time where you blamed the drink."

At the moment, he much preferred something he could sink his teeth into—or his fists. "You're right. But, for now, I need action."

Laylock gave a nod, accepting his decision. "Take care, my friend."

With impatient swiftness, Morgan took sure and steady steps down the swaying plank. Glancing to the right and then the left, he turned on a booted heel and marched down the cobbled street. Not many were up and about at this hour of the morning. Debutantes lay snug in their beds and would not be up until noon. Business owners just now rose and would soon open their establishments. Where should he go first? Nothing to do but walk and keep his eyes open.

He would find Juliana. If he had to search every corner of London . . .

As he stepped from the corner of a tall building, he heard a woman shout. Morgan cocked his head in that direction. A light-skirt having a bit of fun? Then he heard a shrill scream.

Damn.

He ran down the alleyway and spotted two men toying with an unwilling woman. One man held her while the other grinned through blackened teeth and rubbed one hand against his crotch.

Blood and the devil.

"Are you in need of assistance, madam?"

Both men stopped in their tracks. The woman continued her struggle to get free.

One man spoke. "Who the bloody hell are you?" The lady fought and twisted, and still, the brute held her.

Morgan took a stance that came as natural as breathing. The dark devil he had tried to bury soared to the surface. He had given up that life. The one where cold ruthlessness governed his actions. The life where unscrupulous characters were taken down without a moment's thought—without a moment's hesitation. Ruthless impulses and reflexes sprang to life. Muscles flexed ready for action. His mind vaulted to the place other men feared to go—where no mercy was given.

He looked directly at the frightened woman, completely aware of both men. "I asked if you needed assistance."

"Please help me," the woman shrieked.

"She don't need no assistance from you," the shorter man said. "Ya best be on your way, guvnor."

Shoulders taut, Morgan sized up his opponents. He could take them both in a matter of minutes. "Unhand her."

"I think you got ballocks fer brains. Can't you see this ain't none of yer business?"

Morgan advanced one step forward. "I am making it my business."

"What's the gel to you?"

He gave a slight shrug on the likelihood the imbecile facing him would mistake the gesture as though Morgan did not care one way or the other, and relax his guard. "She asked for help."

The other man laughed. "We seen her first. And we're gonna keep 'er."

"Please," the woman begged, and that time when she jerked, her arm came free. The second man grabbed her before she could take two steps.

Morgan glared at him, then turned a threatening gaze on his mate. "I will say this only once more. Let the lady go."

"Or else?"

"I am done with words," he ground out.

"Done with words, are ye. Did ya hear that?"

"Yeah, Augie. I think the bloomin' man is an—" He never finished his sentence.

Morgan struck.

Chapter 3

Kat could not believe a man could move so fast. One minute he stood a few feet away, confident strength emanating from every inch of his broad-shouldered frame, and the next she was shoved to the ground. Her knight in shining armor fought like a devil. He used long legs to kick, and his fists punched in succession, creating a blur. Muscles bunched as he moved. What a sight.

With one lout sprawled on the dirt, she cheered her protector. While his back was turned, the man called Augie pulled a knife from his boot.

"Look out!"

Her champion jolted at her cry. He turned around too late to protect himself. Augie buried the blade in the man's side. Without slowing, his face a mask of pure rage, her knight fought his attacker. Grunts and growls echoed in the alley as the two men charged like animals. Kat heard an ear-splitting crunch, and then Augie's head rolled to the side, his body flopped on the ground.

Kat pressed her fist to her mouth in horror.

A scream surged to rip from her throat, but died an instant death at the sight of blood pouring from her rescuer.

"It would appear I have been stabbed." He stumbled and dropped to his knees before he fell with a thud onto the packed earth. A heart-stopping moment passed as she stared at the unmoving man.

When she regained some of her scattering wits, she ran to his side. Her rescuer now needed rescuing. Kat raised a trembling hand to his forehead. Of course, he would still be warm, even if he was dead. She pressed two fingers just below his jaw, as she'd seen one of the men at her uncle's stable do to another who had taken a bad fall from a horse. Yes. The little blue vein gave a slight jump. If his heart still beat, this gent must be alive.

She tried rolling him onto his back. Great day, he was heavy. Struggling, she finally turned him over and discovered her hands covered with blood. She stared at the sticky mess on her fingers. So much red. Her hands shook. A heavy odor overwhelmed her senses causing bile to rise in her throat. She wiped her hands on the front of her gown, scrubbing the image from her mind.

Taking a deep breath, she regretted her action as once again the fresh smell of blood hit her. She covered her nose with the fabric at her elbow, and calmed her breathing. She focused on the man lying helpless on the ground.

How can he still be alive with so much blood draining out of him?

Boots hammered the earth. Kat's head jerked. Two men ran in her direction. Her heart pounded harder. What should she do? What *could* she do? She was a mere woman, and alone. Surely, they were not after her? Would she have to fight for her life again? She fisted her hands and hardened her resolve—and prayed they were here to help her.

She rose as they rushed forward. These men were much larger than the first two who grabbed her. A beard covered the older man's face. His dark scowl made Kat take a step backward. He may have had a few gray hairs, but he did not lack muscle. The younger man, a bit taller, also flexed bulging muscles. Flowing blond hair enhanced his blue eyes. But the look he gave seared her to the bone.

The bearded man dropped to his knee and placed two fingers on the side of the injured man's neck. "He's alive."

The younger man eyed Kat. "What happened?"

She could not make the words come out of her mouth. Were they friend, or foe?

"She's got blood on her hands."

Shocked, Kat stumbled back against the wall.

"It's her."

"Don't be getting any ideas, Missy. You stay right where you are," the bearded man said. Then his hands moved over the unconscious man, jerking Kat out of a daze.

"He is hurt."

"I see that, girl."

"He was stabbed."

For a fraught moment, the man's hateful glare landed on her. "By you?"

Kat's gasp sounded loud to her own ears. "No! By him." She pointed at Augie.

The younger man strode to the limp body. "Neck's broke. Himself musta done it." Then he moved to the other attacker on the ground. "This one's still breathing." He returned to the bearded man's side, leaned down and whispered, but Kat heard him.

"She's the one."

Fear rose in her throat suffocating her. What did he mean 'she's the one'?

A shout sounded and Kat jerked up to find another man bearing down on them. *Oh, God.* She was alone. Would these men be any nobler than the first two? Panic set in. Gathering her skirts, she fled.

Running footsteps sounded behind her. Blood pounded in her temples as if the mighty Thor did the hammering himself. Her lungs forced air in and out, the pain in her chest excruciating enough to bring her to her knees. Kat ran for her life.

They followed.

She had to get away.

She picked her way through the maze of buildings and raced along a stone wall, searching for a place to hide. Her chest burned as her heart pumped, but she could not slow down.

The crunching sound of pebbles sounded like thunder bolts in her ears, as loud as thunder cracked. Turning her head, she glanced over her shoulder for the two men. They were not in sight. Her legs shaky, she sprinted around a corner. Gasping for breath and ignoring the pain in her side, she ran on . . . until her boot caught—

The world abruptly went still.

Her body moved slowly, as if she were drifting above it, watching, waiting to hit the ground. Where were her arms? She tried to reach out, to break her fall. God, please. No. Don't let me . . . her hip slammed . . . then her shoulder bounced, hitting the ground, knocking the breath from her lungs. She saw stars and waited for the world to right itself.

My God!

Get up, her mind screamed.

She cocked her head, listening for sounds of the thugs behind her. An eternity later, she heard voices. Voices wafting far enough away to give her barely a moment of relief. They could find her any moment. Her leg muscles cramped, she struggled to her feet. With shaking hands, she pulled her cloak around her and clutched it tightly to her bosom. Gathering all the courage she could muster, she plunged onward.

Crazed with fear, her chest rose and fell at a furious speed. She sucked air through her nose and willed her brain to function. Her steps forced, she made her way along the row of buildings lined down the street. As she rounded another corner she found a small passageway and slipped into the tight space in between the walls. She turned her head inward not daring to look back. Closing her eyes seemed foolish, but she did it anyway. She gulped a mouthful of air in fear they would hear her and find her safe haven. She tried to slow her racing heart while she strained for any sound that would tell her they had gone. With her cheek plastered against the wall, she heard nothing but the thumping pulse-beat of blood pumping wildly through her veins. Kat prayed her pursuers could not hear her pounding heart.

Suddenly, a hand came over her mouth, startling a strangled cry with no escape from her throat. Desperate, she clawed at the arm that confined her. Cold terror fell away, replaced by hot anger. Her muscles swelled with purpose and her mind vividly pictured her next course of action. Recalling her brother's teachings, Kat bit her attacker's hand. She ducked as she had been taught, then aimed a violent knee at his ballocks.

"Damn, Jeremy. The little wildcat's trying to kill me. Grab her."

Jeremy jerked her arm with such force she thought he had pulled it off. Then the other man grabbed her from behind and placed one hand around her throat. Tears threatened as they overpowered her. Kat fought with every instinct she possessed for survival. She opened her mouth to scream.

Sudden pain pierced her temple.

Darkness descended, weighing her down, until . . . there was . . . nothingness.

She dreamed of men's voices. Floating in a cloudy haze, she could not open her eyes. Someone was carrying her. She was so sleepy. Was she dreaming? She didn't think so. Her limbs leaden, she could not move. Sleep. Blessed sleep.

Lightning struck across the sky and thunder cracked, shattering the silence around her. She woke with a start. Voices shouted and she heard weeping. Climbing from her bed, she threw on a dressing gown and ran toward the sounds. She heard disorder and confusion among the staff. Katherine ran down the stairs and found her mother's personal maid wailing, like the hounds of hell had found her. What is it? Where is mother? Silence filled the air and all eyes turned to her. She took a step backward as the woman ran toward her with outstretched arms. She pulled Kat tight against her bosom, cradling her while she moaned nonsense over and over. Kat pushed her away. She did not want to hear it. Not her parents. No. It was not true. They were fine. Where were they? What was everyone looking at? No. Nooooo.

She leaned over, grasping the reins and raced like the very wind, enlivened by the powerful strides. With a satisfied grin and words of praise, she urged the mare to a faster pace. Freedom. She was wild and free, as free as a fourteen-year-old could be. Her parents would be horrified . . .

"Now, Kitten. You know a ship is no place for a young girl. I will take you to live with Aunt Elizabeth and Uncle Albert."

He told her goodbye. He really is leaving without me. He is walking out of my life. It was too soon after losing their parents. "I cannot lose you too. You cannot leave me here alone. It's not fair. Don't you want me?" Kats arms locked around him, tears streamed down her cheeks. She would not let him go. "Please don't go. Please. Take me with you." She would do anything to stay with him. "Please, Stephen. Do not do this." She clung to him. He pried her fingers from the death grip she had on his shirt and forced her hands away. "Don't leave me. No, Stephen. Nooooo."

Kat drifted, struggling to come out of the fog around her. Surely the haze would lift sometime. She struggled to open her eyes. Bright light made her squint. Her temple throbbed like the very devil. With great effort, her lashes lifted while her eyes tried focusing on her surroundings. A bedchamber. A high bed, big enough to get lost in, with a mauve coverlet made of the finest silk.

Struggling to sit, she rose slowly hoping to ease the hammering in her head, and lowered her feet over the side. She placed a hand on each side of her body for balance—arms braced, her fingers clutched at the covering. She took a deep breath, inhale in, exhale out. Her hand weighed heavy as she smoothed the mass of hair out of her face. With the greatest effort, her leaden arms tried to wrap themselves about her torso.

Blinking against the brightness, she went over what she could remember. She struggled with the blurred images in her mind. Were they real, or simply dreams?

This was real. She was in a bedchamber she had never been in before. She recalled the tall man who had come to her rescue. Then the tormenting vision of a head rolling limply on a broken body hurtled reality right in her lap.

Oh my God! What kind of nightmare am I in?

She flexed her shaking fingers, then her arms and legs, trying to get the blood circulating through her lifeless limbs. The memory of a man's hand over her mouth and the terror shooting through her entire body made her heart constrict as though a hand squeezed it. Moisture formed under tight lids as she fought the dark image forming in her mind. A cloud of despair made her want to weep in misery.

No.

Her fingers swiped at tears and she cursed, using words she'd heard from some of the men back home—when she wasn't supposed to be listening. Crass as they may be, those very words seemed appropriate at this moment.

Self-recrimination changed to utter confusion. Where was she?

She had been abducted, that was obvious. What did they want with her? She remembered the man's words.

She's the one.

Surely, they could not believe that she stabbed her rescuer.

Apparently, they did. But he had saved her from those horrible ruffians. However, these men would not know that. If they thought she had stabbed him, then what would they do with her—to her? She prayed he had not died. Her only chance would be if he still lived.

She ignored the murkiness in her brain and stood, finding her legs none too steady. She slipped to the door. With her hand on the knob, she leaned against the hard wood, and listened. Hearing nothing, she tried to open the door.

Just as she'd thought.

Locked.

Blinking away the tears that threatened, she inspected the bedchamber that—evidently for now—served as her prison.

And what a prison. The luxuries around the room made it obvious the proprietor believed in solace. Colorful tapestries hung on the walls giving the room a welcoming warmth. Hand woven carpets covered the floor inviting and offering comfort. This room loomed much larger than her bedchamber at her aunt and uncle's. Everything had been done in bold colors of dark pink and rich hues of gold making her think this was a lady's room. A large bed with four reeded posts held a canopy of shimmering silk draperies trimmed in the same brilliant shades.

A set of matching mahogany tables adorned each side of the bed. And by one wall a dressing table etched with deep carvings, such a beautiful creation the likes of which she had never seen. The lovely mirrored vanity reflected bottles of perfume lined on top and other trinkets scattered about. Next to it stood a large stone hearth with a fire already burning. Two cozy high-backed chairs in the same rich colors facing the fire, and a round table between them holding a large vase with what looked like various freshly cut flowers. As she neared the table, she inhaled their fragrance—Honeysuckles, Lilies of the Valley, and her favorite, Blue Cornflowers. Their sweet syrupy scent reminded her of her uncle's country home. Such an elegant room. She would never have expected her prison to be this grand. Kat closed her slackened jaw. Why would anyone put their captive in such lavish surroundings?

Turning toward the massive hutch, she spotted a washing bowl of excellent porcelain, with a matching pitcher. After sponging her face, Kat reached for the dainty towel hanging on the silver rod. Just as she touched the towel to her face, she heard the sound of heavy booted footsteps stopping on the other side of the door.

She stood still, the cloth clenched in her fingers.

A hard knock echoed.

Chapter 4

K at's heart thumped. She was not sure if she was supposed to answer. Before she could decide what to do, it opened slowly and a petite woman appeared. Certainly not what she had expected. Surely this woman had not made the footsteps she had heard. The maid stared agog, then dropped her gaze to the floor. The tray she carried had a tantalizing aroma that made Kat's mouth water. The maid hurried to the round table, sat the tray down, and without looking up, she headed back to the door. When Kat realized the woman was leaving without saying a word, she jumped forward. "Wait."

The maid stopped but did not turn around.

"Please," Kat said.

"Is the room not to your liking?" Kat jerked to the voice of the man standing in the hallway.

The bearded man from the alley. His face dark as a thundercloud. The maid scurried past the man at a quick clip.

So, *he* was responsible for bringing her here.

Where was here?

How long had she been asleep? Her head hurt. Had *he* struck her? Fear bordered on outrage. These scoundrels had acted without a care. Rash, callous and malicious.

Cold eyes chilled her and he terrorized her with a frown. "I am his lordship's right hand man. I'm here to tell you to behave yourself."

"Now, Piers. Is that any way to speak to our guest?" An older gentleman stepped around Piers carrying a black bag, one like a doctor would own. "Pardon his manners. He was raised in a barn."

"Now listen here, Doc. She stabbed his lordship."

What? "I did not."

Doc's brow rose to hide under a shock of blond hair. "Is that so?"

"Of course, it's so," the offensive Piers said.

"No!"

"Run along, Piers. I'll deal with this."

"What do you mean, run along?" Piers mumbled more words as Doc ushered him out the door.

Doc had a kind, yet serious face. Evidently, he did not hold her in contempt as the other man had. Not young, but not too old. A head full of blond hair hung in disarray about his shoulders. He did not seem threatening, but he had to know she was being held against her will. She would not cower before him. She elevated her chin as he studied her.

"Well, well. A little more to the right and you would have a shiner."

"What?" Kat's hand flew to her temple. The spot beside her eye was slightly puffy and sore.

"Yes. You have a kaleidoscope of colors there. Not as pretty as a rainbow, I'm afraid."

Everything came back in a flash. Her face heated as blood rushed to the surface. "Oh, dear."

"Yes. Oh, dear."

Was he mocking her?

He placed his bag on the bed, his eyes glinting with conjecture. "Does it hurt?"

If she were sporting a bruise, what did he think? Yet he had gentle eyes. She could not understand her instant liking of this new man. Maybe he initiated biting wit as his physician's bedside manner.

If he is a doctor.

She screwed up her face and spoke with sarcastic scorn. "It feels like someone hit me in the head."

He neither confirmed nor denied. Several moments passed as he stared. The silence lengthened, and she became uncomfortable under his scrutiny. Nothing could be gained in angering her captor, but some days she had no control over her sassy mouth. "Have you never seen a woman with a multihued face?"

"You didn't do it, did you?"

Was he crazy? "Do what? Hit myself?"

His expression never changed. "Stab him."

Oh. Did this *Doc* believe her, or was he testing her? She wished she knew. "No. I did not." Surely, he had to believe her. And if he was a doctor . . . "How is he?"

Doc gentled his expression. "The fever is keeping him unconscious. However, he is a fighter."

"He certainly is." She mumbled under her breath, "I have never seen the likes of him before."

Doc's eyes narrowed. "What do you mean?"

Kat shook her head back and forth while she searched for words to describe what she had seen in that alley. "He moved faster than lightning flashes across the sky. He used his feet. He kicked and knocked one of the thugs out cold." The image popped into her head again, where she saw her defender twisting Augie's neck. Cold chills raced up her spine as a slight wave of nausea filled her stomach. "He . . . he . . ."

"That's enough for now. Come over here and have a seat." Doc picked up the black bag and pointed to the set of cushioned chairs. "I want to have a look at your eyes."

She hesitated, wondering if she should trust him.

What choice did she have?

Trying not to appear too frightened, she gathered her courage, moved the necessary steps, and sat.

He pulled an object from the bag and held it to her face. "Now. Look at me. Follow my finger." He moved a single finger back and forth. Her eyes followed the motion. After a few moments, he stepped back. He must have sensed her distress. "I don't see any sign of concussion."

"Are you a real doctor?" Kat cringed. The question flew out of her mouth before she could think about it.

He chuckled. "As much as any other one, I suppose."

She bit her tongue to keep from asking what he meant and prayed for courage to ask her next question. Steadying her nerves, she straightened her uneasy backbone. "May I go now?"

Blue eyes bore into hers. "Even if you did not stab Lord Whetherford, there is still the matter you stole from him."

"What?" she squeaked.

Doc picked up his bag. The cold look in his eyes could have frozen her. "Do not take my kindness for dull-wittedness. Or mistake my calm nature as weakness. Whetherford is my friend. Surely you do not expect me to take your side. No amount of tears, suggestive offers, or willing promises could turn my head." His voice lowered to a growl. "I've seen them all."

Kat gaped at the man in astonishment. He returned her stare as though branding his words in her mind. Leaning back, he gathered his things in his bag and left. Unable to form a coherent thought, she stayed mute, the closing of the door the only sound in the room.

Staggered beyond belief, she started to shake—this time in anger. *Stole from him?* What the blue blazes was he talking about? *Lord Whetherford.* Her protector was a nobleman? They thought she had stolen from him? And if he was unconscious, he could not very well affirm her innocence.

What was she to do?

"Hold on, Doc." Piers approached as he closed the door. "What do you think you're doing?"

"Pardon me?"

"Don't go giving me fine airs. I want to know why you were being nice to that bloody female."

Doc took a deep breath. "That bloody female, as you call her, has a black and purple mark on her face."

The fight went out of Piers like the wind suddenly stopped blowing a ship's sails. "Couldn't be helped. Jeremy didn't mean to hit her so hard."

"Jeremy? *He* struck the woman?" Doc could hardly believe it of the boy.

"Nothing else we could do. She acted like a wildcat." Piers shrugged.

"Two men bearing down on a woman. What did you expect? Of course she panicked."

"Don't think so. You better watch out, Doc. She used Toby to get the Whetherford jewels."

He thought on that for a moment. "Young Toby? He's the one who helped her?"

"Young buck. Let his tallywacker do his thinkin'."

Doc smiled. "Toby had a lapse in wisdom. A fledgling boy's fantasies. A beautiful woman took advantage of his unseasoned youth. Surely you have not forgotten the urges of your untried years."

"No woman ever got her hooks into me," Piers grumbled. "The Eastcote chit probably had him salivating for a simple kiss."

"You should not be so hard on the boy." Doc stepped around Piers and strode down the corridor to Morgan's room. He slowly opened the door and stepped inside.

Morgan lay unconscious on a massive bed with a sheet pulled just above his loins. A large white bandage stuck to his side with strips of cloth wrapped around his middle, contrasting with the dark hair covering his chest. Where he'd previously been pale, color filled his cheeks.

"When will he wake up, Doc?" Piers asked from behind him.

Doc took a deep breath. "Hard to say. He's lost a lot of blood."

"Jeremy and I thought he would bleed to death afore we got him home. We couldn't take care of him and fight a she-cat at the same time."

He glared at Piers as he grated his words. "So, you beat her?" Even if the woman stole from Morgan, she did not deserve to be manhandled. Doc drew the line at laying a hand on a woman.

Piers looked aghast. "I told you—" The moan coming from the bed drew their attention.

"Get me some water," Doc said quickly.

Piers hurried to the jug on the table. He poured fresh water into a cup and handed it to Doc. Morgan groaned again.

"Morgan. Can you hear me?" Doc asked.

Eyes roamed under closed lids. At long last, they fluttered open. The glassy film covering them confirmed Doc's suspicion. He raised Morgan's head and pressed the cup to his lips. He barely took a sip before his eyes closed and he went limp again.

"That's a good sign, ain't it, Doc?" Piers shuffled his feet.

"Yes. But he lost a lot of blood and will require time to recover." Doc put the cup on the bedside table and wiped the sweat from Morgan's brow. "The fever is gone, thank God."

"He's been in worse scrapes."

"The cut went deep." Doc turned his gaze on Piers. "That girl didn't do it."

"Hell, Doc. We know that. A mite like her can't get the best of Himself."

Doc glared at Piers. "You let us believe she stabbed him."

Piers frowned. "She was fightin' like a bleeding wildcat. Some of those moves a lady don't know by herself. She's been taught."

"How could you possibly know that?"

"I tell ya she's been taught. By a sea-faring man, if I had my guess. She kicked and struck me where no lady would." His hand lingered just below his belt, demonstrating.

"Anyone could have taught her a maneuver to get free if she was restrained." The door opened catching their attention. Mrs. Beasley came in with a tray.

"Brought the master some broth."

"Take it away, Mrs. Beasley, and bring me some real food." Morgan barely croaked the words, but all three turned in surprise.

"Praise be, my lord," Mrs. Beasley cried.

"Welcome back to the living," Piers said. "You gave us a good scare."

"Doubt it was as bad as I feel," Morgan rasped.

His eyes were still closed and his breathing a bit labored, but his words were balm to Doc's ears. "Bad enough. Broth for you for a day or two."

Morgan's eyes creased open, but his voice came out a rough whisper. "How the devil do you expect me to regain my strength without food?"

"At this point, I don't expect you to keep anything down. So, take it slow." Doc turned to Mrs. Beasley. "Broth for him until I say."

Mrs. Beasley shot a glance to Morgan then nodded her assent to Doc.

"Good. Now I need to check that dressing."

"And I'll be about my business." Piers opened the door and waited for Mrs. Beasley to precede him.

After the door closed, Morgan spoke again. "A traitor in my camp."

"Mrs. Beasley knows what's best for you." Doc gently prodded the puckered skin. The hole in his side had to burn like the very devil. Morgan gritted his teeth as if to prove it. "He did some damage with that knife."

"It feels like he cut out my insides."

"He nearly did," Doc said. "I can give you something for the pain."

"I would rather have a bottle of brandy," Morgan said in a low rumble.

"I'm sure you would," Doc uttered. "You lost enough blood to make me wonder why you're still alive. You need rest. And do not get out of that bed. If I have to get Piers to tie you down, I'll do it."

Morgan's eyes cracked open.

"Yes, Morgan. When I said it was bad, I did not exaggerate."

"Bloody hell. I cannot believe I let him stick me. Should not have been . . . in that alley." His words grew weaker and then drifted off.

"You can tell me about it later. You're weaker than a kitten denied his mother's milk."

"It's not her," Betsy rushed into the kitchen.

Agatha Beasley stared at the girl while she told her startled heart to slow down. That girl must have a bee in her cap. "What are ya talking about?"

Betsy set the tray down with a clatter. "She ain't the one what was here afore."

"Lord Eastcote's daughter?"

Betsy gave an unlady-like snort. "She was a she-devil, that one."

The scuttle-butt in the kitchen had been about the lady coming to the manor. None of them had been looking forward to the return of the young miss who moved in while the master was gone. She had been impossible. But Agatha had worked for the master's father, and she loved Whetherford Manor. She did what she was told and took care of the guests—even if she had to chew her cheek raw while in Miss Eastcote's presence.

"Are you saying the lady upstairs is not Miss Eastcote?"

"She's got the same red hair. I don't know who she is, but it ain't *her*, thank the good Lord."

"Now, Betsy," Agatha Beasley scolded.

Betsy stepped back and put her hands on her hips. "What? You didna like her neither and don't be denying it."

"Never mind about that."

"Wonder who she is? And they keep her locked up."

"She stabbed the master." Agatha was sickened at the thought that the last remaining heir hung on by a thread. The staff had waited years for the new Lord of Whetherford to return home, and dwell in the manor. It was a shame what happened to his parents and elder brother. But the young master could not cope with his grief. No one had been gladder than her to see the young lord finally come home.

"She ought to be tarred and feathered," Betsy grumbled.

Agatha was not a violent woman, but she did agree the girl should not be treated as a house guest. Why should she show any patience toward a woman who had stabbed the master? "Maybe I'll give her some burnt toast for lunch."

Betsy continued, "Why don't you season her food with a little rat poison?"

"If that's what you are serving for dinner, I think I will decline."

Both women jumped at the sound of a deep voice. A guilty flush heated Agatha's face.

Doc entered with a friendly smile. "Did I interrupt the making of a new recipe?

Chapter 5

Kat stood by the window, her gaze following the insufferable man heading to the stables. She longed to go with
him. Well, not with him, actually. Kat had no true desire for the
daunting man's company, simply his destination. If she could
get to a horse, she would be long gone before anyone could
catch her. As far as the eye could see, miles of endless lush green
draped the landscape and swathed the deep sweep of the valley.
Surely there must be someone out there who would help her.
She had been kept in this room, and given food. She did not
know whose clothes were in that clothes closet, but at least she
found a gown that fit. The only fresh air she received came
through her open window. She'd already considered that avenue
of escape. But she preferred to keep her body intact. She disliked
broken bones—which is what she would end up with, foolishly
falling from this height.

Her heart warmed at the spirited grey prancing into view.
How she loved horses and missed the freedom of riding on the
back of her own mare.

She shoved away from the window. What was she supposed
to do with herself?

Four days she had been sequestered, and the Lord of
Whetherford had yet to make an appearance. It was intolerable.
With each passing day, the fear of his death gnawed at her, and
the waiting fueled her anger—she had no idea if he lived or died.

When her meals were delivered, the bearded man stood guard while the maid brought in a tray, gawking at Kat with something between confusion and abhorrence. She'd done nothing to the girl.

Except try to kill her employer.

Like the others, the maid must believe Kat guilty of stabbing the lord of the manor. Did he know these men kidnapped her? Did he know they kept her locked in this room, in his home? Surely, he had discovered their error by now. The very thought sparked her temper.

A brisk knock sounded on the door. She glared at the wood wondering if she could singe the person on the other side with fire from her eyes. She had seen the *right hand man* below her window. So, it was not him.

"Come in."

Doc opened the door. "Good morning."

Kat released the breath she'd been holding. It might be a good morning for him. "As you can see for yourself, my bruising is gone. I am fine. Unless you've come to release me from my prison, I have no use of your services."

He gave a brisk laugh. "That is exactly why I've come."

She shook her head to clear her hearing. "What?"

"I thought you might like to escape the confines of your room. Pardon me. Poor choice of words. Temporarily leave your room to go into the sunshine. Perhaps for a walk?"

"What of Lord Whetherford?"

"What about him?"

Willing her legs to hold her steady, Kat gathered the courage she needed to ask the question haunting her mind. She leveled her gaze and slowly inhaled a silent lungful of air. "Has he . . . recovered?"

Doc settled his gaze on hers. "Luckily for you, he is a strong man."

Kat's anger returned. "Then why am I still here? Why am I locked in this room?"

"In due time, Lord Whetherford will answer your questions."

"In due time?" All apprehension suddenly fell away, replaced with boiling ire. Too impulsive for her own good, she lashed out like she did when someone angered her beyond all reason. "How can you say such a thing? How can you keep me here? Surely, he has told you I did not stab him. Or is he able to speak? You have no right to keep me here." Kat's fury brought tears to her eyes. "This is preposterous. Where is he?"

The doctor's cold stare made her burst of bravado sizzle, like flames of a burning fire doused with a bucket of cold water. "I will give you one hour to compose yourself. At that time, if you want to refuse my offer of a visit to the garden, a simple no will do."

Kat stood speechless as she watched the door close behind him. Oh, why couldn't she control her temper? He had given her a chance to get out of this room. Once again, she must suffer the result of her unguarded tongue.

Time moved at a snail's pace. She paced the floor for what seemed like hours before he returned.

The door opened.

It was not Doc.

A tall man with golden-blond hair entered. Judging by the way he stood, the expensive cut of his clothes, he appeared to be a nobleman. Tall, strong build, a handsome man with a smile that did not reach his blue eyes.

"Good Morning. Allow me to introduce myself. Wesley Montgomery Hathridge."

Warmth flowed through her limbs as his gaze ran up and down her body. Her teeth worried her lower lip, while she stood uneasy under his inspection.

Suddenly, he smiled like a cat that had lapped up all of the cream, making her wonder if she should be afraid of him. Shoulders erect, she stood as straight as her bones would allow, and returned his stare—not about to let him break down her wall of self-preservation.

"Are you ready for a stroll out of doors?"

Kat swallowed her mounting fear. "Do you mind telling me who you are, other than your name?"

"A lady in your position should not ask so many questions."

"Where is Doc?"

"Ah, another question," he said dryly.

Don't let your tongue test his patience. "Doc said he would return in an hour. I simply wondered if he would still come."

"I have come in his stead. If you are ready, I will escort you." He stepped to the side, and with an elegant swerve of his arm, he motioned to the doorway

Kat considered her options. After a moment's hesitation, she arched her neck, hoisted her chin, and stepped past him. He ushered her through the door and down several corridors giving Kat her first glimpse at the house and its extensive wings. She had little opportunity to take in the impressive dwelling as he steered her down the stairs and out into the sunshine.

The garden, as Doc had called it, was a massive maze of color, full of the most beautiful flowers she'd ever seen. Amaryllis, Bluebonnet, Iris, Queen Anne's Lace—too many to name. Eyes agog she spun around, ignoring the presence shadowing her. So excited to be out-of-doors, she did not care her patronizing *escort* surveyed her every movement.

Vibrant fragrances assailed her senses. "Blue Cornflowers, my favorite."

She took a few paces down the path and stopped beside the extravagant blooms. Closing her eyes, she breathed in the sweet fragrance. She would love to snap one stem for her own. Tempted, she glanced back at the man who followed. He spread his arms and shrugged. "I am merely here to keep you company."

To make sure I do not get away. How much longer would she have to wait before the lord of the manor fully recovered?

With Hathridge only steps behind, she followed a path leading to a water fountain. The few clouds above were not enough to block out the sun's sparkling reflection. She studied the water trickling into the pool, the hair on her neck tingling, as though someone watched her closely. She glanced at Hathridge. He stood with his arms crossed, a smirk of arrogance on his face. No. What she felt at this moment was peculiar, different from Hathridge's watchful regard—like a predator monitoring its prey waiting for the right moment to strike.

She searched the area, her gaze taking in the walkway, the flowers and the trees of the dark forest beyond. Nothing. No one else—only the two of them.

She angled her head and eyed the giant stone structure with its many wings aimed in all directions of the atlas. She looked intently at each window, not knowing what she searched for. A shadow? The hair on her scalp prickled as a strange awareness settled over her. Someone watched. A shiver very much like dread overtook her body.

Morgan stood by the window in the darkened room. As if his thoughts conjured her up, she appeared next to the fountain.

He could not take his eyes off the figure standing beside the stream of running water.

Juliana.

Long flowing hair, a vibrant shade of red with a chestnut hue, surrounded her shoulders. The unusual color had caught his attention years ago, when he'd first laid eyes on her.

He curled his fingers into a fist and a muscle ticked above one eye. She was here. Bitterness and resentment filled his soul. His grim smile had nothing to do with cheerfulness, and everything to do with retribution.

The unfortunate scene in the alley had delayed their meeting. Morgan's hand went to his side, caressing his wound. He gave no thought to ask what happened to the girl he'd saved. He supposed his men saw her home or paid her off. Juliana had been the only thing on his mind since Piers told him they had brought her to Whetherford.

What would it be like when they came face to face? Would she plead with him? The way she had at their last meeting—when she wanted to be the next Lady Whetherford and he'd laughed in her face. He made it clear he never accepted the title and had no intention of taking a wife.

Those were the days when his dark soul commanded his movements. The boy with loving parents and a brother he worshiped disappeared the day his family sailed to a watery grave. Nothing and no-one mattered. A woman was simply a tool to ease his lust.

He shook the unwelcome memories away.

Juliana had wanted a titled lord, then. He wondered if she ever got one. Would she strut through the door as if she were the lady of the manor and act as if she owned the world? He remembered how Juliana had tossed her flowing red hair about her shoulders and sneaked a glimpse of him from beneath her eyelashes, sending sexual innuendos with every female propensity in her curvaceous body.

Maybe he would let her entice him again, before he threw her out.

Bloody hell! The head that sat atop his shoulders could not allow the head that lived within his trousers to govern. He needed to think of his mother's necklace. The heirloom that had been in his family for centuries.

Morgan moved toward the bed and grimaced as he reached for the bell pull. To hell with Doc's orders of bed rest. His body had healed enough. It galled him to call for help, but he needed to be dressed for this. He would not allow his weakness to interfere with what must be done.

It was time.

Kat had been summoned. *He* had *requested* her presence, not demanded. Beckoned, as if she were an invited guest. The irony of it all.

Her stomach was tied in knots—had been ever since she received his *invitation*. She tried to slow her breathing. She swallowed, but the lump that lodged from her throat to the center of her chest never moved. Her head throbbed. The pulse in her temples pounded with every beat of her heart. So loud in volume, she feared surely someone could hear it. Glancing over her shoulder, she saw the blond man's smirk, which was becoming all too familiar. He waited for her to enter the *lion's den*. She faced the huge solid oak door, the only thing between her and her impending fate.

The vein in her neck throbbed. she must calm down or she would be at *his* mercy. And that would never do. She could not allow him to know how defenseless she believed herself to be.

Lord Whetherford should have absolved her by now. If he were any kind of a gentleman, he would have set her free. She hesitated another moment outside the door. *He* was at fault—not her. She would demand to be released at once. Her body as taut as a tightly-drawn corset, she knocked on the wooden door.

Hearing his utterance, Kat smoothed her hands down the sides of her gown and squared her shoulders. Knowing Hathridge studied her, she summoned the courage to enter with a confident determination she did not feel.

She opened the study door.

He stood by the window, facing the sunlight, his back to her. A large, dark, muscular man, in all his finery, with broad shoulders and a commanding stance. Inky black waves hung thick and unruly. Tresses just long enough to curl over the neck of a white shirt peaking from the collar of his black suit coat. This man stood as tall as her brother, and Stephen loomed well over six feet. Even from the back, his broadness showed plenty of muscle. Remembering his fight with the ruffians made her sigh, marveling at the instant craving that pierced her torso.

The latch of the closing door generated a spike in her already rapid pulse. No chance to flee since Hathridge, quite possibly, barred the door. She lifted her chin and forced her arms by her side. Not knowing what to say, or if this man expected her to say anything at all, she waited. He remained motionless, taking his darn sweet time to acknowledge her presence. Why did he ignore her? The silence drew out so long she thought her unsteady legs would not hold her much longer.

Finally, he spoke. "Would you like a drink, my dear?

She had forgotten the low deep timbre of his voice. The rich baritone sent surges of awareness down her spine. An unexpected, distinct wakefulness. She resisted the urge to clasp her hands and entwine her worrisome fingers. Kat answered in a voice she hoped would not crack. "No, thank you."

She nearly jumped out of her skin when he whirled around like the lash of a whip. He did not speak. He stood like stone, the same as she. Smoldering dark eyes seized hers in a heated, locked gaze, drowning her in their penetrating force. She had not been prepared for the dark threatening expression—threatening in the way that she felt something move within her.

Time stood still.

Nothing else in the room existed but the two of them. His hypnotic pull seared her, sending a tingling sensation beginning in her stomach, then flowing down the back of her knees and extending through her limbs making it impossible to move.

Her throat tightened.

If those eyes could shoot fire, they would sear holes right through her. But the expression on his face . . . he looked like he'd just had a good kick in the teeth.

Chapter 6

Morgan felt as though someone had just punched him in the gut—hard. His breath caught at the sight of the stunning creature before him. Lost in amazing green eyes—adrift in their sparkling jade and mystique sensuality. He scanned her high cheekbones, her soft creamy skin, and let his gaze slide down to fasten on luscious lips. Suddenly his mouth was dry

A cloud of vibrant red hair floated around her shoulders—like the brightest sunset at the end of a day, resting on the shimmering ocean. Luxuriant masses of thick curls inviting a man's hands. He flexed his to keep from reaching for her. The movement reminded him of the snifter in his palm, which brought him some sense of stability.

He took in her exquisite form, stared at the more-than-generous swell of bosom, letting his heated gaze linger there. A notion popped in the back of his mind telling him to breathe. He tightened his jaw to make sure his mouth did not hang open. His hungry eyes moved lower, perceiving a slim waist before the folds of her gown hid the rest.

She is exquisite.

She stood straight and tall with her chin at an angle in challenge. Even with that rod in her backbone, he sensed her vulnerability. A pang of concern struck his chest.

"You," he whispered. *What the hell is she doing here?*

An explosion went off in his brain. *Holy Mother of God! Those fools. They must have brought her here thinking she was Juliana. Blood and the devil!*

Morgan's heart kicked and landed somewhere in the bottom of his gut. Choking on the words for this unsettling circumstance, he compelled himself to speak hoping his voice would not betray him. "I owe you my profound apology. There has been a horrendous mistake, madam. And I fear that I have made it."

Those beautiful eyes blinked. She stared at him as though someone had taken over her senses. Was this woman a simpleton?

He hurried to the sideboard. Even though she could quite possibly be in shock, he ignored the stronger spirits and poured a generous amount of sherry. Not enough to knock her on her bum, just bring some color back into her face. He strode back to the unknown beauty and placed the flute in her hand.

Changes came over her face. Stupor—awe—surprise—and . . . anger. Although Morgan was not a patient man, he waited.

Her eyes flamed with fire. "Did I hear you correctly? Mistake?"

Morgan stopped the oath before it left his mouth. "Yes. I believe your being here is a mistake."

"A mistake." She echoed with a stupefied look, unseeing the crystal she held in her hand. "That is what I thought you said."

She raised the glass and downed the liquid in one swift movement. Tears came to her eyes as she tried not to cough. She marched to the side table and he feared she planned to get more. Instead she set the glass on the table top. When she faced him, her hands were fisted and the fire in her eyes burned brighter than the flames in the hearth.

"Mistake?" she snapped. "I was kidnapped! I have been a prisoner in your home. Forced to come here and forced to remain. I have been scared out of my mind. Every day I worried if you still lived. I agonized over what would become of me if you died. Then I walk in here and you have the audacious daring to tell me it was a *mistake*?"

Morgan ran a frustrated hand through the mane on top of his head. He wanted to drain his glass of brandy and hurl it at the wall.

"Your actions are reprehensible. Explain yourself. Why was I taken if this was only a *mistake*? They were your men, were they not?"

Morgan saw black. The sudden pain in his jaw came from his clenched teeth. What a deuced dilemma. He needed to sit. His body weaker than he realized, he stumbled.

"Oh, dear. You have not healed." The woman ran to his side.

"I assure you, madam, I can make it on my own."

She jerked back. "Very well. Be stubborn."

Morgan fell, more than sat, in the leather chair. Pain shot through his side. He took several deep breaths. "If you will allow me, I will try to make some sense of this."

"I do not know you. I have only your actions to determine my opinion of your character. And thus far, they have not been principled."

"Would you take into consideration my actions when I came to your rescue?"

She braced her hands on her hips. "Being held a prisoner in your home is what you call rescue?"

He held out his hand and gestured to the twin high back chair facing him. "Please. Sit." Seeing her uncertainty made him painfully conscious of every second as he wondered how in the hell he was going to explain anything to this woman.

"Please."

Without another word, she sauntered over to the offered chair and sat, keeping her posture erect.

Taking another deep breath, he began. "My name is Morgan Hurashune Langston, Earl of Whetherford. Whetherford Manor is my home. Would you allow me your name?" He counted the seconds before she answered.

"Katherine Radbourn."

Shaking his head, he continued. "I'm not sure where to begin."

"How about at the beginning?"

He scrutinized her sparkling, fierce gaze. Her beauty vanquished every sane thought in his head. His fingers tightened on the glass in his hand. Never before, had he been unsure of his actions, but he had no idea what to do next.

"I am deeply sorry for any suffering I have caused you. Until this moment, I did not know you were here. When you came through that door, and I heard your voice, I realized you were not the woman I had expected."

She made no sound to interrupt.

At her silence, he continued. "You see . . . the woman I expected to be here, Juliana Eastcote, took something from me. Something which belongs to my family."

He rubbed a frustrated hand down his clean-shaven face. *Good God, how I have bungled this.* "I went after her." Morgan marveled at the similar, yet distinctive variance as he studied the young woman's features. "You do look a great deal like her."

She bristled at his observation.

Good God. He had to be more careful. Upon closer inspection, Miss Radbourne bore only a slight resemblance to Juliana. The high cheekbones, the same arched brows, and the long auburn hair. Only this woman's hair possessed a deeper, more intoxicating shade of red.

Another man might think they looked the same. Not he. A slender nose, rounded on the end. Full cheeks giving a slant to her amazing green eyes. Winged brows, further accenting the arch of her curving lids. Skin so creamy smooth, the impulse to touch peaked his longing. Ahh, and a pert little chin, showing strength.

"The last thing I remember seeing was you, just before I hit the ground. Then everything went black until I woke up in my bed."

"Didn't anyone tell you they brought me here?"

"My men assumed you were Juliana. They believed that I had found her, and was bringing her—that is you—back, when we were accosted."

Morgan looked down at the amber liquid as his fingers clutched the glass. He wished his hands were wrapped around Juliana's neck. She had started this unforeseen chain of events.

"So, all this time I have been locked up in a room, you thought I was this other woman?"

Like a pocket watch wound too tight, his innards coiled—a spring ready to snap. Damn his weakened body. He placed the snifter on the oak table beside him, and with years of practice—mechanically controlling his emotions—he forced himself to continue.

"My embarrassment and humiliation at this moment could not come close to what you must have felt. My deepest regret is I let that bloody idiot stab me when I should have prevented this entire situation." His eyes bore into hers, willing her to see his concern to be real.

"I have been here for days." Her eyes softened and her voice took on a desperate beseeching tone.

Morgan shook his head. "I concede my apology is not enough. And my injury is not an excuse. But, I was unconscious. My men assumed you were she. I was instructed not to leave my bed. Thank God, I did not follow Doc's orders or you would still be locked in your bedchamber."

"You would have kept this other woman under lock and key?"

By the shock on her face, she must think him an animal. "Please let me explain. No, I would not normally consider such a thing. This other woman invaded my home while I was gone. She stole from me. I went to London to retrieve my family's property. As I walked past that alley, I heard your scream." He shrugged and grimaced as the pain in his side reminded him of the gaping hole there. "The rest you know."

"Ahh. That explains something Doc said."

Morgan's gaze flew to hers. Even the crease across her brow was lovely. "What did he say?"

"You know you could scare someone half to death with a look like that."

Hiding his surprise, Morgan relaxed his features.

"That's better. Doc, as you call him, is an interesting man. Your men thought I was the one who stabbed you."

"What!" *Bloody hell.*

"I am glad I saw your heroism before I was brought here. You can look quite menacing, you know."

He frowned.

"There is no need to pout."

The insult stung. "Madam, I assure you, I never *pout*!"

"It is amazing, really."

The woman boggled a man's mind. "What is amazing?"

"You appear most menacing, but I do not feel threatened at all." Her dainty nose sloped upward and her words so soft, he pondered if she meant for him to hear them.

He inhaled slowly to calm his vexation and tried again. "What did Doc say to you? And where did he get such an outrageous idea?"

"Oh, well, you see, blood was everywhere." As she talked, her hands fluttered about in explanation. "When you fell to the ground, I think I returned to my senses. I must have been in shock or something. I ran to you. You were face down in the dirt. I tried to roll you over. You are a very large man, by the by."

Good God. Would she quit looking at him with those ravishing eyes. Such scrutiny had him fighting the urge to touch her, to run his finger across her cheek—across those full lips.

"It was difficult. But I managed, and that's how I got blood all over my hands."

He'd allowed his mind to wander. "Blood on your hands?"

"Yes. You were bleeding profusely." Holding out her hands, she studied them. "So much blood. So fast. It poured . . ." Her voice halted. Her eyes grew round. Good God, the woman was reliving the scene in the alley.

Afraid she might go into shock again, he interrupted. "As you can see, I am fine."

Her hands fell to her lap as she studied him. Concern etched her brow. "Are you? Really?"

Her gaze captivated him in a way that astounded him, but he was not used to being questioned. "Of course I am."

"But, earlier . . . I saw you stumble."

She had to remind him. What a bitter pill to swallow. God, he hated weakness. If he thought he would not stumble again, he would get up and stomp around the room just to show her.

Bloody hell. He pressed a hand to his side, thinking he best keep his arse right here in this dammed chair.

"What happened next?"

She blinked and leaned forward as if judging for herself whether or not he had recovered. "Does it hurt?"

"It damned well doesn't tickle," he spouted before he caught himself. "My apologies."

She actually chuckled. The sound stirred designs up on his insides—which he'd been desperately trying to keep at bay. A rare and intriguing woman, indeed. Beautiful beyond comparison.

Thinking his house guest was Juliana, he had been primed and ready to unleash his wrath. He had wanted to make her squirm, beg, plead. He'd anticipated the pleasure of seeing fear in Juliana's eyes. Instead he'd gotten the wind knocked out of his sails. Guilt ate at him like acid.

Morgan cleared his throat. "Please, go on."

"As I said, there was so much blood. When your men saw me beside you, and then they saw my hands . . ."

"They assumed you stabbed me?" How absurd. His men knew better. A mere woman would not have the strength. But, a beautiful woman, same lustrous red hair—he understood how Piers and Jeremy would have mistaken her for Juliana.

Her teeth chewed her bottom lip. "Yes. And when I realized what they suspected, I ran."

Morgan could cut his arm off for putting her through such a set of circumstances. "You ran?"

"They caught me."

"Obviously."

"Then, when Doc came to my room, he simply stared at me. Of course, I had a colorful bruise beside my eye."

"A bruise?" Damn, she must have fallen when she ran away.

"The younger one clobbered me."

What!

Rage flooded his sanity. Surely, he'd heard wrong. He would kill those bungling fools.

"There is that threatening look again. Although I wanted to at the time, you do not need to kill him. He is ashamed enough as it is."

By God she patted his knee.

"Now, getting back to Doc. He stared at me for a long while, and came to the conclusion I did not do it. Stab you, that is. When I asked him to let me go, he said 'there is still the matter you stole from him.' Imagine my confusion."

His mind spun. So many truths came to light since she'd made that statement, he'd forgotten Doc had said anything. If only he could undo the damage already done—but he did not deal in 'what ifs.' He learned long ago not to count on anything but cold hard facts.

He swallowed convulsively. "Miss Radbourn. While you are in my home, you will be shown every courtesy. Please know you are safe here. You are my guest. Anything you wish is yours."

A guest? How could Kat wrap her mind around that? It was bad enough his deep voice penetrated the nerves in her spine. And his devilishly handsome features scattered her thoughts. But his piercing gaze compelled the butterflies in her stomach to flurry more like hornets buzzing around a bee hive.

"I will make arrangements for you to return to your home as soon as possible," he said. "However, there is one more thing we must discuss."

Warning signals went off in her brain. She raised her chin. "And what, pray tell, might that be?"

His voice deepened. "I fully accept all responsibility for everything that has happened. My home is secluded. No one outside of the grounds knows you are here. There is no one to carry the tale of your presence to malign your name or damage your comportment. I do not tell you this to make you uncomfortable or to feel intimidated. Only to assure you, this incident will remain as quiet as you wish it to be."

"Thank you."

"However, you must realize your disappearance from London has undoubtedly become public knowledge for the gossips of the ton. I will offer you my name and my protection to make sure your reputation is untarnished."

She blinked. *What?*

She had survived her fear, and fought despair, only to have the rogue tell her—*oh, beg pardon, madam. Just a whit of a mistake.* And now he offered his name?

"Are you sure you did not hit your head when you fell?"

Lord Whetherford's eyes darkened. "I will do whatever it takes to right this wrong. Your being here leads to only one conclusion. Marriage."

Kat's head whirled. Too fast. *This is not happening.*

She pinched her wrist to make sure she was awake. "To save my reputation?"

"Of course."

Her chest tightened. She clenched her hands together, fumbling for words. "Lord Whetherford, you need not go to such lengths to . . ."

"How can I not?"

Taking vows with the man responsible for her abduction? It was unthinkable. Kat prayed she would not lose her temper. What if he had a temper to match? He certainly looked threatening in that alley. And the dark scowls he presented today should have sent her screaming. Even given their situation, she must not insult an earl. To do so now when she barely knew this man, secluded in his home, in the middle of nowhere—he could possibly follow through on his threatening glower. "I hope such a thing will not be necessary."

"I would gladly and most eagerly beg your forgiveness, and those of your family. Too much time has passed. Nothing short of marriage is acceptable."

Oh no, no, no!

What a set of circumstances? She had avoided proposals, found ways to get her uncle to decline offers on one pretext or another, only to be trapped into a loveless marriage? Even if the blasted lord did look like the man in her fantasies.

And she had to find Stephen.

"You do not understand. I cannot marry you."

He tried to hide it, but she knew she'd surprised him. "Are you promised to someone else?"

She chewed on her lip, knowing she must be honest. "No."

A hint of a smile extended one corner of his beautiful mouth. "Am I such a bad catch? I have money and a title. Surely your parents would not object?"

Her parents?

A touch of sadness pierced her chest. "You cannot want to marry me either."

Now she'd gone and done it. Admitted she did not want to marry him. *Not want to marry a titled lord?* Not only would he be insulted, he would think her a complete blockhead.

Kat jumped from her chair. "There must be another way." She paced across the floor. Her voice rose with each word she spoke. "You can take me home or . . . or. . . send me home. You do not have to marry me."

"Surely you must see this is the only way to salvage your reputation. You will be ruined if you return alone."

Drat and double drat! The most arresting man she'd ever met just offered marriage. For one wild, crazy moment she wanted to jump and yell *yes*. Had they met in London, perhaps at a ball, she could give serious thought to her flight of fancy. But Lord Whetherford had been forced—his honor as a gentleman—to correct an impulsive mistake. The mistake of his men.

It was his fault. And one day he would blame her. She would not be forced to accept a loveless marriage. She stopped her pacing and faced him. Desperate, she nearly screeched. "You have done this to me. You must think of something else?"

There was that scowl again. "There is no other option. If you would like me to meet your parents before we speak our vows, I will agree. But, Miss Radbourn," his eyes pierced hers, "we will wed."

Each word he spoke sounded like the resounding toll of a death knell.

Chapter 7

"Wool-gathering?"

Morgan looked up from the numbers in his ledger. "What the hell are you doing here?"

Arms crossed, one shoulder propped against the door frame, Giles' casual stance looked entirely too comfortable. He cocked a dubious brow, shoved away from the door frame and stepped inside. "It is good to see you, as well."

Giving him a momentary glance, Morgan merely grumbled.

"Do come in, Giles. Oh, thank you, Morgan." Giles mocked. Morgan ignored him as he stepped inside, closing the study door behind him. "Your manners, as usual, are impeccable."

Morgan rose from behind his desk. "Shut up, Giles, and sit down." He strode to the side table. Picking up the decanter, he poured a glass of brandy for each of them.

"What has gotten you in such a snit?"

Morgan looked into his friend's shrewd eyes as he handed him a glass, thinking he could almost smile at the slipshod attitude. In all the years that he and Giles had been friends, they shared a number of things. Together they'd fought bandits, thieves, cutthroats, and each had thankfully dodged more bullets than those that found their mark. Saving lives had been at times a thankless job, where they received swollen eyes and bruised knuckles for their troubles. Still, they had become solid friends—each willing to give his life for the other.

Giles took the offered glass.

Morgan threw back his head draining his drink. With a slight grimace, he marched back to the table and reached to pour another,

"Bad as all that?" Giles asked. "You knew I would be here once I heard you were back."

Morgan's steps were soft as he strode across the carpet covering the wooden floor. He gazed through the windowpane. This side of the manor faced the maze his grandfather had built. He saw nothing but the thoughts running rampant through his mind.

Giles' voice pierced through his preoccupation. "I heard another interesting piece of news."

Morgan raised his glass and took a hefty swallow.

"Is it true?" Giles asked.

"Mind telling me how the hell you found out so fast?" Morgan asked over his shoulder.

"It appears one of my groomsmen has taken a fancy to one of your kitchen maids."

"You don't know the half of it."

"Enlighten me . . ." Giles made himself too damned comfortable.

How in hell could Morgan explain his state of affairs? An instant pang of guilt hit him square in his belly. Piers and Jeremy may have brought Miss Radbourn here, but *he* was responsible for their foolish mistake. Now he had to spill his guts, for Giles would not have it any other way.

Morgan reluctantly took the seat behind his desk and told the tale of how he now had an innocent young woman in his home.

A victim. Who had been kidnapped. Snatched off the street. Abducted and forced to come to Whetherford against her will.

"Good God, man! Why the deuced hell would Piers remotely believe a mere female had done you in?" Giles shook his head. "I've heard of sweeping a girl off her feet . . . but Jeremy actually struck the chit?"

"You have an irritating manner." Morgan raised his glass and found the snifter empty. He headed to the sideboard for more brandy.

Once Morgan returned to his seat, Giles narrowed his eyes over his sharp stare. "How could you let this happen?"

"Let?" Morgan echoed.

"The woman was held captive for days. Surely someone may well have identified her sooner—before you made it necessary to offer for her."

His arm stilled. His throat constricted at her image. His attraction to the lovely object of this entire business beyond his control. Her extraordinary green eyes had a bit of a slant, framed by long luminous lashes and set off by gracefully winged russet brows. A sun-kissed curl hugged her cheekbone. Her small chin hinted at willfulness with full, pink lips that beckoned a man's caress. Creamy smooth breasts, made him think of soft pillows and satin sheets.

Morgan shook the vision from his mind. Good God. He had no right to lust after her. She'd made it clear enough she scorned their betrothal. She more than likely despised him.

When had her opinion of him become important?

Determined to do everything in his power to atone for the pain he'd inflicted on her, he would give her his name and live in the trap of his own making.

"And what do you know about this girl—other than she is a replica of Juliana?"

Morgan did not like having to explain himself. He ground out, "Damnation, Giles. It was supposed to *be* Juliana."

Giles went on, flaying Morgan with his every word. "But that is not the lady's name, is it?"

He did not need Giles to point out that tidbit of information. Hell, he'd already beaten himself up a hundred times. Giles could not deliver over any more torment than he had already bestowed upon himself. "How the hell was I supposed to do anything while lying unconscious?"

"You obviously regard the lady in high esteem. Are you convinced she is an intelligent, honorable woman?"

"Do not be condescending. You think I would not know the difference?" Morgan combed his fingers through his hair.

"Don't you think you should find out before you leg-shackle yourself to her, for God's sake?"

Warranted or not, Morgan did not like being under Giles' scrutiny. "Miss Radbourn is different. She is a beautiful young woman. And her beauty goes deeper than the skin." A muscle ticked in the side of his cheek. He resented the knowing expression on Giles face while he looked down his nose.

"Maybe guilt and remorse clouds your judgment. Are your men continuing the search for Juliana?"

Morgan studied the contents of his glass. "I've called a halt to finding her until I can go myself. To be sure nothing like this happens again."

"Done in by a damned look-a-like." Giles shook his head, then drained the last of his brandy. "So, the question is not if you are going to marry the girl—but when. You are going to marry the chit, aren't you?"

Morgan trusted Giles' judgment, but at the moment, he wanted to throttle the man for laying him open and pouring salt on his wound. The smile he allotted his friend was grim indeed. "Yes. It appears to be so."

"Well, old man." Giles stood. "Am I invited to dinner?"

Morgan scowled as he got out of his chair and stepped around the mahogany desk. "Why? Are you hungry?"

"Like I said. Impeccable manners." Giles set his empty glass on the side table. "Mayhap I should meet this houseguest of yours who is the paragon of Juliana, before you turn into a poor besotted fool."

"And like I said. Irritating." He tossed back the brown liquid and set his glass down with a whack. "I guess there is no way to prevent you from meeting her."

Giles slapped him on the back. "Well then, let's be about it."

Alone in the parlor, Kat brooded over the events of the last hours. She turned when she heard a distinct voice not belonging to her host.

Whetherford stood well over six feet, muscular build, broad shouldered, dark hair, and dark eyes. The gentleman standing next to him stood a bit taller, about the same muscular build, with noble features and eyes a light grey in color that glittered with a hint of mystery—or from an intense interest in her. His demeanor suggested distinguished authority.

"Your Grace. Katherine Radbourn, my guest," Whetherford said. "Miss Radbourn. His Grace, the Duke of Nethersall."

Good Lord. A Duke. Kat nearly gaped, then quickly dipped into a deep curtsy befitting any grand ballroom. "Your Grace." *Such impressive connections. I wonder if the duke knows how his host acquired his houseguest.*

"How delightful. And such a beautiful guest. I am charmed, Miss Radbourn."

She noted his courtly manner, yet his close scrutiny made her wonder at the thoughts behind his searching eyes.

The duke gave a formal bow, and extended his arm, his gallantry beyond reproach. "If you will allow me."

Kat's eyes darted to Morgan and she saw him frown before she accepted the proffered arm. Heat warmed her hand as she touched solid muscle concealed under her fingers. The duke escorted her into the dining hall with the conviction and confidence of his station. A perfect gentleman, he waited for her to take her seat, then moved around the table and pulled back a chair directly across from her, a twinkle in his eyes.

He had the devil's very own smile, which put her on her guard. She steeled herself against his discerning stare. His intense scrutiny—not particularly unpleasant—felt penetrating, nonetheless. His dynamic stare probed as though he were trying to determine her secrets—the ones she had hidden in her very soul.

Kat could hold her own with the *grande dames of the haute ton*. Hadn't Aunt Elizabeth made her spend hours becoming skilled at conversing and achieving just the right demeanor in the parlors of lords and ladies?

The conversation started out discussing the activities of any normal given day. His Grace asked what she thought of Whetherford Manor. The tone of his voice had a deep rich quality—not as deep as Whetherford's—but with a trace of mild sarcasm, laced with charm and a projected authority of which his position entailed. Their exchange lulled her into a relaxed state. Then, he came right to the point.

"It would seem our host has more than . . . inconvenienced you. The situation is somewhat problematic."

Whetherford made no move to speak, nor showed any reaction. *Inconvenience? Problematic?* Certainly not words she would have chosen.

"Even so . . ." He gave a long pause before he continued. "You are here. And my good fortune to be in such charming company."

"You are most kind to say so." Kat dipped her head as she'd been taught.

"I am much encouraged. You are behaving most admirably, considering this set of circumstances."

Kat lowered her eyes just enough to appear demure. "How would you have me behave, Your Grace?"

"You are certainly entitled to be angry, even bitter. Why, were I in your unexpected situation, Miss Radbourn . . ." The duke hesitated and gave her a discerning look. "You are being too gracious by far, bearing in mind your predicament, through no fault of your own."

The man had a way with words. Of course, it was not her fault! Was he really appalled or making fun of her? Surely, he did not think she was responsible for her own capture.

He continued with questions. "Is your home in London, Miss Radbourn?"

Kat picked up her fork and stabbed at her meat. "Brighton. I live with my aunt and uncle. They have no children of their own."

"Might I inquire the names of your aunt and uncle? Perhaps I know the family surname." He put a morsel in his mouth and chewed waiting for her answer.

The Duke's attention, together with Whetherford's lack of comment, unnerved her. His Grace had not said anything wide of the mark. He was quite captivating even though this felt like an inquisition and he the firing squad. Whetherford sat there brooding.

"You must have experienced much of the world in your travels," she answered. "I seriously doubt our families would be in the same political circles. I hardly imagine my meager family would be of interest to you, Your Grace. However, they are Albert and Elizabeth Thornton. My parents were . . ."

When she hesitated, he asked, "Were?"

Kat lowered her eyes to the silver clutched in her hand. "I lost my mother and father in a carriage accident when I was a child."

"I do beg your pardon." The duke became sympathetic. "Please accept my sincere condolences and my humble apologies for being so crude."

Kat raised her chin. "Thank you. There is no need to apologize. My aunt and uncle are caring people. They gave me a good home and loved me as if I was their own."

"They sound most admirable. And their home is in Brighton?"

She wondered again if perhaps the duke pretended the empathy he portrayed or if he had another purpose altogether in asking her these questions. "Actually, it is Chelmouth. A small community about three days ride north from the coast of Brighton. You probably have not heard of it."

The duke cleared his throat. "I have not traveled that far north of Brighton. I do, however, know every port along the coast."

Sadness pierced her breast. "Odd, that you should mention ports. My brother is captain of his own ship and has docked there every year until the last two."

His gaze darted to Whetherford, and then back to her. His expression grew shuttered. "Your brother?"

She noticed the calculating glint in his eye. "Yes. My brother took me to my aunt and uncle after our parents' death. Then he left me."

Again, the duke cast a look toward Whetherford in silent communication. "He left you?"

Kat remembered the incident as if it happened yesterday. She struggled to keep her voice from cracking. "He thought it better than taking me with him to live on his ship."

The duke's voice grew softer. "I quite agree. I am sure he had your best interests at heart."

Kat met his stare. "I know that now. But in the mind of a child, he deserted me."

Morgan's gut twisted at the pain in her eyes. "Giles. Do you think we may find more pleasant conversation? Not dwell on how Miss Radbourn came to be here. It smacks of my lack of finesse." *And stupidity.*

"Finesse?" Giles gave a bark of laughter. "Good God, man!" Catching himself, he immediately directed his next words to her. "I do beg your pardon for my outburst, Miss Radbourn."

Morgan swallowed his frustration when she simply tilted her head in a graceful bow in exoneration. Giles was a pain in the arse.

"A beautiful woman like you, how is it you have escaped so long without a husband? I assume there is no husband since a nuptial is pending?"

Her shoulders straightened and she bristled like a little peacock. "No. I am not married nor promised to another."

"Well, now. There are a lot of aristocrats in London. But then you have landed a titled lord and wealthy land owner in our host."

Morgan's exasperation had grown to its limit. "I don't think it is necessary—"

Giles interrupted. "It is not necessary to make the lady even more uncomfortable than this predicament already forced on her." Giles completely ignored the menacing glower Morgan tried to send him. "However, I cannot ignore the young lady's unfortunate situation." He then tuned his gaze on *the lady*. "Be assured, my dear Miss Radbourn, you have my protection."

Morgan had to swallow the retort that came to his tongue. He glared to keep from leaping across the table to pound his fists into the very face of the one who dared to insinuate himself in her favor—and after putting her through an inquisition.

Mrs. Beasley came in with a breeze, offering one of her most delicious confections, saving him from his own folly.

Kat's lips slanted in a perplexed smile directed at Giles. "Do I need your protection?"

"Not from me you don't," Morgan quipped. Deuce, how absurd that sounded. She would not be in this mess if not for him. Why would she trust him? Better yet, why would she trust Giles? She just met him, for God's sake!

Giles paid no attention to Morgan's discomfort and entirely too much to his lovely houseguest. "I hope it will not be so. All the same, you have it."

"'Tis rare to find a gentleman gallant enough to offer protection without expecting certain . . . liberties in return," Katherine said.

Morgan gave a cynical snort in his friend's direction. That ought to tighten his cravat a notch or two.

"I'm sure *you* have no such expectations, Your Grace." She gave a dramatic sigh. "The protection of a Duke. My Goodness. I would be the envy of every young maiden. Oh, dear. Did I assume correctly, there is no Duchess?"

The damned girl was trifling with him. Watching her face, Morgan agonized whether she was near to accepting the offer or simply amused.

Giles did not help matters by leaning toward her and speaking in a conspirator whisper. "You are correct, Miss Radbourn. I am a lonely man."

Teeth grinding, Morgan refused to acknowledge the green monster dancing on his back.

"Hmmm. A Duke." Miss Radbourn actually cooed. "Are you willing to make the same sacrifice as Lord Whetherford?"

Giles coughed and cleared his throat as though he swallowed mud instead of the wine in his goblet. The blasted woman presumed a proposal from Giles? A familiar red haze swam in Morgan's brain. "Are you refusing my offer for a better one, Miss Radbourn?" Morgan asked through clenched teeth.

She met his gaze. "Surely you would not deny me the title of a duchess, my lord—if the Duke is offering?"

The little minx fluttered her lashes and swept her glance to Giles.

Blood and the devil!

Before Giles could get his tongue out of his throat, she continued. "Let me warmly give you my gratitude, Your Grace. I sincerely appreciate your kindness. I would never refuse your protection."

Morgan's breath caught. The damned woman accepted Giles proposal—which he had not intentionally made. The damned sod. How in hell had this happened—and right in front of his nose? Silence stretched for several moments while Giles hid his shock. He'd been in worse situations. No doubt he would recover from this one, too.

"I believe a man should stand by his word," Katherine stared pointedly at Morgan. "A man's word is everything, is it not?"

Then her gaze returned to Giles. "I must respectfully tell you, before you offer, I have already accepted Lord Whetherford's proposal."

Morgan sucked air into his lungs and savored the warmth spreading through his chest.

Giles calmly folded his linen napkin and placed it beside the china plate. "Forgive me, Miss Radbourn. I am afraid I forgot my manners. How thoughtless of me." He took a long breath. "A man's worth is his word. How noble you recognize and honor a man's word. And *you*, a woman."

The peacock was back. Her shoulders stiffened and she sat taller in her seat. Fire flared in her eyes while she kept a serene smile on her lips. Giles should have learned his lesson when he offered his protection. Kat's sharp wit and intelligence matched his own. And she had a delightful way of speaking her mind.

"Never say you believe one's word is for the male gender only, Your Grace."

"Ha. He would never say such a thing. Would you, *Your Grace*?" Morgan taunted in his direction.

Giles gave him a hard look, which did not bother him in the least.

Then facing her, Giles laughed. "You, my dear, are a delight. You stimulate a man's mind." He hoisted his goblet. "If you are set on marrying my friend here, may I propose a toast?"

It was unbelievable at how fast Giles had gone from Miss Radbourn's adversary to her champion. And if he kept smiling at her like that, Morgan was going to put a fist right in the middle of his cocky face.

Chapter 8

"Are you satisfied?" Morgan accused as soon as they were in the study.

"I thought I was quite charming." Giles calmly responded.

"Charming while you were drilling her." Morgan gritted through his teeth.

"Merely inquisitive."

"Hell, Giles. It was more than inquisitive," he threw over his shoulder as he strode to the liquor table.

Giles settled himself in one of the leather chairs. With an elbow propped on each chair-arm, he put his hands together and steepled his fingers.

Morgan studied his friend. "Well. What is going through that intrusive brain of yours?"

"She really is quite charming. After the enlightening story you told me, I did not expect her to be so appealing." Giles' voice held a trace of awe.

"I did try to tell you." Morgan pulled the glass knob from the top of the decanter.

"You know, Morgan, you can learn a lot about a person just by listening to them talk."

Despite his annoyance, Morgan relented when his friend frowned. "And what did you learn?"

"A diamond of the first water. Here is a lady of quality and breeding. I found her gracious. As well-mannered as any hostess of any well-respected home. A true lady in every definition of the word. It is obvious she has been reared with nobility. It is also evident having the finer things in life are second nature to her."

"Yet you behaved like a bloody interrogator in there."

"Of course. How else was I to get to know her?" Giles speared him with a glare. "I was acting in your best interest."

For a moment, Morgan wanted to pour the contents of the bottle on Giles' head. Regretfully, he did not. Instead, he picked up a second glass.

"Have you not wondered about her family? Did you not question if she were someone of the upper crust or just who her family could be? Perhaps, it may well be someone in Parliament?"

"Come now, Giles. She was in an alley without a chaperone." After handing Giles his drink, Morgan turned to the matching chair and lowered his large frame onto the worn leather.

"It is a possibility. It would be one hell of a bloody dilemma if you just happened to kidnap the relative of one of our friends."

Good God, what if it were someone they knew? This woman's family may not only have his hide, but they could be a formidable enemy. His self-assurance took a hard fall. Giles pointed out what he should have considered. "No, it never crossed my mind."

"What about this brother she spoke of? Where is he?" Giles asked.

"That's the first time I heard of him." Morgan wondered why she had not mentioned a brother. Well, hell. Why would she? Between his guilt and falling all over himself to make amends, she never had the chance.

"Why is he not here storming down your walls, demanding you release her? Why has he not come to rescue her? If she has a brother, where the devil is the bounder?"

"How would I know?" Morgan took a long swallow. He had not considered a raging brother, or anyone else defending her honor. Nor did he want to think about the possibility of coming to blows—or worse—with a member of her family.

"Yes, well. I still have to wonder why he has not come for her." Giles raised one booted foot to settle on his opposite knee. "Good God, Morgan! A bloody brother! If she were my sister, I'd have your head. After I cut off certain other parts of your anatomy."

Morgan silently agreed with him.

"Then there is the uncle. Thornton," Giles said.

"Thornton. Yes, I've heard the name. I believe it was in London."

"Thornton, is connected with Glenshire."

Morgan lowered his arm, all instincts on alert. "The devil you say."

"Come now. I know it was many years ago, but never say your memory is fading, old man."

Guardedly, Morgan searched his friend's face. "Refresh it for me."

Giles ambled to the sideboard to refill his drink. "The funds. The assistance. The mystery man who made the rescue for Glenshire possible. It was Albert Thornton, although that information was never made public." After filling his glass, he held the bottle out to Morgan in a questioning gesture. Morgan shook his head in reply. Giles returned the decanter to its rightful place, then resettled himself in his chair.

"I met the man once. Rotherford held a discreet meeting with a few members of parliament. Thornton was there. Afterward,

Rotherford told me it was Thornton who provided the means necessary for the mission to be successful."

"Where was I when this meeting took place?"

"You retired. Remember? You left the service and all your dark deeds behind."

Like ripping a scab off an old wound, vivid images rose haunting Morgan's thoughts. Tormenting exploits of his past actions. Dangerous endeavors and suicidal missions. Not for one moment did he regret leaving that life. And now he was the Earl of Whetherford. If he were to carry on the family name and honor his father's legacy, he had to move forward and consider his future—the future of Whetherford Manor. "You suppose *that* Thornton is *her* uncle?"

"Good God, I hope not." Giles tipped his glass for a hefty swallow.

Morgan frowned. "Would he remember you?"

Giles brow rose in reservation. "Of that there is no doubt. Beyond being near untouchable, his mind is sharp as a quill. There were other enlightening things about the man which made me wonder the depth of his involvement or the extent of his knowledge on other matters of fact. So, it's best to think the girl's relatives having the same name, is merely a coincidence."

"Anyway, I take her home in the morning," Morgan uttered. "Her family will be expecting us."

Sprawled in the chair, Giles studied the brandy that remained in his glass. "So, the next time we meet, you will be a married man?"

"If her relatives desire a hasty wedding." Morgan squared his shoulders. "It doesn't matter in the least to me." After all, he planned to marry someday. He needed a wife to provide a Whetherford heir.

"I would be worried about the brother."

An angry man would be expected. But an incensed, protective brother would be doubly grievous.

"Apparently, Miss Radbourn is not any more taken with the idea of marriage than you. Her words agree, but her eyes tell another story. She may very well put a dagger in your heart on your wedding night."

Morgan sighed as if the weight of the world rested solely on his shoulders and turned his eyes to the blue flames of the fire. His insides twisted to such an extent, a smarting ripped through his body. "I have wronged this woman. I am prepared to give her anything she wishes."

Giles seared him with a look. "Anything?" He set his tumbler on the oak table and leaned forward with his elbows on his knees giving Morgan his full attention. "I understood when you said you needed to come home and accept your duty. I understood when you said you were tired of the life we led. I too grew weary of the constant danger, even before my father died and left me a dukedom. I know you need to marry. But, be careful, my friend. Do not promise what you are not willing to give."

Kat stared at the massive structure of her uncle's country home. Her heart raced. Her anxious mind would not calm. How could she breathe a sigh of relief when her world was about to be turned upside down? Nothing she said had changed Whetherford's mind, and she didn't really want to be ruined. She should be excited and happy of her betrothal—instead of dreading the moment she must introduce him as her husband-to-be.

The carriage ride had been unbearable. They'd ridden in silence while Whetherford's gaze bore into her. She somehow managed to keep her breathing steady. His dark brown coat and trousers matched the dark scowl of his features. With his arms crossed and his legs stretched out, he'd appeared relaxed, yet he was no simpering lord. Not with bulging muscles and a body made of steel.

She spent most of the trip wondering how she might prevent the marriage of her forced engagement. Then there were the moments when she did not think of her upcoming wedding—she was compellingly aware of him.

Even sneaking peeks had been a trial to her composure. Her gaze returned more than once to the stray lock hanging over his furrowed brow. The blue-black strands beckoned a woman's fingers to caress their length. She could not remember ever wanting to run her fingers through a man's hair. The enthralling need to reach, to stroke . . . His smoldering gaze ensnared hers, making her jerk.

What had the blasted man been thinking? If he did not want to marry her, why did he offer? Whetherford's will was made of iron.

She had to try once more. Turning to him, she took a deep breath. "Please. I beg you to reconsider. This is not necessary."

His eyes narrowed. "How do you know your uncle—at this very minute—does not have a shotgun or a clergyman on hand?"

"You are being ridiculous."

He elevated that cocky brow. "Am I?"

The carriage stopped and a footman opened the door. She groaned in desolation.

Whetherford stepped out and extended his arm to assist her from the carriage. His hand covered hers, activating a leap in her pulse as they took the steps together. The front door already open, her uncle's butler bowed in greeting and took Whetherford's hat.

Instead of allowing the servant to assist her, Whetherford helped her with her redingote as if he had every right. And weren't they here to announce their betrothal—when she wanted nothing more than to kick the overbearing man out.

Come now. Did she really? He may be arrogant, but there were times when he simply took her breath. Like now. He stood too close. His tangy scent assaulted her senses. Nerves ran amuck. Clearly there was something wrong with her—wishing he had dispensed a real proposal, wishing this had been a love match.

But it was not.

His gentlemanly honor. He cared enough to set things right, to protect her reputation. Considering how she fought the idea every step of the way, there was no use considering such foolish notions now.

Aware of his gaze on her, she shoved her traitorous thoughts aside. Whetherford stood with his arm aloft, obviously waiting for her to place her hand on his sleeve. She stuck her nose in the air and marched forward.

"Katherine. Thank the good Lord!" Aunt Elizabeth opened her arms. Kat rushed across the room and straight into her aunt's warmth. Tears ran down her cheeks.

"There, there, child. You are home, at last. There, there." Aunt Elizabeth held her until her sobs quieted.

Uncle Albert took out his handkerchief and handed it to his wife. "You are home, safe and sound."

Her uncle's voice drew her to him. His caring arms enveloped her. She absorbed his warmth and comfort, while her aunt took the offered linen and dabbed at her own weeping eyes. Whetherford cleared his throat. For a moment, she'd forgotten him.

"Katherine."

Good Lord he'd used her Christian name. Whetherford's voice had the ring of authority, and indicated he would not be put off.

A wide range of emotions came over Uncle Albert's face. How in the world would she explain Lord Whetherford?

She kissed her uncle's cheek. "Uncle, this is Lord Whetherford. Lord Whetherford, this is my uncle, Lord Thornton and my aunt, Lady Thornton."

"Lord Thornton," Morgan said as he gave a slight bow. Then he turned to her aunt. "Lady Thornton."

"Thank you for bringing our niece home," Uncle Albert said. Kat watched as the two men studied each other, trying to distinguish the other's merit.

"Yes. Thank you, Lord Whetherford. We've been so worried." Aunt Elizabeth twisted the cloth between her fingers as she looked over at Kat. "Dear, are you all right?"

Seeing the worry in her aunt's face, Kat's heart cracked. She grabbed her small hands and squeezed in reassurance. "Aunt Liz, I am fine. Really I am."

She chewed on her bottom lip wondering if she should just blurt out she was to be married. Guilt-ridden, she imagined Aunt Liz sensing her need for confession. The anxious look in her aunt's eyes made Kat cringe in remorse, and at the same time made her want to rant at her *betrothed*.

"If you are sure, dear," her aunt said. Then she turned to Morgan and clapped her hands to her cheeks. "Please, Lord Whetherford. Forgive my manners. Come into the drawing room. I will ring for refreshment."

Kat wanted to put off the inevitable as long as possible. "Uh, Aunt. Uncle Albert, we have traveled a long way."

"Of course, my dear. Why don't you and Elizabeth go upstairs? I am sure you want to rest. Lord Whetherford and I have much to discuss."

This is not what she had in mind. Who knows what Whetherford would tell her uncle.

"Lord Thornton, I . . ." Whetherford started.

Oh my God! He could not be so cruel as to announce their engagement now? She loudly interrupted, "Maybe our guest should be shown his rooms. I am sure Lord Whetherford is also tired."

Whetherford's scowl was back and even darker. "Katherine, don't you want to tell them our news?"

The blasted man got the words out before she had a chance to stop him.

"What news?" Aunt Elizabeth's brow creased in anxious curiosity. "Katherine, what is it?"

Drat. And double drat. "Nothing Aunt. There is nothing to worry about." She glared at Whetherford.

"I should say not. Good news, in fact."

Good Lord, she had to shut him up. Kat looped her arm through her aunt's, trying to steer her to the stairs. "Uh, what Lord Whetherford means—"

"Katherine and I are engaged."

Chapter 9

Thornton ambled over to the majestic oak table and raised the lid to a leather box. Pulling out a pipe, he added tobacco. He looked over his shoulder. "My wife puts up with my vices. She countenances me having a puff of my pipe now and again. May I offer you a cigar?"

"No thank you," Morgan replied.

Thornton struck flint and held it over the top of his pipe. The flame bent down, crawled inside and danced up again while wafts of smoke curled into the air. "You don't smoke?"

"I prefer a cheroot at times, out of doors." Morgan studied Thornton as he calmly strode across the carpeted floor. His frame portrayed a man of confidence and power. He'd not given any indication of his thoughts to the scene in the parlor, where only moments ago, Morgan had bleated his betrothal like a bloody sheep. He could still see the shock on Katherine's and her aunt's face when he burst out *their news*. Bloody hell. If Katherine would have given him time to think, he would not have done that. But she'd been determined on getting him out of the room—the exasperating wench. Her relatives had needed to be told, and waiting would not have made it any easier. Being a man of action, he did not dawdle. She already had him frustrated as the very devil. He refused to drag his feet when it came to announcing his intentions—whether the female was willing or not.

And that is what got his gourd. The bloody woman did not want to marry him. The look that had come to her face could have sent his soul to hell.

Good God! He had a title. He had wealth. He was willing to correct his mistake. What the deuce did Katherine want? Blood?

"Not in the house?" Thornton's voice jolted from his tirade.

It took him a second to recover. "I like looking at the stars. Somehow, the combination of the two has an incredible calming effect on me." As a matter of fact, he would much rather be outside right now. Instead of standing here like a lad ready to receive a lecture.

Thornton gestured toward a decanter. "Care for a brandy?"

This is what is called going the long way around the barn to get to the door. Thornton had an objective, and he would take his damned sweet time getting there. Morgan was in no position to hurry the man. Guess he deserved the dressing down that was sure to come. Why hadn't Thornton been more outraged, or demanding?

"Forgive me," Morgan said. "But, I am a bit surprised you accepted me so easily into your home."

"You brought my niece back where she belongs." Thornton raised the bottle, silently offering the drink again.

"Yes, thank you." Morgan gave a slight nod of assent. He admired Thornton his calm reserve.

After handing Morgan a glass containing a generous measure of amber liquid, Thornton took his seat behind the large oak desk. He settled back in comfort, with the ease of a man ready to unwind. Morgan half expected the man to prop his feet upon the desk. His expression shuttered, he gazed toward the sun shining in the double set of windows.

"It took some doing to calm Elizabeth down, once she discovered her niece gone."

So, his tactic was to instill guilt, as if Morgan hadn't already dealt with self-reproach. Thornton, playing the card of throwing his wife's distress into the mix was obviously a maneuver to gain an edge.

"Lord Thornton. I am beyond remorse for what happened. Please accept my word as a gentleman, your niece was not harmed and I will do everything in my power to make it up to her. There is no excuse, but I ask that you allow me to explain." And what explanation could possibly excuse him from this debacle. If he had been the one in Thornton's chair, he would have tarred and feathered the scoundrel for taking his niece. Not invite him to his damned study for a cigar and brandy.

Thornton put the pipe to his lips. He inhaled, opened his mouth, and a whirl of smoke drifted into the air. With his gaze still on the gray cloud he replied, "Very well."

Thornton appeared relaxed and without a care. But Morgan had spent enough time honing his own skills to recognize a man on his guard. This man hid secrets. And he would not willingly divulge anything, unless he wanted to share. The shrewd expression on Thornton's face matched the man Giles had described. Morgan chose his words carefully.

"I came to London looking for a certain female. A lady who took something from me. She bears a remarkable likeness to Katherine." Since they were to be married, he supposed her uncle would think it suitable for Morgan to use her given name.

"I happened to be passing the alley when I heard a woman's cry. I hurried down the backstreet and found your niece. She had not been harmed," he added quickly. "But the two men objected to my interference. We fought. I won, but I was stabbed." Morgan rubbed his side. The wound still throbbed at times.

"I lost consciousness. When my men found me, they mistakenly assumed Katherine was the woman I had journeyed to London to locate." Morgan braced himself for Thornton's reaction to his next statement. "They took her to my home, Whetherford Manor."

One dubious brow rose in question—or intimidation. "They took her?"

"I should say brought her along. She stayed in a guest room." He did not add that she'd been locked up as a prisoner against her will.

With his elbow resting on the arm of the chair, Thornton held his pipe out to one side. Both brows arched, he stared down his nose. "I cannot imagine my niece going along with your men peacefully."

Morgan was not about to explain how correct her uncle was in his assumption. And he still had to deal with Jeremy. Wesley had taken pity on the scoundrel and hauled him off before Morgan was out of his sickbed. "I accept full responsibility for everything that happened, including the actions of my men. I know my duty as a gentleman. I have asked Katherine to be my wife."

"Your duty." Thornton studied his pipe for much too long. "And what did my niece say?"

Morgan resisted the urge to clear his throat. He was not used to sitting in the interrogation chair. Usually the roles were reversed. "She is my betrothed. With your permission, we will be married as soon as arrangements can be made."

"Well now," Thornton said as he leaned forward. "That is quite something."

Morgan frowned. "Sir?"

Thornton placed his pipe in a grey and white marble dish, then locked his gaze with Morgan. "You see, Whetherford. I imagine Katherine did not accept your proposal any more calmly than when your men spirited her away."

Blood and the devil!

What the hell was he supposed to say to that?

Thornton's eyes stayed sharp as his rigid features softened. "We love Katherine very much. But that girl gave us every grey hair we have on our heads."

Baffled by Thornton's calm attitude, Morgan kept his confusion hidden. Moments ticked by.

"Don't worry, my boy. I know who you are." Thornton reached for his pipe and fingered the stem. "If your reputation is to be believed, you are never distressed."

From years of habit, Morgan's instincts kicked in bringing every nerve in his body on alert. How fitting Katherine's uncle turned out to be the very man Giles had warned him about. *Good God he was that Thornton.* Giles had indicated this man was of considerable importance. Thornton had to be involved in controlled confidential circles if he knew anything of Morgan's exploits.

"And what do you know of my reputation?" Morgan dared to ask.

"I know you vanished years ago, and returned home only recently. I know you are an honorable man."

Evidently the man had learned—and now concealed—more information than he let on. And it didn't have anything to do with Whetherford Manor or the Earl. "My title does not make me honorable." At Thornton's steady gaze, Morgan added. "Although, I am an honorable man."

Thornton's lips lifted at the corners. "You may rest easy, it will not be necessary to announce an engagement."

Morgan checked to make sure his mouth did not hang open. "I beg your pardon?"

"You do not need to protect my niece. We kept her disappearance quiet. As far as the *ton* believes, Katherine was in the country with her friend, Viscountess Roxborough. No one would dare question the Viscount. Elizabeth and I retired to my country estate immediately to give credence to the tale."

Morgan took several moments to digest this information.

Not necessary?

He waited for the feeling of disappointment to fade. Marriage to Katherine would be no hardship. He could spend the rest of his life feasting his eyes on her beauty. Not to mention the thought of her in his bed. That idea was unwise for many reasons.

Morgan shook his head and found his tongue. "Astonishing how you managed to keep her absence a secret."

"The Viscount was accepting of the tale to appease his wife." Thornton lifted his pipe to his mouth, then after a long drawl, leaned his head back and sent a spiral of smoke to the ceiling. "His wife has been Katherine's confidant ever since my nephew brought my niece to us."

There was the mention of her brother again. Presenting a calmness he did not feel, Morgan braced one ankle over the opposite knee and casually asked, "Katherine's brother?"

Without giving away his thoughts, Thornton answered with a shrug. "Yes. Stephen prefers water to land. Anyway, you don't need to worry about him. He knows nothing of her disappearance."

Thank God for that!

"Since no one knows of her . . . indiscretion, and you have given your assurance my niece was in no way compromised, it is not necessary on your part as a gentleman, to enter into a marital arrangement."

Morgan was not sure if the weight on his chest had just lightened or grew heavier.

Indiscretion?

Compromised?

"My niece can be very stubborn. When she sets her mind on something, she is worse than a bull charging after a red flag. And in this instance, her emotions ruled her hasty actions. You see, her brother pondered heavily on her mind." Thornton took another puff on his pipe.

Morgan watched the gentle swirl of the white cloud, belying the tension in the room.

"Katherine has put off suitors for years. There has been more than one spurned swain offering marriage, I'm afraid." Thornton let out a deep sigh. "It's my fault. I agreed she would be allowed to choose her husband." Thornton put his pipe to the side, then he propped both arms on the large desk as his body leaned forward.

Now we were getting to the matter.

"I appreciate your integrity, Whetherford. But, she did not choose you."

Morgan blinked. Thornton surprised him. Again. The man had a way of commanding attention and getting his point across. Morgan could only imagine the sway Thornton had in Parliament.

"Your arrangement with my niece obviously developed because of your moral sense of obligation. Your willingness to save her reputation has earned my regard, and raised your character even higher in my esteem. But, you see, I want my niece to be happy."

Morgan focused on the words *even higher in my esteem*. "You are releasing me from my promise to marry Katherine?"

"Come now. You were forced on each other. Her disappearance has been kept quiet. There is no threat to her, and no need for you to forfeit your freedom due to her willful action—although quite understandable."

Willful action?

"Are you sure Katherine will agree to rescinding my offer? I should not want her to feel slighted." Katherine had voiced her disagreement quite strongly. *Hell.* She was still trying to talk him out of the bloody proposal as the carriage pulled up to Thornton's front door.

Thornton's brow rose in disdain. "We *are* talking about my niece."

Apparently, he knew his niece well. Morgan suspected she would be quite pleased with this outcome.

He drained the brandy from his glass. "Very well. If Katherine agrees, we will not announce an engagement."

Thornton started to rise. "Thought you'd . . ."

"However," Morgan's fingers tightened on his glass. He weighed his options as Thornton slowly settled himself back in his chair. "There is another matter I would like to discuss."

Thornton's face darkened, reminding Morgan that the man could be a notable enemy. One he would rather not engage. "Does this involve Katherine?"

"No sir. It does not."

Although cautious, Thornton did not give his emotions away.

"You seem to know me—or should I say *of* me. The Duke of Nethersall is a close friend."

Thornton eyes flared with speculation. His lips compressed as he leaned back in his chair, distancing himself. "Ahh. I understand. The duke told you of our meeting."

I must be getting soft. This habit Thornton had of shocking him assaulted his certainty. Being put off guard was more than he could swallow. Thornton had again taken control of their conversation. Morgan narrowed his eyes and pressed his lips in a tight line. "He mentioned it."

"Do you think I would let a man in close proximity to my niece, let alone allow him to walk into my home, without learning every detail of his history?" Thornton asked with complete ease.

This grew more interesting by the moment. He could not imagine how Thornton could be any more on guard than he was now.

"That explains your calm manner when I delivered Katherine home. It also explains why you are prepared to quash a marriage proposal, and why you are willing to accept my word. What did you mean by 'Katherine's willful act was understandable?'" Morgan would not make the mistake of underestimating Thornton. But he believed the man would not act without listening and carefully exploring his options.

Thornton clasped his hands, placing them in the center of his desk. "Katherine is quite close to her brother. He captains a ship. Owns two more. He has been absent for some time. She must have overheard me telling my wife of Captain Danvers' ship docking. The captain made a few inquiries for me, asked around about Stephen, that sort of thing. Katherine has a mind of her own. That is why I did not tell her. I knew she might try to go to the docks for any information on her brother. Which is exactly what she did. I later discovered she was on her way to Captain Danvers' ship which coincided with the night you happened upon her."

"You mentioned my offer to save her reputation earned your regard. You know the duke and I were involved in undercover operations. Some of them were not necessarily noble."

With a slight turn of his head, Thornton's gaze pierced his own. "I know you risked your life to save others."

No more needed to be said on the subject. Obviously, the man knew everything. "With respect, Lord Thornton, it puzzles me how you came by your information, for the duke would not have been your source."

Thornton stood. His desk was massive, but Thornton dwarfed the oak when he braced his weight on his forearms and leaned forward. "I grasp your curiosity. You prefer to leave your dark past behind, hmm? More prudent not to probe secrets best left buried. Let's just say I trust you because those I know gave me assurances. And leave it at that."

Chapter 10

On her second morning home, Kat stood in front of her gold framed mirror reflecting on her whirlwind engagement. As exhausted as she was, she'd been unable to sleep. For a tall, brooding man with dark penetrating eyes invaded her thoughts.

The door to her bedchamber flew open and Charity came running in with her skirts flying about. She threw her arms around Kat, weeping in relief. "Thank, God! I feared for your life!"

Kat returned her hug like a drowning victim who had been thrown a survival line. She knew her best friend would come when she found out Kat was home.

With a tearful sniff, Charity leaned back. "Are you alright? I was so worried. Tell me quickly before I collapse from sheer apprehension."

Kat had no time to answer before her friend rattled on.

"Never do that again, worry me so. You have been gone for weeks. No one could find you. Everyone assumed I knew where you were and was keeping your secret. Once they realized I had no idea, things around here really heated up. I thought your uncle was ready to sport one's canvas. Your poor aunt looked done to a cow's thumb. Everyone had to keep your disappearance a secret until we determined if you'd been kidnapped, held for ransom, or . . . Oh, Kat. It was too horrible to think you'd been taken." Charity's nerves always did make her a chatterbox.

Kat tried to reassure her. Especially after seeing Charity's increasing waistline. Kat's mind spun from trying to absorb the information that her friend was expecting another child. "I'm sorry you had to go through that. I am home now, and as you can see, I'm fine. You look ready to fall on your feet. Come. Sit." She led Charity to the wide box beneath her window. With a thick cushion and plump pillows, it was Kat's favorite place to daydream while in her chamber.

Charity pulled at her gloves. "Just a little short of breath from running up the stairs." She unpinned her hat and tossed them both upon the counterpane. "Do not mention this to Byron. He watches me like a hawk. He thinks I should stay in bed with my feet up like a good little-mother-to-be."

Mischievous as a young girl, Charity had grown into an elegant woman. She lived in comfort and had adjusted to life as a viscountess in a short time. Her husband believed his job was to sort out the problems of the world, and his wife was to do nothing more than be beautiful. He spoiled her, pampered her. He had an abundance of servants to take care of the household and he'd hired a governess to care for their son.

"He let you out of the house?" Kat said, half-teasing.

"Byron is overprotective. You would not believe the things I have to do to get around him." Charity waved her hand as though it were more of an inconvenience rather than any real aggravation.

Kat smiled, knowing the viscount was unquestionably and most assuredly wrapped around his wife's little finger. "Your cheeks are glowing. How are things with little Ethan?"

"He thinks his mama is getting fat." Charity patted her belly.

"Wait a few months." Kat laughed.

Charity's face wrinkled in concern. "I have really been worried. When your uncle came to Byron and asked for his help, I nearly swooned. Where have you been? Tell me exactly what happened."

"You never swoon." Kat pointed out as she sat beside her friend. "I hardly recognize the girl who used to instigate our adventures. You've turned into an old married lady."

"Pishaw. Old—never. Married—very." Charity put a finger to her chin, tilted her head just so and studied Kat closely. Too closely. "If you want to change the subject ... there's something you're hiding. Well, do not think you will hide it from me."

Her friend knew her too well. Many times, they'd been involved in hair-brained escapades. But nothing like the unbelievable incident which turned her life upside down; the fateful night and the disastrous *mistake* which started this bizarre chain of events.

Charity's interrogating features fell away, quickly replaced with anxious concern. "We used to talk and tell each other everything. Surely, that has not changed?"

No. They had always shared everything. "Thank you for covering for me."

Charity reached over and squeezed Kat's hands. "What else would I do?"

Loyal to a fault, her friend's voice, so soft and so full of warmth, Kat wanted to confess all. Share her burden. Not only the tangible events, but her feelings—the ones she should not have. Feelings for a man who had offered his name in protection. A man who plagued her thoughts like a ghastly disease. Once introduced, the infection spread slowly and with surety.

"I decided to find Captain Danvers."

"I figured that much out for myself. I know something happened besides the obvious. You disappear and the dashing Lord

Whetherford brings you home, which I find very interesting." Charity's eyes possessed a teasing sparkle. "Why didn't you take someone with you? You know better than to make such a mistake."

"A mistake." *A word which continued to rear its ugly head.*

"One that got you kidnapped," Charity added.

And got me engaged.

Kat remained silent while she thought about her abduction. And the mysterious Lord Whetherford. Her lids fluttered closed long enough for her to imagine dark probing eyes. A little thrill of excitement tingled down her spine.

"Are you sure you're all right? Let me see your eyes." A spark of recognition lit Charity's face while her intense gaze searched for secrets.

"Good grief." Kat threw her hands up and rose from the bench, bounding across the floor. "I took Alice and she turned into a petrified mouse."

"Alice?"

Kat spun on slippered feet and paced in the opposite direction, moving her hands as she spoke. "You know I wanted to speak with Captain Danvers. Well, I took Alice with me and she panicked and I sent her home."

"You should have returned with her. I told you I would go with you."

"With your protective husband? Anyway, I would have been fine if those two drunkards had not accosted me."

Charity shrieked. "Two? Oh, good Lord." She waved her hand in front of her face as if she had the vapors.

Kat swallowed her remembered fear from when the two men forced her deeper into the shadows of that bleak alley, then quickly brushed it off. "They did not hurt me. My rescuer didn't give them a chance."

Giving a suspicious glare, Charity asked, "Lord Whetherford?"

"Yes." When Uncle Albert sent word to the Viscount, he must have included Lord Whetherford's name in the missive. Again, his image sprang to mind. Tall, broad shoulders, and black waves surrounding his tanned face. Gleaming dark eyes and his mouth lifting in a slant on one side of his full lips.

Maybe it would be easier to forget him if he did not scourge her thoughts every moment.

"He was quite dashing. He came to my rescue like a knight in armor without his steed. He told the drunkards to let me go. When they refused, he fought them."

Charity gasped. "He fought them?"

"He was fierce. And fast. One minute he stood there with the look of the devil, and the next, the men were on the ground. One of the brutes stabbed him. I shouted a warning but it was too late. And still he fought off his attacker. Then he fell to the ground, and I knew he was badly hurt."

Kat shuddered, remembering the blood on her hands. Blood everywhere. So much blood.

Charity's hand landing on her shoulder startled her back to the present.

She took a deep breath and started pacing again. "His men found me leaning over his body. They scared me and I ran. But they caught me, and . . ." She decided to leave out the part about the punch to her face.

"They what? For crying out loud. What?"

Fury embraced her as gripping as when she woke and found herself locked in a strange room. Vulnerable, but not help-less. She whirled around in anger. "They took me to Whetherford Manor and kept me prisoner." Her hands fisted, knuckles white. Blood rushed to her face. "Lord Whetherford was unconscious for days and they kept me locked in a room."

"Heavens above! How cruel. How awful for you. How did you survive?"

"Quite well, actually. Until Lord Whetherford recovered and told me I was a mistake."

Charity's mouth hung open, but nothing came out.

"Stunned speechless?" Kat asked. "So was I."

Eyes blazing, Charity rose. "Hold on a moment. I think you left something out along the way."

Kat shrugged. "As it turned out, they thought I was someone else."

Emotions flittered across Charity's face. Bewilderment, uncertainty, irritation, and then anger. "Someone else? They would have imprisoned this other person? Who are these criminals? And they are associated with Lord Whetherford?" Charity appeared as frustrated as Kat had been when she'd reasoned it out. "I don't believe it. Who does he think he is? A lord simply does not kidnap a woman and lock her up. I don't care if it was his men. It is not done. They kept you a prisoner? What did they feed you? Bread and water? All this time we waited and fretted. We were right to worry. That horrid, horrid man. What did he do to you? He restrained you for weeks. I cannot believe a titled Lord held you in captivity. Against your will. Wait until your uncle hears of this. Wait until I tell my husband."

"Stop!" Kat shuddered to think what would happen if her family learned those details. The last thing she wanted was a confrontation between her uncle, Lord Whetherford and Byron. "I told you, Lord Whetherford's men thought I was someone else."

Bolted from her harangue, Charity stared with big rounded eyes. "That is no excuse. It simply means they would have apprehended some other poor woman and locked her up."

Kat scowled and crossed her arms over her chest. "Do you want to hear the rest of my story or not?"

Charity sealed her lips in a grim line—for all of two ticks of a clock. "Did you believe him? Do you have a twin out there somewhere?"

"Supposedly we have the same *lustrous red hair*." Kat twined a curl around her finger.

More lines crossed Charity's brow. "No one has the same shade of red as you."

"Must be very close. The color of my hair is why they grabbed me."

Charity flounced over to the bed. "I do not like hearing how they seized you."

"How do you think I felt?" Kat pivoted waving her hands in the air. "Anyway, once Lord Whetherford explained everything . . ."

"Explained?" Charity's stunned expression turned to annoyance. "What reason could he possibly . . ."

Kat continued, "It was already too late. Besides, there was nothing I could do."

Charity's chest rose and fell in exasperation. "Well there certainly is something we can do now." She grabbed her hat, flounced off the bed, and sailed to the door.

"Wait!"

Charity hesitated long enough to secure her bonnet. "Lord Whetherford will deal with my husband."

"There's no need," Kat rushed on. "He insisted on offering for me."

If her intention was to shock Charity again, she managed. After several moments, Charity's shock eased to acceptance. "Well, why didn't you say so?"

"Lord Whetherford decided—*he* decided, mind you—we would marry."

"Please do not tell me you refused him?"

"Despite the fact that he is exceedingly handsome, and not at all an ogre, he is an aristocrat. An English nobleman. He became an overbearing, pompous villain when he announced his decision—without my acknowledgement or consent. You have no idea how relieved I was when he broke the engagement."

"He broke . . . I need to sit down." Charity returned to the window-box-seat.

"It was not a real betrothal," Kat hurried to explain. "But he did make an announcement to my aunt and uncle."

"He . . . never mind. Continue."

"Oh, he had every intention of marrying me. He convinced me my reputation would be ruined, so I reluctantly agreed."

"Reluctantly?"

Kat took a deep breath. "He did not want to marry me anymore than I wanted to marry him. Your falsehood saved me from a gruesome fate."

"Hmmm," Charity voiced. "Come here."

Kat joined her on the window seat. Charity took her hands and squeezed her fingers in empathy. Her eyes squinted while, once again, she tried to read Kat's thoughts. "Are you sure? Oh, I know he did an honorable thing, but his proposal endangered your freedom. You find him attractive, you cannot tell me otherwise. I think something else happened."

Kat remained silent.

"What a ferocious scowl. You will get wrinkles." Charity's voice lowered to a soft hush. "What is it you're not telling me?"

Against her will, Kat felt her face flame. She tried hard not to blink.

Moments ticked by. She swallowed.

"His eyes could be dark as storm clouds or bright as the stars shining in a night sky. Confidence and strength encircled every inch of him, from his thick black curls right down to his shining black hessians. He had an . . . almost dangerous aura. Threatening—yet compelling." Even now, his image made her weak in the knees. "I cannot explain it. It seemed as if I was spellbound. Mesmerized."

"Ah, I understand," Charity nodded.

Kat wondered how, for she had no idea why her emotions were at sixes and sevens. She had finally managed to meet a man who interested her. Of course, she had been forced into his presence, and nearly forced to wed. It wasn't like he had noticed her and approached her out of any attraction. How could he possibly have a fondness for her after such a calamity?

"He offered his name to protect my reputation and crush any scandal." She turned away and her voice rose in volume. "If it had been an earnest proposal, a real engagement . . ."

"Do I sense a touch of infatuation?"

Pulling her hands free, Kat stood. She padded to the balcony door and stared through the lace curtain, examining her emotions. She could not identify her feelings. Enchantment? Attraction? Infatuation?

Something pulled her. Allured her. She spoke her thoughts aloud.

"It's too new."

Chapter 11

Heat from the flames of the roaring fire enveloped the parlor, chasing away the morning chill. Yet the heat in the room could not reach inside to warm the alcove of Kat's soul. Even though her eyes glimpsed the shining sun and the cloudless blue sky, she could not see beyond her own fearful imaginings.

Not only had her brother plagued her mind, now the dark lord entered her every waking thought. What would it be like to have Whetherford for her husband? Her skin tingled at the idea. If only she had met him in a ballroom. If only his proposal had been from the heart and not one of duty. If only . . .

Guilt assailed her. How could she entertain such thoughts when her brother was missing?

"Aunt Elizabeth, why hasn't he come? You know Stephen would never stay away from me this long. Does Uncle Albert think something happened to him?"

Elizabeth set down her embroidery and removed the spectacles from her nose. "You need to stop worrying." Her gentle voice always soothed. "As your uncle said, Stephen was traveling a little farther this time. Most likely, he has been delayed."

Kat's stomach fisted into a knot and she could barely speak for the lump clogging her throat. "But it's been two years. And if Uncle has Captain Danvers searching, he must be worried too? Stephen's ship may be lost. What if he's hurt?"

"Perhaps there might be another reason." Even though her aunt tried to hide it, the tension in her voice displayed her unease. "Stephen is a handsome man and you know he is getting on in years, my dear. He cannot sail the seas forever. It is possible . . . he may have met a young woman he cares for. One day he will have a family and . . ."

Kat groaned, interrupting her aunt, "Oh, Aunt Liz, please do not bring my spinsterhood up again."

Elizabeth sniffed and cocked her head at an angle. "I was speaking of *your brother.*"

"You know the focus would have turned to me, as it always does." This was one of their sore topics. Aunt Liz hinted every chance she got that Kat should be thinking about marriage. Even though this woman was her aunt, like any parent, she wanted grandchildren. Kat rolled her eyes and flung up her hands. "You continue to beat a dead horse. You are once again pointing an accusing finger at me."

Aunt Elizabeth's eyes grew round and her hand flew to her chest.

Instantly ashamed, Kat bit her lower lip. Usually a brow-beating was all it took to coerce her into behaving properly. Her temper, and this repeatedly tiring matter of her state of matrimony had Kat's tongue issuing words out of her mouth before her reasoning could stop them.

"I'm sorry, Aunt Elizabeth." Why couldn't she understand? "I am not ready." They'd had this discussion many times before. Only this time Kat seemed to be convincing herself. She rather liked the idea of marriage to Lord Whetherford. But she wanted to marry for love., and Kat was not about to tell her aunt that. How foolish she would look. "I want to experience the world. I want to be free to travel as my brother has."

"A lady does not have the same freedom as a man. You have become such a lovely young woman. Yet you turn down every suitor who asks for your hand. Including Lord Whetherford."

Why did she have to include *him*?

Kat went to her aunt. Kneeling down, she placed her hands on the arm of the cushioned chair.

A soft, gentle, loving look flared in her aunt's eyes. "You need a life of your own, dear. A home, children . . ."

More emotions filled her gaze. Love, yearning, longing for Kat's happiness. Sadness for the loss of Kat's mother and how proud her mother would be of the young woman Kat had grown to be. Sighing, she covered Elizabeth's hands with her own.

"I have not met anyone who I am attracted to, let alone someone I might want to be with for the rest of my life."

Liar.

The audacity of Lord Whetherford, taking charge, expecting her to follow him like a lost lamb. Kat changed the direction of her thoughts. "I know you think at three and twenty I should be married with a brood of children. Everyone thinks I am past a marriageable age. I guess you think I should have held Lord Whetherford's proposal."

Elizabeth's face took on an inquiring look, as though she waited for Kat to suddenly admit her feelings. "You did seem eager to accept his proffer to beg off."

Several contradicting emotions assaulted Kat at once. Aunt Liz knew her too well.

"Come sit, my child." She patted the cushion beside her.

Kat climbed up from her squatting position to sit beside her aunt. Warmth enveloped her as Aunt Liz's slim fingers grasped her own.

"Katherine dear, it would make your uncle and me very happy to see you wed. Albert has agreed he will not force you to marry someone not of your choosing. And he saved you from a forced marriage to the Earl. I must admit we were rather excited when your handsome Lord Whetherford brought you home and said he was your betrothed."

"He is not my handsome Lord Whetherford."

Elizabeth arched her brow in mock surprise. "You do not think he is handsome, dear?"

"You know what I mean."

A sparkle came to her aunt's eyes. "Of course. Even in my day, I would have swooned for such a specimen of a man to show interest in me." She patted Kat's hand. "Don't tell your uncle, dear."

Kat chuckled. "Why you wily, shrewd . . ." at her aunt's vaulted brow, she quickly altered her words, "uh, clever, sweet, dear woman."

"Thank you. Now. I believe you are waiting for something that sets one man apart from all the others."

A face made of granite, until it softened when his gaze raked down her body. Blue-black strands beckoning a woman's fingers to caress their silken length. Full lips, slightly parted, that made her mouth go dry.

Dark. Powerful.

He is the most mysterious man I have ever seen.

When she noticed her aunt's sharp look, she swallowed hard, glad this woman could not read her thoughts.

"Albert and I have been married for thirty years and I feel blessed to have every single one. With the right man, you can have that too."

"Do you really think I will find a special someone?" Had she already? Whetherford offered for her hand. But, he'd been put in a position where his nobility and honor dictated his actions. No sentiment had been involved. He had not been looking for Kat when he found her. What a crazy idea, thinking Lord Whetherford may possibly care for her, especially after she snubbed his offer of marriage.

What was this other woman to him? He said she stole from him, but what kind of relationship did they have before she fled? Surely, he had feelings for her if he'd been so consumed with finding her. Had she been his lover? Why did the thought bring a pressure unknown to Kat's chest?

"Of course, you will, dear." Elizabeth cupped Kat's face with gentle hands. "Darling, I just want you to be happy."

"Aunt Liz, I am happy," she hastened to reassure her. After a crushing hug, she whispered, "I love you so much."

With unshed tears in her voice, Aunt Elizabeth replied, "I love you too, my dear. Albert and I are so glad you came to live with us."

"So am I, Aunt Liz. So am I."

"Now, go dry your eyes. And take a nap. You don't want to appear at the ball tonight with puffy eyes and a red nose."

Morgan handed his hat and overcoat to the doorman. He could not believe he'd hied off to London in search of Katherine. One minute he avowed to banish her from his mind and the next he possessed the fanatical urge to see her. As he entered the crowded ballroom, dancers floated past in a twirling blur of motion. He looked for a way around the mass of chattering young maids—some corner where he might view the entire room without having to converse with fluttering feather-headed girls and husband-hunting mamas.

Before he reached a place of refuge, Lady Farsdown bore down on him. He allowed himself a final glance for Katherine then he greeted the hostess of this fine gathering.

"Lord Whetherford. How dapper you look." He wore a new suit of clothes his tailor had advised was the latest gentlemen's fashion.

"Good evening, Lady Farsdown." He gave a formal half-bow.

"You do your parents proud. Please accept my sincere empathy."

He hated balls and he hated pity. Since he had inherited the earldom, he had to appear in public. And he knew he'd have to deal with commiserations as well. "Thank you. Such a lovely affair."

Her smile equaled the illuminations reflecting from the chandeliers. "I am pleased you were able to attend. Your presence has been missed. It is good to know Whetherford Manor has an earl again."

"Hello, Whetherford," A clear-cut voice came from behind.

Aha. If he's here, she is here.

Straightening, Morgan swiveled toward the masculine voice.

"Good to see you, my boy," Thornton said.

"Lord Thornton." Turning his gaze to the woman beside him, Morgan bent from the waist. "Lady Thornton."

"Back in London so soon?" Thornton asked.

"I have business demanding my attention." He did not add their niece was the demanding business that brought him back so speedily. The lovely redhead played havoc with his mind. He could not get any work done for thinking about her day after day. What was wrong with him? She was just a woman. His damned guilt must have him pining after her.

Pining? Surely not! Katherine had charmed him. With those mesmerizing green eyes.

"Lord Whetherford, we are delighted to see you," Katherine's aunt presented her hand.

He smiled at the elder woman. "May I say you are quite fetching, madam." As pink flooded her cheeks, he regarded Thornton. "I see you also have returned to London."

"My wife and Katherine desired to finish the season."

Morgan mentally groaned at the mention of desire. Once again, his gaze searched the ballroom, and found her. His throat went dry. His chest tightened. His lungs constricted. Yet he indulged himself, admiring her from afar. As expected, a collection of followers surrounded Katherine. Laughter echoed from those standing in her circle. He marveled at her regal beauty as one gent took her hand and led her to the dance floor.

Morgan's gut clenched while one after another claimed the woman who was becoming his obsession.

An impeccably dressed swain swirled her about right in front of him, the damned man amazingly light on his feet. He swore a cloud of her fresh fountain scent lingered behind, wafting to his nose, teasing his senses. Her partner had access to the ripe curves that lay hidden beneath the gown clinging to her shoulders and falling in an elegant sweep to the floor. A sudden jolt of envy robbed him of his breath.

Morgan weaved his way through the throng of dancers.

Katherine's heart gave a leap in rhythm, which caused her to miss a step. *What in the world is he doing here?* His strapping form stood taller, above the dancing couples, his breathtaking masculinity unmatched by any other man in the ballroom. Sweet Lord. How her eyes had craved the sight of him. Before, he had looked dark and rugged in his handsomeness. Tonight, he appeared more dashing in his fitted trousers of charcoal gray and a waistcoat of silver brocade with a white cravat and black coat for the occasion.

With great strength, she tore her gaze away.

Her mind reeled. For three long weeks, she'd fought her attraction to Lord Whetherford. Through hours of darkness, she'd been tormented by his handsome image. After his and her uncle's meeting, he had taken himself away fast enough. Without a backward glance, not even a word of goodbye. She loathed the man, she really did.

She accepted another dance partner and intended keeping her focus on the steps. But her eyes strayed to him again, and again. Another dance ended and Kat gave a heart-felt sigh. The best way to keep her partner from stepping on her toes would be to send him for a glass of punch. Then she could dash over to Aunt Liz—like a lady, of course.

"Good evening."

Katherine stiffened. *Drat.* Just the sound of his vibrating tone had her insides churning. Heat flooded her face. *Great. Right when she thought she had finally managed to strike him from her mind.*

Who was she kidding?

Her dance partner seemed none too happy. "Hello, Whetherford. Didn't know you were in London."

"Gainsford." Lord Whetherford nodded to the man standing beside her.

Gainsford tilted his head toward her. "May I introduce . . ."

"I already know Lord Whetherford." Kat gritted through tight lips. Her gaze shifted and lingered for a lengthy moment. Black waves curled around his face with an unruly lock fallen forward over his brow. Eyes dark as midnight heating her body to her very soul. Remarkably wide shoulders, a virile physique that roused a yearning within her. Kat took a deep breath, hating her giddy reaction.

Gainsford did not hide his surprise as he looked from one to the other. "Ahem."

Kat resisted chewing her lip between her teeth.

"Hello again, Miss Radbourn. May I have this dance?" Whetherford kept his voice light, but his eyes threatened the man standing beside her.

Nonsense. Just because she had dreamed of him did not mean he had given her the least bit of thought.

Gainsford touched two fingers to his brow in a casual salute, and took his leave. Kat widened her eyes in surprise. Whetherford's gaze followed only a moment before he offered her his arm. Kat placed her hand on the curve of his elbow and he led her to the floor.

She placed her fingers lightly on Morgan's shoulder. "You scared my partner away."

Drawing her closer, his arm locked about her waist. A soapy scent of pure masculinity assailed her nostrils. Her head spun—and not because he swept her around the floor in a circle. Ever since she noticed him standing at the end of the ballroom, her breathing had grown labored. Now that she was in his arms, she was increasingly more aware of him.

From beneath her lashes, Kat weathered him a glance. The man was maddeningly attractive. She struggled to keep from smoothing the unrestrained curl from his brow. He stared, causing a wave of heat, streaming from her breasts to roast her face. She dropped her head hoping he would not notice her flush.

"May I say you look exceptionally lovely this evening." His voice sent pangs of anticipation along her senses.

She glanced at him and wished she hadn't. Black eyes seared her. Another eruption of heat exploded in her chest. Goodness it was hot in here. She managed to reply, "Thank you."

She wrestled with her sanity, mentally knocking some sense back into her head. He seemed too perfect. Not considering the fact his men had kidnapped her, and his dominating arrogance telling her—not asking—they would be married.

As the music ended, Whetherford guided her toward the open French doors. Kat considered her options. If she went with him, others would see. She'd already been in one compromising situation, even if she had been saved by her uncle. It wasn't that Whetherford would be a bad choice for a husband—she had not been allowed to choose. He had forced the decision upon her. The idea of marriage to the lord had not been so appealing when he had done so simply to save her reputation.

Before she thought further, she found herself on the patio with a gentle breeze caressing her face. A three-quarter moon shown above—a moon for sweethearts. Capturing her hand within his, he led her down a set of stone steps. Curiosity made her follow without argument. Sluices of light flickered from lit torches along the path. Couples strolled in every direction. Quite a few with their heads together, giggles floating in the air mixed with hushed whispers.

Kat inclined her nose upward. "Lord Whetherford. Do you not worry you may find yourself forced to offer for me, yet again?"

She felt more than heard his sudden indrawn breath. He stopped, causing her to stop as well. "I was not forced."

"How can you say that? Of course, you were."

"Miss Radbourn. I have never been *forced* to do anything in my life."

Kat swallowed. Then why had he offered his protection. Could it be he might actually care? Impossible. "You did not know me. You'd never met me before that night. You had no interest in me whatsoever."

His gaze intensified, and he stepped even closer. "No interest?"

If she thought her breathing strained before, it was nothing compared to the desperate need for air now. The way his eyes swept over her left Kat feeling as if she'd just been stripped of her gown. His gaze lingered on her breasts, arousing a burning within her bosom.

She opened her mouth to speak, her voice less than steady. "What . . . what would a man of your station possibly want with me?"

Whetherford's head lowered ever so slowly—closer, closer. Her lips parted. Her eyes drifted closed. Suddenly, his lips pressed against hers. She stilled, more from curiosity than from shock. Warmth flooded her entire being. She leaned into his embrace. His arms enveloped her and he slanted his face across hers. Pressure, moistness swept across her mouth.

His tongue.

Fire leaped in her belly.

His groan jerked her back to reality.

Good Lord. She had lost her wits. Kat pushed out of his arms. "Lord Whetherford. You forget yourself."

He sighed and stepped away, then beamed a smile of pure satisfaction.

She wanted to slap his face. She stomped her foot instead. "How dare you."

The smile immediately left his face. "You seemed to enjoy it well enough."

"My curiosity got the better of me. I did not like it at all."

"The devil you say." He grabbed her arms and molded her to his chest.

Kat lost all thought. She went limp in his arms, and an instant later she was kissing him back. His tongue teased her lips open. She gasped in pleasure at the fierce stroking as it laved and danced around in her mouth. Heat flowed through her body, so hot, her bones melted. When her lungs were near to bursting, he finally ended the kiss.

It took a moment for the fog to lift and her senses to return. Lord Whetherford came into focus and his hands were the only thing holding her up. Then she saw his grin. That cocky, swaggering, full-of-one's-self grin. Embarrassed and furious, her impulsive nature took over. She struck out.

The slap cracked—sounding like thunder to her ears. The shock on his face matched the astonishment she felt. She had actually hit him.

Whetherford's jaw twitched. His eyes flared. His hands fisted, opened, and then fisted again. The icy glitter in his glare set her back on her heels. Fearing she'd gone too far, she grabbed the hem of her gown and fled.

Chapter 12

Morgan slammed the front door of his London townhouse so hard the walls shook. He charged through the entryway and sprinted up the steps, two at a time.

"What the devil!" A voice roared from below.

He halted in his tracks. Looking over his shoulder, he stared below. A tall form appeared from the receiving room.

"What the hell are you doing here?" Morgan bellowed.

Wesley shoved his hair out of his face. He'd clearly been roused from slumber. "I did not anticipate a warm welcome, but neither did I expect to be thrown out."

Altering his course, Morgan descended the stairs at a much slower pace, his dark mood evident in every footstep echoing on the stairs. He wondered if his face showed the infuriating anger he felt. This evening was just getting better and better. He strode past Wesley without another word.

Wesley gave a bark of laughter. "She must have turned you down."

Morgan swung around on sharpened reflexes. "What?"

Wesley quickly held up his hands. "Hold on. I figured some light-skirt turned you down. There's a first time for everyone. Including you."

"Devil take you." Turning on his heel, Morgan advanced to the cabinet that housed the port. Bending, he opened the cabinet door and pulled out a bottle of whiskey.

"Planning on sharing that?" Wesley had the uncanny habit of presenting good humor, which this evening irritated Morgan beyond all reasoning.

"Sit down. If you need to open your mouth, do it only to absorb liquid."

"I'm all ears." Wesley reclined in the soft upholstery looking like a cat ready to receive a full bowl of cream.

Morgan placed two glasses on the table and popped the cork in the bottle. He poured a hefty amount in one, lifted it and downed the burning liquid in one swallow. The glass landed with a smack. He swiped his mouth with the sleeve of his arm, then poured again, filling the glass once more and then splashed whiskey into the second tumbler. This time, he handed one to Wesley before draining the contents of his.

"Although you are hospitable with your brandy, your welcoming skills are lacking. Must have been some thrashing to put that thundercloud on your face."

If he only knew.

Morgan filled his glass a third time. He strode to the opposite chair and lowered his frame.

"Why are you here?"

"A letter came from my father. When I arrived, he was still in Parliament. So, I came here looking for you."

"At this late hour?"

"I will admit I fell asleep. I'd had a long ride. Fatigued more than I realized, I suppose."

"Do you know why your father sent for you?"

"Perhaps another assignment. I've been lax these past few weeks." Wesley swirled the liquid in his glass. "Did you find her?"

Morgan stared into the honey colored liquid. *Her?* He rubbed the side of his cheek. The damned wildcat? "Yes. But not the one you think."

Wesley frowned and lowered his snifter. "Care to explain?"

"Not Juliana."

"Then who the hell are we talking about?"

Moments ticked by while Morgan stared into luminous amber liquid. Katherine, resplendent in the moonlight. Red waves shimmering under the stars. Her beauty pulled him into her spell. He could no more control his actions than the desire that flamed between them. Green eyes dazzled with passion. Gleamed with horror when she had struck him. He lifted his hand to his face.

"The last time I saw that thunderous look on your face, a cock-sure redhead made a cake of you. Right after you'd made a mull of abducting her.

Morgan's gaze shot up. The tightening of his jaw made his teeth grind together. He loosened the hold on his glass before it shattered within his fingers. "I did not abduct her."

"Oh, forgive me. I thought the girl was held hostage at *your* home? Surely you cannot be faulted for that."

"Rot it, Wesley."

"Then tell me, my good man, that you have not done something just as outlandish?"

Morgan's face heated. He quickly upturned the tumbler and emptied its contents.

"By gum, it's worse than I realized. Snap out of it, man. I've never seen you lose your head."

"I have lost my bloody mind." Morgan sprung from his chair.

"Can we back up a bit here?" Wesley asked. "I think you'd better tell me what happened."

"Tell you what?" Morgan's frustration made him shout. "What a fool I am? Why I've lost all reason? Damned if I know." The damned whiskey was not helping. Not yet anyway.

Wesley held his glass for Morgan to refill. Once done, Morgan carried the bottle and settled back in his chair, feet out, boots crossed at the ankles.

"How, after years of avoiding emotion, could I have allowed sentiment to enter my brain? I came here—came to London mind you—to find the chit, at a damned ball." He tilted the bottle over his glass.

"Good God. You actually attended a ball?" Wesley snickered while shaking his head.

"I wanted to see her." Morgan grunted. "She stuck that pert little nose in the air and danced away as if she didn't know me."

"Bet that stung," Wesley's smile held no sympathy at all.

Morgan swore under his breath. *Blood and the devil.*

His mood and the drink loosened his tongue. "When I saw her tonight, it wasn't enough. I had to touch her."

Wesley narrowed his eyes and issued him a leering grin.

"If you would like to keep your teeth, cover them," Morgan growled.

Wesley fisted his hand over his mouth.

The rotter.

"It was only a kiss," he blurted. But what a kiss. Pliant in his arms. He could still smell her heavenly scent. Still feel her soft curves. And for a moment, he'd felt . . . what—peace? Comfort? An emotion of some sort? *Damn.* He would not allow it.

"So, you are lusting after her?"

"Of course it's lust! What else could it be? The damned woman drives me insane." Morgan tossed back the drink.

"Then why do I have the feeling there is more to this. The darker side of you has been at rest. You were breathing fire when you came barreling through that door."

Morgan showed his teeth. "Rest? The sinister devil always lingers just beneath the exterior."

Wesley's eyes pierced him. "Then tell me what has made him surface tonight?"

Morgan's temper had certainly flared this evening. "Over a bloody female." Hearing his voice made him realize he'd spoken aloud. He scowled at his friend for a long intense moment. He took a deep breath, and another. He stared at the bottle in his hand.

Wesley persisted. "You have yet to mention an incident. Something happened. What was it?"

"You harp like a damned woman." When Wesley continued to stare, Morgan knew his comrade would force the issue. Damn his pride stung. "She slapped me."

"What!" Wesley's eyes bulged. "You jest." He gave a shout of laughter. He quickly thought better when Morgan shot him a glare. He coughed instead. "No, I see you do not. Good God, man. Did you strike her back?"

"Hell, no. What do you take me for?" Morgan pushed out of his chair and stomped across the carpet to the side table and slammed the bottle on the surface. Palms down, breathing heavily, he gripped the wood until his knuckles whitened. For years, he'd allowed the devil to govern his movements. Steady breaths and sheer force of will kept his inner demons confined. Until he faced the gates of hell. He cared not to go there again.

Morgan shoved his hands in his pockets and strode to the window. He looked out into the dark night, seeing nothing but a past he would rather forget. "It's time I remember why I returned home."

"You were tired of your other life."

Morgan's spoke over his shoulder. "And to marry and produce the required heir."

"Emotions should not enter into it." By the clink of a glass, Wesley poured another drink.

Morgan frowned. "Katherine would make a fine wife, if she were not so bloody headstrong. I do not need that particular quality in a wife."

"That is twice you have mentioned her name and wife in the same sentence."

Morgan whirled around. "What are you saying?"

"Are you considering marrying her?"

"Blood and the devil. I need an obedient wife. Katherine would defy me to my dying day."

Chapter 13

Time moved at a snail's pace. Watching her aunt, Kat wished she had invented an excuse—maybe a headache—for she would surely have one at the end of this soiree'. She glanced from one woman to the next. Lady Marsden prided herself as the queen of gossip. Most of her guests, the scandalmongers, attended with purpose. No doubt the tales would be repeated as soon as the blabbermouths cleared Lady Marsden's door—with embellishments, of course.

Steam rose from the china teapot on the table in the center of the room. High-back brocade sofas and several cushioned chairs completed a circle. Gold filigree plates with dainty slices of sweet-cakes made Kat's mouth water. After all, she'd forgone breakfast this morning. She glanced up and wondered if anyone would notice if she grabbed the plate and stuffed her mouth with one of the sugary confections. With her aunt sitting beside her, the idea was unmanageable.

On the other side of her aunt, Paige Tillingdale saw everything and listened closely to every word—no doubt for her gossip paper. Anything they discussed would be in her column the next day.

Kat could clearly see the caption. *Guess what guest at Lady Marsden's soirée' stuffed her face with sweets like a starving dog?*

"Lord Whetherford is looking for a wife."

Kat's ears tingled. Her hearing affixed on his name like a bee drawn to the pollen in a flower.

"He looked rather splendid at Farsdown's ball last night. Wonderful event." Lady Delgrave gave a self-absorbed nod to Lady Farsdown.

"That poor boy. Losing his family all at once."

What?

"Yes. Horrible." Mrs. Cockrell gave a shiver. "Lord and Lady Whetherford were such an admirable couple."

Kat paid closer attention.

"The entire ton felt their loss," Lady Marsden added.

"I believe he was at Eton at the time?" Lady Delgrave glanced to each patron seeking confirmation.

"Yes," Lady Farsdown corroborated. "Then he disappeared."

Disappeared?

"Just vanished. No one knew where he'd gone."

"Or if he would ever return. The Whetherford estate remained empty with no Earl."

"The boy was just too young." Lady Delgrave gave a disheartened sigh.

"That boy went wild," Mrs. Tillingdale said with vigor.

"Oh, Millie. You invented that for your paper."

"I invented nothing."

"Well, you must forgive him. He'd been given a shock. He had to mourn." Dignified and demure, and with starch in her corset, Lady Farsdown settled the matter.

"He's been gone for years. So many, we wondered if he would ever come home?" Lady Delgrave showed compassion for him.

The women buzzed like a bee hive. Each giving her opinion of his absence. The scuttlebutt was Lord Whetherford was a boy at Eton, his parents were killed, he ran away, and came back a man. Where did he go?

"Lord Whetherford has turned into quite a man." Lady Palfrey rolled her eyes with gleaming interest.

Kat agreed with her. A manly man. Not like the dandies gliding about the ton.

"It would appear the new earl has returned to carry out his duty," Lady Farsdown said.

"And what duty would that be?" Mrs. Cockrell asked.

"Why, to sire an heir, of course. And he put in his first appearance at my ball." Lady Farsdown gave a boastful arch of her spine any peacock would be proud of.

Lady Delgrave's daughter, Felicity, gave a shudder. "I think he's rather frightening." The girl was so silly, Kat mentally called her *Flighty* Felicity.

"When he stormed out, he looked like thunder," another lady said before she shoved a piece of cake in her mouth.

"Lord Whetherford seemed pleasant enough when he arrived," Lady Farsdown spoke up. He complimented my home and gave praise, saying it was a fine affair."

Several women bobbed their heads in agreement, making their latest fashionable hats come dangerously close to losing some of their adornments.

"Well, something set him off," Mrs. Tillingdale said. "And I missed what. That would have been a fine bit of natter for my column this morning."

Oh Good Lord.

Mrs. Cockrell, not to be outdone, said, "My husband said Whetherford looked ready to kill someone."

Heat crept up Kat's neck and her cheeks grew hot. As the ladies spoke, one after another, she sat in complete silence, hoping no one knew she was the one responsible for Lord Whetherford's murderous expression.

"Of course, you've heard of his dark past?" Lady Marsden continued.

Kat paused with her cup at her lip. Holding her breath, she strained to hear with urgent interest.

"What dark past?" Mrs. Cockrell asked.

"They say . . ." Lady Marsden paused, Kat was sure, for dramatic effect.

"What do they say?" Lady Delgrave asked.

Lady Marsden met each lady's eye, making sure she had everyone's attention. "When the young Lord Whetherford disappeared . . ." She placed her china cup on the table and waved her linen napkin about her breast. "I shan't say for it will simply give me vapors."

"Everything gives you vapors," Mrs. Tillingdale said sourly.

"He must be remarkably brave. Do you think he could have been a pirate?" Kat glanced at Mrs. Cockrell's daughter. *Silly goose.* The girl dreamed of the day when a pirate would steal her away and she would live happily ever after. What a romantic notion.

"He seems fierce enough if the threatening look on his face was anything to go by," Lady Delgrave added.

"He is not a pirate." Lady Farsdown spouted with all the conviction she knew of what she spoke.

Kat's head spun. Voices came from every direction. She wished they would all be quiet and Lady Marsden would finish what she'd been about to say.

"It is suspected he worked for the government . . ." Lady Marsden captured their attention again. She leaned forward and spoke in a conniving whisper, "as a spy."

"Oh, Clara. How on earth would you know?" Kat almost gasped at her aunt's retort.

Lady Marsden pointed her nose in the air. "I'm not at liberty to say."

"I know how," said Mrs. Tillingdale. "You keep your ear to your husband's library door."

Lady Delgrave came as close to snickering as one could at her lofty station, and said, "Snooping."

Mrs. Tillingdale chuckled.

Lady Marsden puffed up like a primed peacock opening its feathers. "Is that not like the pot and the kettle? Just how do you get *your* bits of drivel for your editorial?"

Mrs. Tillingdale glared back at her.

Mrs. Cockrell spoke. "I heard if you want the job done, Lord Whetherford—before he accepted the title, of course—was the one to do it."

"What job?" someone asked.

Lady Palfrey leaned toward the circle of women and spoke in a hushed whisper. "You know. *The* job."

"You don't know either," Mrs. Tillingdale harrumphed. "But, I suspect something illegal."

"My husband would not have accepted Lord Whetherford into our home if he was not an honorable man." Several pairs of eyes turned to stare in her aunt's direction.

A hush fell over the room. It was as if the world had suddenly stopped. Tea cups suspended in mid-motion. Mouths hung agape. Gazes sped to Kat, Aunt Liz, and Kat again.

She silently counted to ten.

"Your home?" Lady Marsden was the first one to speak. Her tone made Kat want to crawl under the Persian woven rug.

Flighty Felicity squeaked, "You had a pirate in your home?"

"He is not a pirate," Lady Palfrey rebuked.

Ignoring them both, Mrs. Tillingdale asked, "When?"

Oh Good Lord. How could Aunt Liz make such a blunder? Now every woman in this room would want to know why Lord Whetherford had been in their home. Kat's absence would surely come to light.

Aunt Liz looked down her nose and said, "He and my husband had a matter to discuss." Then she squared her shoulders and very smartly dismissed the onlookers as she sipped her tea.

Apprehension slowly ebbed from Kat's shoulders. *Thank you, Aunt Liz, for keeping me out of it.*

"Besides." Aunt Liz placed her cup on the delicate saucer, her spine rigid. "You should not listen to gossip. Those tales are apt to be false."

Too late. For Kat's suspicions had already been roused.

Every day, Lord Whetherford created disorder in her mind. Her thoughts of fancy had been just senseless moments of lost reason. But now she looked at the man in a whole different manner.

Dark past. Secrets. Mysterious. Spy.

If any of this was true . . . Could it be possible? Lord Whetherford may well be the very person to help her find Stephen.

Chapter 14

Morgan looked at the mahogany surface covered with papers still needing his attention. Commanding his eyes to focus, he forced his concentration on getting some work done. He was in a hell of a fix. In the quiet of his study, there was no hope of concentrating. A number of things needed his consideration and a certain redhead was keeping him from it.

Katherine.

Even her name was lovely. She would be here soon. At Whetherford.

A lump caught in his throat.

Kissing her had been intoxicating. Headier than any other woman he'd shared an entire night of invigorating kisses. She may have slapped him, but she had been just as involved as he in that kiss. Her sweet mouth had begged for more. The thought of teaching her other pleasures made his chest tighten.

He attempted to go over the ledgers again. Within minutes he shoved them aside and picked up a letter from his comrade in Parliament. After reading the same paragraph four times, he still hadn't absorbed the words. He tossed the quill across his desk and pushed out of his chair. Balancing his weight, he braced one arm on the wall to the right of the window. The same spot he had been standing when he first laid eyes on her.

A knock sounded on his study door.

"Enter," he said.

Frederick opened the door. "My Lord. Lady Thornton and Miss Radbourn have arrived."

She's here.

Morgan's muscles tightened. Remembering their last encounter, his hand lifted to rub his cheek.

"Thank you, Frederick. Ask Mrs. Beasley to bring tea."

"She is seeing to it now, my lord."

Morgan flexed his hands and forced his dry throat to swallow. He should send her away. Deny her. Rebuff her the way she had turned her nose up at him in London.

He couldn't wait to see her.

He imagined kissing the wildcat again. The next time he would see her eyes darken with desire. The next time he would give her what she craved. For he had no doubt, if he kissed her again, the passionate creature that he knew lurked underneath would come to life.

He strode out the door and down the hall. Voices drifted through the open parlor doors.

"Katherine, do sit down. You do not want Lord Whetherford to find you pacing his floor like a lioness. What will he think?"

He thinks a lioness is a perfect comparison.

"I don't care what he thinks."

Is that so?

"You have forgotten your manners."

A meek, "Yes, ma'am," echoed.

He took the remaining steps necessary for his eyes to rest on the very thorn that pricked his mind. Kat sat on the settee beside her aunt.

"Good afternoon, ladies."

Kat's head jerked his way. From the blush staining her cheeks, he could only assume she was also envisioning their last meeting.

She was even lovelier than he remembered.

"Lord Whetherford," Lady Thornton greeted him.

Morgan dragged his gaze away and gave a slight bow. "Lady Thornton." He turned his gaze back on Katherine. Her eyes wide, their jade sparkled with intensity. He longed to release the pins holding her crimson curls, allowing long tresses to fall about her shoulders—reminding him of the lioness her aunt referred to. The idea of taming the unruly feline into a purring kitten thrilled him more than he cared to admit. The corner of his mouth twisted at the prospect. "Miss Radbourn."

Katherine dipped her head. Her tantalizing scent assaulted his nostrils, a steady pull on his senses. Not the overpowering aroma of flowers. Her fragrance was less sweet and more like the fresh air after a rainstorm. Enticing. Making his mind crave more of her mystical essence.

"Welcome to my home. I trust your journey was pleasant." At that moment, Mrs. Beasley entered carrying a silver tray with a pot of steaming tea. "Thank you, Mrs. Beasley."

After she departed, Lady Thornton gave a speaking glance to her niece. Katherine asked, "Shall I pour, Lord Whetherford?"

"Thank you, Miss Radbourn."

Her fingers curled around the slim silver handle.

He swallowed. His vision blurred while he imagined her fingers curling around his neck, sliding through his hair. Smooth hands gliding over his skin, pulling him closer. He glanced up to find her gaze locked with his.

"My uncle asked me to deliver his letter in person." She withdrew an envelope and held it out. On the front Morgan's name was written in bold script.

Taking the paper, he placed it upon the mantle to read later. He moved to sit in a high-back chair across from the ladies and propped one leg on his opposite knee. "I am delighted that he did. Whetherford Manor gets too few visitors. I hope to correct that in the near future."

Lady Thornton sipped her tea. "I understand, Lord Whetherford, that you have been away for some time."

"Much too long, I'm afraid. Now that I am firmly ensconced in my family home, I plan to stay." Morgan glanced to Kat.

She chewed on her lower lip. She fidgeted like a lad bursting with a secret. She wanted to say something. What held her tongue?

"Thank you for your hospitality," Lady Thornton spoke, drawing his attention. He would find out what bee Katherine had in her bonnet later.

"Please do not give it another thought, Lady Thornton. I am happy to open my home to guests. Perhaps you will come again, and your husband can join you."

"Albert would have come this time, but important business kept him in Town."

"Sometimes, we men take our political business rather seriously. Look at this as an opportunity for you ladies to enjoy a holiday."

Several more pleasantries were shared over tea and when Lady Thornton declined more tea, Morgan stood. "I suppose you would like to rest before dinner. Your rooms are ready."

Frederick suddenly appeared as if he'd been summoned. "Ah, Frederick. Please see the ladies upstairs." He swept his arm toward the doorway. "This way ladies. Each of you will find a maid waiting. If you need anything, merely let her know what it is you wish."

While Kat climbed the stairs, his eyes caressed her backside—the soft sway of her hips, a trim ankle as she lifted her skirts with each step. He mentally circled her form with his hands and his breathing constricted. He would never tire of looking at her.

Morgan swiveled around and headed straight for the envelope resting on the mantle. What could be in the letter from Thornton? And why had he sent Katherine? He ripped open the missive and read the words written. He blinked. He read the words again.

Gripping the missive, he turned and strode down the corridor to his study. He walked around the solid oak desk and pulled the right drawer open. After placing the letter carefully inside, he shoved the compartment closed. With a grin on his lips, he strode over to the side table, his eye on the crystal decanter filled with amber liquid. He poured a generous measure into a glass and took a healthy swallow.

So, Thornton needed his niece out of his hair for a few days.

Giles handed the butler his hat and cane. He glanced up the curved mahogany staircase and wondered why he'd been summoned. The signature on the communiqué had been such a surprise, he'd thought of nothing else since receiving Thornton's directive. He followed the servant through the hall and waited before a set of doors as the man announced Giles' presence.

"His Grace, the Duke of Nethersall."

Thornton stood by a large stone hearth smoking a pipe. The room held a pleasant aroma nix of Cavandish, and sweet Molto Doice. He pulled the pipe from his lips and gave a nod to his butler, then greeted Giles. "Your Grace."

"Lord Thornton," Giles replied.

The steward left, closing the door behind him.

"Please, come in." Thornton gestured with his pipe. "Would you care for a drink?"

As soon as he could, he wanted to dispense with formalities and find out why the man had sent for him. But, being a duke called for proper protocol. Certain standards had to be respected. "Thank you."

Thornton strode to the sideboard containing a silver tray with a crystal decanter and two glasses. After pouring a generous portion into both, he handed one to Giles.

"I'm sure you are wondering why I asked you here."

Asked? More like commanded. But then Giles was a curious sort, and one to get answers, so he had eagerly anticipated the meeting. "I pondered whether you invited me as a duke . . . or if something else was underfoot."

As with most men of Parliament, Thornton's stone features gave nothing away. He angled his head and penetrating eyes looked over his spectacles. "I see no need to dally. We have met before under, should I say, dubious circumstances."

Giles held his tongue. He'd learned from experience—when you kept your mouth shut, you learned more.

"I wanted to see you for a precise reason." Thornton spoke as he walked over to stand in front of one of the two leather chairs. He gestured to the other. "Please."

As Giles lowered his tall frame into the cushioned seat, he contemplated Thornton's words. "I gather this meeting has some serious significance. You have my attention."

"We have mutual friends," Thornton said.

Giles studied the amber liquid in his own glass before he answered. "I thought as much."

"And have those friends told you anything about me?"

Thankfully, his voice remained even. "I'm sure you know a man in my position never gives information. Of any kind."

Giles' jaw twitched from tension. He took a deep breath, concentrating on the air going into his lungs, expanding, willing his muscles to relax. "That being said, you were among those who met with Rotherford. So, I know you are to be trusted. I understand you were the one responsible for funding a certain rescue. I have speculated, upon occasion, if other missions had a connection to you."

Thornton's gaze bore right through him. At the same time the man appeared completely relaxed.

Giles continued. "I would never ask or seek answers where it is not necessary."

With his elbow resting on the arm of his chair, Thornton held his pipe to the side. "And here I expected you would glean every statistic down to the last detail."

"I know you are a private man, as am I. Discretion and secrecy made many operations successful. I would not interfere in your solitude."

Thornton nodded as though he accepted the words as honest. "I need a man of your particular skills. There are only two men I would consider for this task, and one is you."

Giles knew without asking, the second man was Morgan. Thornton's eyes seemed to acknowledge that thought. What the hell could Thornton need from the man Giles used to be? "I am no longer at a point in my life where I live for danger."

"Yet you risked all to find your friend," Thornton said.

Damn. How had he known about that?

Giles took a hefty drink. Bloody hell. Did he need to ask? Thornton was like a ghost—haunting, privy to all worldly beings. He could probably read a man's mind. Giles shook off the thought. "Proceed, Lord Thornton."

Thornton rose and stepped over to place his pipe in a marble bowl. Giles felt like a lad in the presence of one who commanded a room just by being in it. Thornton had most likely headed many of their assignments. Giles and Morgan were in the field, so to speak, while Thornton and other men of significance secretly gathered information and set the wheels into motion. How did someone send a man on a dangerous undertaking that held no guarantee of success? No assurance the candidate would return. How did a man sleep at night when he sent another on a mission that could end his last breathing act?

Giles' empathy grew to unknown bounds. He sure as hell wouldn't have wanted to be in Thornton's shoes.

"Very well." Thornton returned to his chair. "Now, the reason I called for you." He leaned back and exhaled a deep breath. "An unfortunate matter. It's my niece, Katherine."

Giles paused with the brandy inches from his lips. With years of practice, he managed to mask his feelings.

What the bloody hell?

Was he about to be sent after Morgan?

Chapter 15

Morgan stared out the glass-paned window. He had no idea how long he stood there when he heard a rustling of skirts. He turned, and his heart lurched at the vision before him. The most beautiful sunset could not compare to the effervescent colors in her hair, or the persimmon gown covering the generous curves of her body. Before his lower region could be allowed to bloom, he squelched his desire, and then frowned in confusion. He'd not expected to see her again so soon.

"If you have a moment, my lord, I would like to talk to you," Katherine said.

Her wringing hands displayed her nervousness. He pushed the annoying lock of hair from his forehead and forced his muscles to relax. "Of course."

When she took a few steps forward and stopped, Morgan gestured to the chair across from him. "Please."

"Do you mind if I close the door? My aunt is asleep upstairs. I do not want her to overhear if she awakes."

"Miss Radbourn. Do you plan on putting me in a compromising position?" His lip curved as he thought of how he'd barely escaped by the skin of his teeth the last time.

"Don't be ridiculous. I let you off the hook." Kat glared at him.

"Off the . . ." Morgan shook his head at the exasperating female, and moved to close the door. Once again, he held out his arm and motioned to the twin leather chairs. Katherine perched on the edge of one cushion, her body erect. Giving her time to gather her words, he took the chair opposite and leaned back in comfort.

"I am short on time so I will come right to the point."

What was the minx up to now? He narrowed his eyes and studied her. "Very well."

"How much power do you have?"

Morgan's fingers tightened on the arm of the chair.

What the bloody hell?

With her naiveté, her question made one think the opposite, for it gave him free reign on his imaginings. His heart gave several beats while she squirmed on her seat. When she looked ready to burst, he answered. "Enough."

She plunged on with her next words. "I want you to help me find my brother."

Brother? He'd almost forgotten. He slackened his grip on the leather he'd been clutching. Anything he might have expected, he certainly had not expected that to pop out of her mouth.

"You want my help. To find your brother." He sounded like a bloody parrot.

"Yes." Her shoulders slumped as if she had been holding her breath.

Morgan watched her chest rise and fall, her ample bosom caused his groin to constrict. Damn, she was lovely. He imagined his hands on her breasts. How he would like to tug the lace covering her generous swells and suckle her nipples like a newborn babe. He wondered what color her nipples would be—dark rose? Or a lighter shade of pink? Suddenly his tongue felt too large for his mouth. And his breeches too damned tight. Katherine was the kind of woman one marries, not someone to dally with. He shifted, then crossed his legs to hide her effect on his body and forced his mind to the topic at hand.

Her brother.

"Is this why you asked how much power I have?"

"Yes."

He sorted through what she'd just revealed, pleased that she had come to him, and relieved she no longer snubbed him. The girl was a mystery. In her uncle's letter, Thornton had been right when he mentioned he feared his niece was up to something. Morgan would be happy to keep an eye on her. And he had her uncle's sanction.

Morgan rose slowly, and proceeded to the assortment of bottles on the oak table. He poured a small amount of burgundy into a crystal flute, and then added a splash of brandy to his own glass. Handing the claret to Katherine, he took his seat. "Now. Tell me about your brother."

She took a hesitant sip of the offered wine, then placed the flute on the round table beside her chair. "I am very worried about him. He's been gone a long time."

Pain etched her face. Clearly, she had a story to convey. He would let her tell him in her own way and in her own time. Sometimes a body had to cleanse—flush out their emotions—their pain—their grief. He listened without interruption.

"Stephen is my senior by ten years. As a small child, I followed him around everywhere." She tipped her head and held his gaze. "I idolized my brother."

Morgan could see the binding love—the bond between a sister and her brother. Pain filled her eyes before she quickly looked away.

"I remember as a child, he was a good and caring brother. He never shunned me or ignored me. How in the world he put up with me tagging along behind him everywhere he went, I don't know. His patience had no limit. Not with me, anyway. Stephen was always there for me. He taught me so many things."

Morgan's heart twisted when her tortured gaze returned to him.

"Stephen taught me to ride at an early age. He showed me how to care for a horse as well as how to ride one. By the time I was twelve, I was a master in the saddle. If I fell, he was there to pick me up. If I cried, he was there to kiss my hurt and wipe away my tears."

The kissing had Morgan thinking he'd like to do some kissing of his own. He wondered what it would feel like to be on the receiving end of unconditional love. To have a woman love him unreservedly. He remained silent, and motioned for her to carry on.

"It broke my little girl's heart when he went away to sea. I did not understand why he left me behind. Why he did not take me with him."

Morgan empathized with the lost little girl who so badly wanted her brother. Katherine took a deep breath and her eyes lit up along with the smile on her face.

His gut took a dive.

"Stephen always came home with presents and hugs. Even when I'd grown, he picked me up and twirled me around until I was breathless."

Seeing the glowing excitement on her face made Morgan wish he could have been the one to put it there. He wanted to give her that stimulating glow. He wanted her to feel that thrill of exhilaration—for him.

Her gazed drifted toward the window. "When my parents died, Stephen insisted I live with my aunt and uncle. I understand his reasoning now, but at the time I was devastated. I thought he was deserting me." Her voice turned raspy as she continued. "You see, Stephen is captain of his own ship. He can come and go as he pleases. At least twice each year he visits me, sometimes more." She faced him. Her eyes implored as she leaned forward to demand his absolute attention. "I have not seen my brother in nearly two years. That's how I know something has happened to him. Stephen would never stay away from me this long."

So, the brother is as devoted to her as she is to him.

Clearly, they had a special relationship. What would it be like to have a woman speak of him with such a loving glow in her eyes?

Blood and the devil.

He would never know. How could he be jealous of her brother, for God's sake?

Katherine shifted in her chair. "You've got to believe me. I know something bad has happened."

"I believe you." The relief on her face eased the tightness in his chest. At that moment he would give her anything, do anything she asked.

"I had planned to look for him on my own."

That got his attention.

"If your men had not grabbed me, I would be on my way to find him."

God's teeth! She had just reminded him again that all of this was his fault. Then the realization of exactly what she had said penetrated his crazed brain. "What do you mean, on your way? You were planning to hire someone, of course. Not alone."

Her teeth chewed on her luscious lip again. "I don't know. I had not gotten that far. I was looking for Captain Danvers."

"Surely you knew better than to go to the docks on your own? This sounds like a matter for your uncle to handle. Not for a young woman. I hate to be reminded of my own ineptness, but what do you think would have happened had I not found you?" He held up a hand. "Don't answer that."

Morgan rose from his chair and marched to the window, anxiety churning in his gut. Knowing what could have happened to a young woman, alone at the docks. Seadoers were an unscrupulous lot.

Thrusting his fingers through his hair, he warred with his conscience. Frustrated that he could not go back and undo the misguided actions of his men that day—not sure he wanted to change the outcome even if he could. Maddened at the idea of her even considering going alone. Alarmed of the possibility she could have ended in a worse situation. He turned and took one agonizing step in her direction.

"Good God, woman," he managed, between a groan and a shout. "There are all kinds of devils lurking about—waiting for the unsuspecting—the innocent! Worse than the two who grabbed you. You could have been . . ." Sheer terror knifed him in the chest. He clenched his hands at the thought of someone hurting her. He would bloody well kill the bastard.

Katherine gaped at him as though he'd sprouted horns. "I know how foolish it sounds."

He scrutinized her, regretting every panicked heartbeat he had caused her. "I apologize for the outburst."

"Tis no more than I would have received from my brother." She smiled. "Actually, he would have done much worse." Shuddering, her face scrunched up as if she saw an unpleasant image. Then, just as quick, the frown was gone and uneasiness creased her face with worry. "Will you help me find him?"

How could he deny her? His fierce need to protect the chit was unbelievable. He took deep breaths to calm his mental anxiety. Used to living by his gut instincts, he'd always been in control. With her, his reactions surprised him.

"You will *not* do anything on your own. Am I making myself clear?" He had no right to make her subject to his vexation after the grief she experienced by his own hand, yet she sat there in accepting silence.

"I need your help." She raised beseeching eyes to his. "I will do anything you ask of me."

Knocked to his toes, a different kind of excitement built inside of him. Did she even know the innuendo of her offer? His mind filled with images of him helping her out of her clothes, his fingers brushing against soft, white skin. He forced his mind away from that line of thinking. He would not exchange sex for a favor.

"I require nothing other than for you to be safe."

"Lord Whetherford . . ."

"Do you suppose we could agree on a more casual address, Katherine? After all, we were engaged."

She rolled her eyes.

"Please. Call me Morgan."

"I . . . I cannot."

His voice deepened. "In privacy? When it is only the two of us?"

She lowered her head and he thought she would refuse, until she softly spoke the words, "As you wish." Once again, she implored him with pleading eyes. "I must find him. I need to know Stephen is all right."

She took a deep breath expanding her well-endowed bosom. No matter how tempting the distraction, he kept his eyes locked on hers. After what seemed an eternity, she spoke.

"Will you help me?"

He took advantage of the silence to calm his racing pulse. If she continued to beg with her eyes, he would refuse her nothing. His gut twisted. With great effort, he concentrated on the situation at hand. "To answer your earlier question, yes, I am a powerful man. You can trust me and I must be able to trust that you will do *nothing* without my approval." He put emphasis on the word nothing, wondering if it would do any good. He would not be surprised to find this incredible woman was used to getting her own way.

He glared down on the beauty seated before him. His fierce look probably frightened her, but maybe she needed a good scare. Either that or turn her over his knee and . . . best not think of her appealing backside. "I will never allow anyone or anything to place you in danger again. I must insist you not do anything on your own to find your brother. If you agree, I will help you. Do I have your word?"

The object of his desire came hurling at him and threw her arms about his neck. "Oh, thank you, thank you, thank you."

Morgan sucked air into his lungs. Christ! He couldn't breathe. Her luscious curves pressed against him were most gratifying . . . for a moment.

She was gone before he could truly savor the sensation.

Chapter 16

*D*amn the man!

Juliana Eastcote paced back and forth on the woven carpet at the foot of her bed. She'd been reduced to this. Forced to stay in rooms at a hostel. She had hoped to be long gone by now, with a sizable amount of cash. But, a *friend of a friend* declared the necklace so remarkable it would be hard to resell. He had said the piece was old and would be recognized as a family heirloom. He refused to buy, claiming a transaction too dangerous—for a memorable piece like that would be easy to trace.

Shaking her head, Juliana fumed. If the imbecile had not been so spineless, they both would have benefited, and she could have lived like a queen.

What was she to do now? Whetherford would find her. Those jewels were worth a fortune, but he cared not. Why should he care about money? After all, he hung the moon—or so everyone thought.

Whetherford would never forgive her for taking what had belonged to his precious mother. If she could not sell the necklace, she would not get money for passage to America. With so many people landing on those shores, she would have been one in a million, like a grain of sand on a deserted beach. She could have disappeared. No matter how many men he sent to look for her, their search would end in defeat.

Riches had been within her grasp. She had waited for the timing to be right.

Her hands rubbed the top of her arms for solace. Glancing toward the bureau, she squinted at the sparkles reflecting off the flawless jewels.

Her uncle's death had been a boon. After getting over the shock, she enjoyed playing the heiress at Whetherford Manor. Frolicking with young Toby had turned into more than she'd bargained for. The young fool made it simple, and then she'd made her move.

Used to getting what she sought, Juliana cursed her current state of affairs. She wanted those jewels gone, replaced with hard coin.

And she wanted out of here. Out of hiding.

Her resentment escalated to new heights. Her life would be forfeit if Whetherford got his hands on her. He'd been gone so long, her uncle thought Whetherford dead. Why hadn't the blasted man stayed gone? Or better yet, be dead. True she had wanted him once. But if she could not be Lady Whetherford, she did not care if the insufferable lord met his demise.

Juliana pulled back the curtain and glanced at the street below. Two men stepped from the curb crossing the cobbled street. *Her spies.* They must have word of his whereabouts. Releasing the thin veil, she turned toward the door. A few moments later, the awaited knock sounded.

"Enter," she said.

A tall man met her gaze as he stepped inside. The second man followed, and closed the door. The first one, Amos, removed his hat. "His lordship has gone back to Whetherford Manor."

"Excellent." With him gone from London, she could breathe easier. At least now, she would be able to go outdoors without the fear of running into him on every street corner. "And the men he hired to find me?"

"Seems something else got his attention."

Juliana glared. She had pictured Whetherford tracing her steps and finding the merchant where she'd tried to sell the jewels. The unknown reason he'd suddenly changed his mind unsettled her.

The second man spoke. "Ya dinna tell us he was the *dark devil*."

Her gaze flew to his. "What do you mean?"

Amos cleared his throat. "Charlie here, thinks he resembles the one they call the 'dark devil'. No way his lordship can be him."

"Who is this dark devil?" Juliana asked.

"No one you'd care to meet. He's a paid assassin," Charlie said.

Amos, the calmer of the two, tried to smooth things over. "Some say he's a ruthless killer for hire."

Wound up, Charlie continued. "If you have the blunt, he'll do any job no matter how dangerous. Tis said he likes killing, whether you pay him or not. He tore a man apart with his bare hands. He's left mutilated bodies where 'ere he's been."

Amos turned his glare on the man beside him. "There's no way the 'dark devil' could pass himself off as a nobleman."

"How about concentrating on the task at hand?" Juliana gave a glare of her own. "Whetherford is hard-hearted, but I doubt he is cold-blooded. Nevertheless, I do not want to be without protection." She studied the two ruffians. They were strong and she'd been told they were skilled.

She knew of Whetherford's fierce temper. Why would her informants think him the *dark devil*? Rumors, of course. Who knew what he'd been up to the last five years. Or why he decided to suddenly come home now? No one expected him back. A foolish mistake on her part, and now she could very well pay the price. Something like panic crept under her skin. If these two brutes were nervous, and Charlie correct in his assumptions, then she better come up with a plan. Quick.

Nothing would keep her safe from the dark Lord's outrage. She flung her hair over one shoulder. Her only recourse—return the jewelry.

Juliana focused on a speck on the wall, her thoughts requiring every brain cell she possessed. She needed leverage. Come Hell or Sunset, she would find a way to save her own skin.

Chapter 17

If curiosity was wicked, Kat would ask for forgiveness later. The manor had so many wings and corridors, she could not resist. Once up the curving staircase, she turned and headed to the far end of the second hallway. In the middle of the corridor she found a passageway with several massive doors. She wandered the long hallway coming to rest at the last one. Looking back, no one stirred. She turned the handle.

Floor to ceiling windows checked one wall. Bulky items covered with white canopies were strewn about. Large stones formed a hearth, so hefty she wondered how anyone managed to cart the heavy things upstairs and then assemble them to form a stunning success. In front of the massive fireplace two covered heaps at an angle faced each other. Lifting the cloth, she found elegant cream-colored, wing backed chairs. For a loving couple? Maybe a husband and wife?

Someone must come to clean the room, for as she removed the shrouds enveloping the pieces, no dust cloud formed to prove the room had been completely abandoned. She found a few marble top pieces that were too beautiful to be covered up and stored away. This chamber displayed a magnitude of wealth. She wondered if painful memories survived this room. Had a loved one been lost? Perhaps children played here while a devoted mother or grandmother read stories to them. A sense of comfort—peace—love—filled the essence of the air. She had no idea why she felt so drawn to this room, but she longed to know its history.

Rays of sunshine streamed through large windows tugging her forward. Endless lush green trees filled the deep sweep of the valley. Whetherford land, she supposed, as far as the eye could see. Puffs of white floated in a clear blue sky. Splendor so beautiful, the tranquil image suppressed her anxiousness of the day before.

She had not seen him since she'd gone hurling into his arms. Had she really thrown herself at Morgan—she could no longer think of him as Whetherford—in thankful jubilation? His stone hard body had sent tingling awareness through her limbs. Just the thought of his fingers on her person made her breathless. She'd always heard about butterflies in one's stomach. The little devils had taken flight throughout her entire being. Her impulsive body had wanted so desperately to lean into the solid muscle of man.

Everything he did fascinated her. The way he moved like a panther with stealth—elegant, sure strides. Graceful movements that seemed improbable for a man of his size. His hands were strong and sure and she believed those hands would be gentle when he caressed a woman's skin. There were times he looked at her as a man looks at a woman. True she was inexperienced, but she *was* a woman. And he a virile man.

"Mrs. Beasley said this is where I could find you." His deep voice sent chills vibrating over her flesh.

Letting out a breath, she turned, taking in his dark form. "I hope you don't mind?" Her voice came out as a breathless gasp.

"What are you doing up here?" His tall, dark form appeared almost sinister.

Excitement bloomed within as he stepped from the shadow. "I am curious by nature, and you have an interesting home. There are so many rooms and wings."

"Yes, some of them were closed off." He examined the room with a forlorn look. His face displayed vulnerability, opening something inside her. "It's been years since I've been up here."

Unsure if she should ask about his family, she decided she would steer away from the subject unless he spoke of them on his own. "There are some lovely pieces in this room. Too beautiful to be hidden."

"I only returned to Whetherford Manor recently."

"Returned?" The word flew out of her mouth before she thought to stop it.

He crossed over to one of the white linens that had yellowed with age. He raised the faded cloth and angled his dark head as he peered underneath. "I had planned to open the estate again. Intended to marry and raise a family in the home where I grew up."

A tightening curled around her chest. Did he have a woman in mind? Had he decided to marry the one who ran away? The tightness turned to pain. It should not, but it hurt to think of another woman—any woman—as his wife.

How ridiculous a thought.

He uplifted another shroud. Seeming satisfied, he removed the covering to reveal a roll top desk. "I've not had the chance to come up to this level since I moved back. I'd forgotten what's up here."

"How long have you been gone?" A mournful expression crossed his features revealing he suffered something painful from his past. She wondered how many of the sinister stories she'd heard were true. He did not threaten her—not in the way of impending doom. But his presence loomed in a delicious forbidden manner, making her susceptible.

"My parents . . ." He hesitated, then started again. "My older brother was to inherit. He took my parents on his ship . . . They had been married for twenty-five years and he gifted them with—what was supposed to be—an anniversary voyage."

She dreaded what was coming next. Hating that she had most likely opened an old wound. With her heart in her throat, she waited, not daring to say more.

"They suffered a storm and the ship broke apart." He turned toward the sun's rays coming through the window. "My family went to a watery grave."

She wished she could take away the remote look of painful remembrance.

"At the time, I was in my last year at Eton. I guess I thought my parents would live forever." His shoulders rose and fell as he took a deep breath. "To lose them both at the same time was . . . quite a shock. To learn my brother was lost as well . . . I was devastated."

Oh God. Her knees grew weak.

When his gaze caught hers, his eyes held a hollow emptiness. "A lad of seventeen years, on the brink of manhood, I became an angry, temperamental scoundrel." He turned back to the oak desk. "I behaved outrageously."

Her heart broke for the boy who was forced to become a man overnight. She held back tears as he ran a finger lovingly over the well-worn wood. He picked up an inkwell and examined it as though looking to see if any liquid remained.

"The Devil took residence in my body, and I rebelled. I sought adventure—the more dangerous, the better. No perilous journey turned down, no threat too great to refuse." He stood like the rock of Gibraltar. Hard, like granite, with a compelling sincerity that drew her toward him. He set the inkwell back on the desk with notable care. "After all, what did I have to live for?"

She could not hold back the surprise of anguish caused by his casual lack of concern for his life. If he heard her gasp, he showed no sign of it. He continued, evading the ghosts haunting his memories.

"Giles, before he became the Duke, he and I met a man who had connections. We involved ourselves in some risky missions. Nothing was too treacherous. Giles had his own demons to fight." Morgan took a deep breath and exhaled as if the weight of the world rested on his shoulders alone.

"By then I was a man of five and twenty. Together, we could do anything. We risked our lives at the blink of an eye, on any whim, and stayed fervently ready for the next undertaking. No mission was too great. There was no such thing as defeat, and we never left a job undone. I lived by my wits."

His hypnotic voice rolled over her in alluring waves. Those lips and his hollow expression—so distracting. She blinked back moisture which threatened to fall. When he swallowed, her gaze fastened on the lump that moved undeniably up and down his appealing throat. That simple motion had her swallowing right along with him. His hands, his fingers, every movement, every action, made her aware of feelings in her body that she had never felt before. She wanted to go to him, put her arms around him, in comfort.

She did not move. Did not breathe.

"I am not proud to say, I was a nasty piece of work. I thought I didn't give a damn. Somewhere along the way, I grew up. I knew I had to accept my duty and carry on the family name."

His gaze swept the space again. "I have not been in this room for a score of years. I came back a few times to check on the estate. Everywhere I looked, I saw my parents. My brother should have been here. If I stayed in any part of the house for long, the walls closed in on me. My guilt . . ."

"Guilt?" Up until now she dared not interrupt. But, she could not hold back her distress when he blamed himself.

He locked his gaze with hers. "I lived. They did not." The emotion behind those words explained everything.

This heart-wrenching story of his life created a need to sooth, to touch. Her fingers strained to smooth the blue-black curl from his sorrowful brow. Her arms ached to hold him, to tell him everything would be fine. "He," she croaked. "I too lost my parents." Unshed tears clogged her throat. "Carriage accident . . . lightning . . ." she hiccupped. ". . . a tree . . . I was f-fourteen."

Morgan held his arms open and she fell into them. He embraced her with soulful tenderness. For long moments, tears rolled down her cheeks soaking the material on his shoulder. She relished the warmth that seeped from his hands into her back muscles, extending through her limbs. How wonderful it felt to be held in his arms. A compassionate man giving her peace, and warmth, and tenderness.

He led her to the linen covered sofa, then motioned for her to sit, never letting go of her hand. He sat beside her, their knees almost touching, and reached into his pocket for a handkerchief. "I'm sorry. When I told you . . . I had no idea."

She dabbed at her tears with the monogrammed linen.

"Please forgive me for bringing up such painful memories." His voice gruff with emotion.

She ached more from seeing the raw concern in his eyes. "There are pleasant memories too. Wonderful recollections."

He squeezed her hand. "Would you share those remembrances with me, Katherine?"

Pleased to see a smile on his handsome face, she gave him one of her own and told him of her love for her parents. How she'd been sheltered, pampered, and somewhat spoiled. Her parents respected each other and she reciprocated their love.

She would never forget the pain of her parents' death. She explained how she had been shattered when she lost them. Holding nothing back, she told him how she relived the nightmare in her dreams, waking in the middle of the night, tears streaming down her face, to find it all too real. She survived the darkness and emptiness until Stephen had come home.

"From the time I was a baby, I got exactly what I wanted. Stephen was never able to deny me anything. Until the day he told me I had to go live with my aunt and uncle."

He listened as though he cared, as if her words were important to him. Her heart opened and more words poured forth. "I begged. I pleaded for Stephen to take me with him. That was the first time he ever denied me."

Remembering what felt like desertion clogged her throat, but she got the words out. "I could not believe my brother was leaving me again." Tears ran down her cheeks in earnest. "I had just lost the two most precious people in the world. It felt like I was losing him too."

Morgan put one arm around her and pulled her head to his chest. She snuggled while her fingers clung to the lapels of his coat. Safe. In the haven of Morgan's strong arms.

She wished she could stay there forever.

Chapter 18

An enormous full moon glowed against the midnight sky, providing the only illumination across the countryside just beyond the Indian border. Parts of India concealed split loyalties. And Giles had landed right in the heart of one. Crossing the ocean had taken less time than the weeks it took to find his quarry.

When Giles had set off on this quest, he suspected to find the man ship-wrecked or in the arms of a willing woman. Not to be. When people were afraid, they kept secrets. Money changed hands in order to get the information they sought. And if their informants were correct, they'd be lucky if they found him alive.

Crouched behind a boulder, he waited, every muscle in his body tense and on alert. Just like the old days. When he and Morgan fought devils incarnate. Instincts sharp and on the ready for any possible threat. His horse and the others blended in the darkness. He glanced around, squinting to sharpen his eyesight. One by one, each man vigilant, equipped and prepared. They followed him—their leader. No one knew he was a damned duke. His title would not help this situation.

He intended to find Katherine's brother if his life depended on it. Morgan needed this more than Katherine Radbourn's uncle.

Once the shock of Thornton's summons had worn off, Giles accepted the nobleman's request with fervor. Being a duke did not have his heart pumping or his reflexes honed like his old life. Giles looked forward to sinking his teeth in a new escapade. If Stephen had fallen into trouble, and he quite possibly had, Giles would get the fella out of any damned mess he may have gotten himself into.

"Damn, it's dark out here. I can't see a blessed thing."

Giles kept his gaze straight ahead instead of looking at the man who'd spoken. "The point is for no one to see us."

"Place looks like a fortress."

With those stone sides, it looked like a prison to him. "That's why we wait here. If the men in there are unsavory characters, they'd shoot us down before we got close to their walls."

"I hear'd tell, there be bad-tempered brutes disagreeable to English blokes. Some don't cotton to having an English colony hereabouts." Piers spoke over the tobacco in the side of his mouth. "Some princes are fearful Brits are gonna take over their territory. And if the India chiefs happened upon *our bloke,* they wouldn't take too kindly to him being an Englishman."

Giles agreed. One of them, most likely, hid within that barricade. "The pieces we found were from an English ship." Which only confirmed Katherine's brother's ship went down. His jaw tensed and his fists clenched. If this stronghold held those offensive men and Stephen had been captured, then he'd already suffered unspeakable torture.

A noise sounded to his left. His hearing sharpened and he narrowed his eyes, trying to make out the form he knew must be there. Elmes slid around the boulder with the stealth of a fiend. Assured his friend was safe, Giles relaxed the tendons in his neck.

"He was here, alright," Elmes said.

They were on the right trail.

Giles heart increased its tempo. He focused on one word. "Was?"

"Some blokes breeched the walls and broke the prisoners out. A rebellious sort disagreed with the chief and ended up in there. The bunch that freed the rebel musta been his comrades." Elmes shook his head as he took another breath. "Some ghastly things went on in there."

Giles unwound just enough to be thankful Katherine's brother had escaped. "At least he's not in that hell hole."

"Don't go getting too excited. One of the fellas was in bad shape. Described him as a giant. Till the Chief got hold of 'em. Some bugger wanted to leave him for dead, but the boss of the lot wouldn't leave without him. Said he had withstood more than another man could take."

That's not the first time Giles had heard Stephen was a large man. Although, if he'd been tortured and probably starved, it was evident he had diminished somewhat in size.

This particular Rajput chief is proud of his social and religious identity, but he don't agree with the Emperor. Tradition and all that. Resents the British Empire. When the captain's ship crashed on the rocks, this chief captured the crewmen who made it to shore. Killed 'em and made their captain watch. Poor devil sounds like our man."

Giles hands fisted tighter with every word. The pain in his neck spread through his head and pounded behind his eyes. *Good God.* He knew from experience, the screams of men under your command cut worse than any knife.

Elmes pulled a twist of tobacco from his pocket and bit off the end. "The louts are looking for 'em. Bloke I talked to, said these men are a breed of their own. They don't go by the Emperor's law. His words—the chief is a 'blood thirsty, evil monster'."

Fury ate at the bile churning in Giles' stomach. Cruel, evil men. Madmen. He'd dealt with this sort before. Clenching his jaw, he sucked air between his teeth. "Which way?"

Elmes spit into the dirt. "Due East."

"Let's ride."

Chapter 19

The garden hedges were sculptured with tunnels that if one were roaming around, one could get lost. Kat moved down the path, expanding her chest as she breathed deep, inhaling the fragrant aroma of each species. She spotted Blue Cornflowers. Reaching out, she caressed the smoothness of a delicate bloom. The petal's softness brought her contentment. Inhaling its fragrance brought her peace.

Only moments ago, she had acted like a little girl with her first crush. Thank goodness, her aunt liked to rest after dinner. Kat needed this time alone. Her traitorous body had taken control of her senses. Her innards knotted just being in the same room with *him*. Hopefully these beautiful flowers would help relax her muscles as well as her troubled mind.

As if conjuring him up, the tingling on the back of her neck made her aware of Morgan's presence. The hint of his breath, just below her ear, was enough to send a shiver of feminine pleasure through her veins. *My heavens.*

When he spoke, it was more of a whisper. Still, the low timbre of his voice sent quivers of awareness down her spine. A hair's breadth away, her body longed to lean back against that massive chest, eager to feel his strength.

Her nerves cried their delight when the tips of his fingers touched the spot between her neck and her shoulder. The gentle contact sent searing heat shooting across her bosom. The instant pounding of her heart robbed her breath. She was afraid to move. Afraid he would remove the hand that settled on her bare skin. A man's hand. The touch of *his* hand. The wicked thought entered her mind that she wanted his hand to touch much more.

Just then he bestowed the lightest of squeezes, Kat thought it could have been a lover's caress. A pleasant pressure formed in the center of her chest and traveled to her lower stomach and settled right between her legs. She must lean against him, for if she didn't, her legs would surely give out. Was that his finger on the lobe of her ear? Kat closed her eyes, delighting in the burning sensation. However, closing her eyes only made the spark of awareness flame higher and blaze into a roaring fire that daunted to consume her.

"Katherine?"

She jumped, right out of the fantasy she had created. A starry-eyed dream that was only her imagination. She turned, a smile pasted on her lips, and found *him* standing a good distance from her.

Morgan gestured toward the stone bench and smiled. With his hand extended, he turned his palm up in invitation. When she placed her hand in his, he curled his fingers around hers, shooting a bolt of fiery warmth up her arm to land in the center of her chest. This was real. The wonder of it all made her legs unsteady, so it was a good thing he held her hand until she plunked, graciously of course, upon the bench.

Taking a deep breath, she smoothed her hands over the folds of her skirt. "Your garden is beautiful."

"My grandfather loved my grandmother and I am told this was his way of showing it. She loved flowers and he gifted her with every bush, every stem, every shape and color imaginable. I understand he traveled far and wide to find the rarest and most exotic flowers. Through their years together, the garden continued to expand. As you can see, it is very extensive."

The pride she read in his eyes pleased and excited her. "And the maze? The hedges?"

"I believe his spontaneity of the hedges were significant to his passion for her. She loved his surprises and impulsive behavior. The maze of flowers and pathways were a game for them. He built the fountain as a center point—a home base, if you will. They would return to the fountain and sit on this bench, sharing their pleasure of the adventure and their love for each other." He cocked his head and smiled. "At least, that is what I was told."

A wave of longing seared her center. "You were told?"

"By my grandfather."

Morgan had the darkest eyes she'd ever seen—or been lost in. She swallowed, hoping her mouth did not hang open. "Don't you believe him?"

"Oh, I believe my grandfather. I am not sure I believe in that kind of love."

Her elation plummeted.

"Although, I do remember how they behaved toward one another. Always kind." Lines furrowed his brow. "Now that I think on it, they were always smiling."

"What of your parents?"

"Hmmm?"

She hesitated, choosing her words carefully. "Did they ... ummm ... love each other?"

"Yes. They did." His expression turned to regret.

She sensed his hurt and shared the pain he suffered. "I'm sorry."

His voice grew husky with concern. "Don't be. You remember your parents' love for each other, don't you?"

She looked at him, knowing her soulful emotions must be exposed "Yes."

His fingers tightened over hers. Then, he turned his gaze to the pathway. Rising, he strode to the fountain, placing his booted heel on the stones.

With his back to her, he spoke over his shoulder. "The future of Whetherford Manor has fallen to me. I have many business interests and investments among which I own a large number of horses. Not too long ago, I went to the Continent to take care of some business. New Orleans, to be exact. I also had the intention of purchasing some good horseflesh for breeding and establish stables at Whetherford Manor. I gained Pegasus in an unusual manner, but he is an excellent addition for what I have in mind."

Kat remembered the gossip—the tale of a man mistreating a white stallion and how the *dark devil* had taken the whip away, and then the horse. The rumormongers told of Lord Whetherford's fierce temper. But the man before her seemed compassionate.

"Someday, I hope to breed the finest animals around." He spoke with pride and his voice soothed her to a state of peaceful longing.

"I told you I returned to Whetherford, hoping to raise a family. Someday, I will marry and share a life with someone." He watched her with interest, as though her reaction mattered to him.

Her heart rose to her throat and she nearly choked. Why did the thought of him married to someone else make her chest tighten and her temples throb?

"The woman you resemble, the woman I sent my men after, when I returned from the Continent I found Juliana and her father had sequestered my home. He died and she had gone. Not only did she leave, but she took my mother's jewel necklace. A gift from my father. A Whetherford family heirloom."

Morgan's eyes took on a faraway look. "I found my mother often holding the necklace to her breast, with a smile on her face just before she lifted it to fasten around her neck. I seldom saw her without it. She even wore it to balls, and what my father called fancy affairs, in London."

A light breeze brushed across her cheek, bringing his scent along with it. She closed her eyes and inhaled deeply. A woozy feeling of dizzy delight spun in her mind. His husky voice reverberated through the air causing tiny prickles to dance across her skin.

"I kept the necklace locked up like a sacred treasure, honoring my parent's memory. The fact that Juliana had touched it at all was enough to anger me. When I found out she'd taken it . . ." Morgan's face grew harsh and his hands fisted.

Kat stood, and on silent feet went to him. She placed her hand on the crook of his arm. "I'm sorry."

He looked down and gave her a smile that melted her already enchanted heart. "Please don't apologize. The matter is over." He covered her hand with his own. "I *will* get the necklace back."

She tried looking away, but his gaze held hers immobile. She'd been told she had expressive eyes and they usually showed whatever her current train of thought might be. At this moment, she feared he would see the longing and know the depth of her yearning.

Morgan placed a kiss on the back of her knuckles, gave her hands a quick squeeze and to her shock, stepped back. "You enjoy being here in the flower garden. I'm glad."

She blinked. Surely, he did not hold back because he thought she would strike him again? Horror still struck her chest when she thought of that. God, how she hated her rash action in London. Horrified that she had stuck him, when she should have aimed her confusion and annoyance at herself. Her foolish, impulsive behavior had infuriated him. A man of his stature would certainly not be very forgiving. "Yes, it is very beautiful."

"Of course, not as beautiful as you."

So, he had forgiven her? He stepped closer, swamping her with his male physique. His penetrating stare started her heart to pounding. A rush of air escaped between her teeth. His face sharpened with hunger.

Kiss me. Kiss me, Morgan.

He stood there, his expression one of pain, for so long she thought she would expire. The vein on his temple stood out. He resisted. He fought something. What was it? She silently willed him again.

Kiss me.

A sigh escaped Kat's lips drawing his attention to her plush mouth. The mouth he'd tasted in London. Lush lips slightly parted as if waiting... The ache in his gut amplified. Hungry for a taste, his tongue hissed behind his teeth, just as he remembered a slap against his cheek—the crack still resounding in his ears.

Morgan pushed away the memory.

Her beauty drew him. Soft lashes fluttered over her eyes, but not before he saw hunger in their depths. His loins reacted. He had to kiss her.

Did he dare?

His gaze traveled down the slender column of her alluring neck and moved farther, lingering on naked flesh spilling from the embracing bodice. His fingers itched to touch the white silken skin and follow the trail his eyes had just taken. So tempting. So lovely. A violent surge of need thumped his lower region.

He stepped closer, his thighs brushing her gown. Sun-kissed tresses fell in waves caressing her bosom. He lifted one strand and rubbed it between his fingers. Raising the silky curl to his lips, he inhaled her scent, then gently returned the fiery strand where it rested over her breast. Her sudden intake of breath gripped him by the gut. She could deny until hell froze, but she was not immune to his touch. Her face flushed, her breathing rapid—making her delightful bosom rise and fall—she was exquisite. His hands ached to feel her softness.

With a feather light touch, he slid one finger across her cheek. Her eyes closed. His thumb traced the line of her bottom lip, from one enticing corner to the other. Her lids fluttered open and she gave a siren's smile. A jolt went through his belly.

"You are very beautiful." Unable to resist, he lowered his head and briefly touched his lips to hers. Soft and so damned sweet, just like he remembered.

His palms gently gripped her shoulders and pulled her into his embrace, meshing her breasts with his chest. The hitch in her breathing had been music to his ears, but her eager response staggered him. He held her mouth open while he plundered the secrets within. Hoping he did not scare her, for she made it damned difficult to restrain his passion, demanding to be released.

Morgan let his lips linger, and then he forced himself to pull back. Encouraged she did not resist him, he placed a gentle kiss on her temple. He kissed her brow, her eyes, her nose. Leaning back, he searched her eyes for breathless moments. What he saw drew him in, ever so slowly, lessening the distance, and once again, he tenderly put his mouth on hers.

Sensations he believed long dead swept through him. His body came thrillingly alive. His lips moved over hers, needing more. When his tongue teased its way into her mouth, her hands tangled in his hair and he caught her gasp of pleasure. A deep sense of satisfaction filled him. He took advantage. Kissing her slowly, leisurely, savoring every drop of her fervent embrace.

Good God. She moaned.

His mind reeled. The sweet sound urged him on. One hand reached for her breast before his mind could tell him he should not.

She gave herself, willingly. Such hunger from an innocent.

He wanted to plunder, take possession. But, he could not lose his head. Her aunt was in his bloody house. With disciplined strength, he pulled away.

An ache spread through his lower region. He studied her. Lids closed, flush from his kisses, he nearly changed his mind. The need to possess—the urge to protect . . .

Blood and the devil.

He'd never been so consumed with a woman. His stomach tensed to rock hardness. She had plagued his thoughts for weeks. He could not lose control now. He loosened his hold.

"What? No whack up side my head," he whispered.

She smiled before opening her eyes. "At the moment, my hands are otherwise occupied. My disposition is such I shall ignore your teasing and enjoy this occurrence."

Morgan exhaled a deep sigh. "You have me at sixes and sevens, Katherine. I never know what to expect from you."

She pulled free. "You should not expect anything, my lord."

"My lord? Why so formal after . . ."

She placed her fingers over his lips. "Please. Don't ruin it." She puckered her lips and whispered, "Shhhhh."

His mouth slightly opened and he drew one finger inside. He sucked the tip while his eager tongue laved her sensitive flesh. At her gasp, his chest lurched and his cock thickened. Forcing his mind to govern his urges, he ignored his baser instincts to throw up her skirts and satisfy his gnawing hunger.

Suddenly, withdrawing her fingers, she blew him a kiss. The damned minx. Then she lifted the hem of her gown and hurried back to the manor.

Chapter 20

Morgan holed up in his study with the insane thought that if he buried his head in paperwork, the effort would keep him from thinking of Katherine. He agonized over every note, every figure, forcing his mind to concentrate on the Whetherford accounts.

It was useless.

She'd been gone three days. Not an hour of the day went by that he didn't ache for her. He envisioned his fingers tangled in her hair, pulling her face closer, closer for his kiss. And what a kiss. Her response had rocked him to his toes. What kept him from taking her there in the garden, he had no idea—for he'd wanted her badly.

He leaned back in his leather chair and scrubbed a hand over his face. Her scent still lingered in the air. He closed his eyes and saw luxurious waves of amber silk. He imagined getting lost in that cloud of velvet while spread across his pillow. He imagined alabaster breasts with aroused beading nipples. Long sleek thighs open in invitation.

Blood and the devil.

He shoved out of his chair with the force of a strong wind. Frustration propelled him out of doors. Determined to push her from his mind, he saddled his stallion. Spirited as ever, Thunder pranced, anxious to make a mad dash across the open field. Morgan gave him his head and they took off at a furious pace, racing until both were exhausted. Orange streaks grazed the evening sky, alerting him to the lateness of the hour.

An owl hooted in the distance. A lonely sound. He clicked his tongue and brought Thunder about. Then, sinking in the saddle, he dropped the reins giving Thunder his head. The stallion knew his way home. With a lazy rhythm, Morgan rocked as hooved footfalls plodded home.

He peered at the stars and wondered if the man in the moon was lonely. He had been lonely most of his adult life. He'd never allowed the feeling to enter his seclusion, at least he'd never admitted his lonesomeness. Looking back, he'd been too busy putting his neck on the line to let the emptiness sink in. But it was there. Pulling at him, enticing him to sink down in further misery. The loss of his family nearly devastated him. Cocky in his youth, he'd thrilled at adventure and spit at danger. What idiocy. He often wondered if his parents' spirit had kept him safe. Watched over and sheltered him from his own folly.

A light glowed from the stables, outlining a man's form. Doc. One of many men Morgan had met while on his road to destruction. Even though he'd been branded a *dark devil*, he managed to make lifelong friends along the way. He tugged the reins and brought Thunder to a halt.

Doc waited with his arms braced on his hips. "Out kinda late. Was thinkin' maybe I ought to come fetch ya."

With a smile, Morgan shifted in the saddle. "Worried about me, were you?"

"Nah," Doc said. "A mite worried about the horse."

Morgan grabbed the saddle-horn and dismounted. Holding the bit, he brushed Thunder's mane. "You hear that, boy? Doc here thinks more of you than me."

"That's cause I know you can take care of yourself." Doc leaned to the side and spit a stream of brown juice in the dirt.

Six years ago, on a grievous mission, Doc had been a contact. Morgan quickly learned the man's worth. When the time came for him to return to Whetherford, he offered Doc a place at his home, which was a good thing, for he'd saved Morgan's hide in that London back-alley.

"You think so? Even after my fiasco in London involving a pretty redhead?"

"You're here, ain't ya?"

"Thanks to you," Morgan replied.

Doc grunted. "Giles' man rode over here a while ago. Left a note at the main house. I'll take Thunder." Doc reached for the reins. "Come on, boy. I got a big bag of oats for ya."

Morgan sharply turned on his heel and headed for the manor. As soon as he closed the door, he yelled, "Frederick?"

"Yes, my lord?"

He came out of nowhere. The man was a damned ghost.

"I understand the Duke's man was here."

"Yes, my lord." Frederick held out a folded parchment with the Duke's seal. Morgan tore it open.

"Good, God." He folded the missive and marched to his study, the sound of his booted heels impatient. He closed the study door and walked behind his desk. Pulling the note from his pocket, he smoothed the parchment open and stared at the words.

We found him.
You'll be happy to know
he's in one piece—barely.
Giles

Albert picked up his pipe and ambled to the hearth. Propping a forearm on top of the ledge, he took a puff from his pipe and lifted his face toward the ceiling. Rings of smoke swirled in the air at a lazy pace, reflecting the heaviness that had elevated from his chest the moment he received the news. Heat penetrated his skin, but the warmth inside came from knowing his nephew had been found. *Thank God.*

By thunder, I knew Giles was the man.

Giles—not the duke—had lived up to his reputation. From the sound of things, he had been the perfect selection. The *duke* also had a reputation. Spotless. Honorable. A nobleman descended from a long line of respectable dukes. Both men, dualistically speaking, were praiseworthy. His first choice, Whetherford was better considered to occupy his niece, so he moved on to his second choice—equally proficient.

Yes, he'd been aware of his niece's obstinate behavior. She had always been an impulsive sort. He prided himself as an excellent judge of character and interpreting a person's body language. His instincts had never failed him in the past. And he had directed many exploits on his correct assumptions.

The door behind him opened.

"Albert. You sent for me?" Elizabeth stood with her hand still on the doorknob. His heart twisted at the anxious look on her face. The love he had for his wife went beyond anything he'd ever imagined. Raw emotions bubbled to the surface. He turned his back to the burning logs.

"Come in, my dear." Albert strode to his desk and placed his pipe in a marble bowl. When the door closed, he held his arms open. He loved this wonderful woman. For thirty years she'd been by his side. They'd shared many blessings, and he considered Katherine one of their best. Even though he and Elizabeth had no children of their own, the love they shared made his life complete. There was nothing like the warmth of a good woman.

Elizabeth slid her hands around his middle. "You are scaring me. Has there been news?"

"Can I not enjoy holding my wife?" Albert pulled her close. "Yes, my dear. I will not make you wait. Stephen is safe."

Elizabeth jerked back. Her anxious eyes stared up at him. "Stephen? You are sure?"

"Yes, Lizzy. He's coming home." Albert caressed her cheek with his thumb. "I hope those are happy tears."

"Oh, Albert." She hugged him fiercely. All the months of keeping her fears in check suddenly dissolved as the floodgates holding her tears burst open.

He held her until her sobs quieted and her shoulders stopped shaking, all the while soothing her with long strokes up and down her spine. When she calmed, she stepped back and brushed at her face.

"We must tell Katherine. Right away."

"Tell me what?"

When Aunt Elizabeth turned, tears shimmered and she hurriedly dabbed her eyes. Kat's blood chilled.

"Oh, God. Stephen." She flung her hand to her throat in despair.

As if her uncle realized her thoughts, he took a step forward with out-stretched hands. "Stephen is safe."

Her eyes darted to his. Once his words registered, she wobbled. "Thank God."

He rushed forward and put his arm around her shoulders. "My dear, Stephen is all right."

Stephen is all right.

"My head is spinning."

"He's coming home." Elizabeth said in a choked voice, swiping at the moisture on her cheek.

"When I saw your tears . . . I thought." Kat rested her gaze on her aunt, and choked back a hysterical laugh. Then she turned to her uncle. "Is it true?"

His gaze softened and he smiled while nodding.

A wave of relief flooded her entire body. She had been so worried. Her mother and father had died. With Stephen being gone so long, she had feared he too had met his fate. She had waited and waited for her aunt and uncle to take her seriously when she had voiced her apprehension. She thought they had ignored her. She did not like being told all was well and she not concern herself. Nor the many excuses she had been given. She never meant to disappoint them with her brazenness, but she had known in her heart that her brother was in trouble long ago. She was not about to sit back, like a prim and proper miss, and do nothing.

If only her uncle had told her of his concern, and not concealed the fact, but that he had acted. That he was searching for Stephen.

None of that mattered now. He had found Stephen. Tears of relief stemmed her eyes.

"You have heard from him? When?"

"Come. Sit. I will tell you what I know." He led her to the sofa and she collapsed. He gestured to the opposite settee. "Please, Lizzy." He guided Aunt Liz over, and then sat beside her.

Katherine's nervous fingers pulled at her skirts. Unable to remain still, she leaned forward on the edge of her seat. "Where is he?"

Trepidation glittered in his eyes. He glanced to Elizabeth, then back to her. "India."

"India?" An uneasiness settled into the pit of her stomach. "What is he doing there?"

Elizabeth placed her hand over Albert's. In turn, he cupped his hand over hers and squeezed. "Stephen's ship crashed upon some rocks in Indian waters."

Aunt Elizabeth jerked her hand, covering her mouth.

"But he survived," Kat said quickly, needing the assurance Stephen was alive.

"Yes," Albert replied. "He was hurt and has been recuperating."

"Uncle. How bad was Stephen hurt? Are you sure he's alright?" Her anxiety grew. "Why did he not send word before now?"

"Katherine, my dear. You can stop fretting. Stephen is well and on his way home."

***

Kat sat on a velvet cushioned stool in front of her looking glass. Had Morgan been responsible for finding her brother? She'd done the right thing in approaching him. And now Stephen was coming home.

One hand held the silver brush, as the other twisted a strand around her fingers. Remembering Morgan's kiss, she studied her lips, noting their fullness. She raised her hand, placing her fingers over her mouth. Her eyes closed and his image flourished clear in her mind. The man sure knew how to kiss.

Dear God, how she wanted to experience his touch again. He made her want to do things. Like kiss him forever. Touch him in ways that a woman would touch a man.

She caught herself. Certainly understandable why young girls needed chaperones.

Morgan.

He fascinated her like no other man she'd met. The London dandies had been more interested in themselves, than in her. Rakes flirted outrageously, and what her uncle called young bucks had gone out of their way to get her attention. Even at her coming out, she'd not found anyone who caught her interest. Of course, she had been curious about kissing, but no one had ever made her desire a second one. Not one fella had made her mind fog over, let alone her toes curl. She allowed one or two the liberty of a kiss. The wet, slobbery press to her mouth had been disgusting.

This dark, threatening, brooding, mysterious man pulled at her heart strings. She'd never felt these perplexing feelings before. Why now? What was different about Morgan?

The man could be maddening. Keeping her locked inside a room for weeks. But then, she should not blame him entirely for the *mistake*. Oh, how she'd grown to hate that word. And it really was not his fault. If not for the blunder in identities, she would never have met Lord Whetherford.

Morgan.

Since meeting him, she'd done her share of naughty thinking. She'd had lurid notions. Shocking ideas. And she just could not help herself. Every moment she spent with him lifted her mind and her spirit, creating a mystical excitement. An awakening within that roused her with burning curiosity.

A sudden image of Charity flashed in her mind, the one where she had that dreamy look of contentment.

It will be something like you have never felt before in your life.

After that kiss, there was no doubt—Morgan was the man she wanted. Never had a man triggered such an impact on her sensibilities. His kiss lured her into a world she had never experienced before. Oh, how she wanted to explore the feelings that had sprung to life. That quivered her flesh right down to her very bones. Morgan was the one she fancied to teach her passion. The one to answer the craving of what she had yet to learn. She knew she would never find this magnetism with another man. With him, maybe she would experience what Charity and Byron shared.

She held the back of her hand against her mouth to suppress a yawn. The lamp cast a soft glow about her form while highlighting her crimson hair reflecting her image in the mirror.

The other woman popped in her head—the woman who she had been mistaken for. Doubts assailed her. Could Morgan be attracted to her because she resembled the one he tried to find in London? What was Juliana to Morgan? Did Juliana have a place in his heart?

Kat shook the unwelcome thought away. She was not jealous. Besides, Morgan searched for Juliana because she stole from him—nothing more.

Kat laid down the brush and padded to the window Pushing aside the sheer covering, she gazed into the darkness seeing dark eyes—black as midnight. Curly blue-black hair—tempting her to run her fingers through its silky softness.

I suppose I should thank him.

It would be the proper thing to do.

Yes, she would go to Morgan and thank him for his part in finding her brother. A note would not do. She must thank him in person.

With that decision made, the next one would be much harder. She strode back and forth across the hand-woven carpet at the foot of her bed. What reason could she invent to go to Whetherford Manor?

None.

None that would satisfy her uncle.

Chapter 21

F rustration of this kind was making him unbalanced.

Up to this point, Morgan had embraced freedom. He answered to no one other than himself. He had taken his pleasure with the thirst of a dying man whenever and wherever he happened to be. For who knew, the next mission could be the end of his cursed existence.

Then Katherine appeared—forcefully—right in the middle of his organized life, disrupting his well thought out plans. He huffed out a breath and braced his boot on the fountain. He had come to his grandfather's garden for solace. Katherine's presence lingered.

Just thinking about her gave him a feeling of contentment. A long-term relationship with her. Here. In his home. Where he could see her every day. Make love to her every night. Her breathtaking body joined with his. Her thighs locked around his hips. Her breathless pants while he stroked in and out of her.

Bloody hell!

Morgan stared at the flowers before him. He caressed the delicate petals and wished her hands were caressing him.

Good God! Was he never to strike her from his mind?

He shoved off the stone and took three furious strides before he came up short, shoving both hands through his unruly hair.

What was wrong with him? He had to get control. She was just a damned female.

One that twisted his guts.

A soft crunch on the stone path alerted him that he was no longer alone. For one insane moment, he thought it was Katherine. He cursed himself for his folly before he turned.

"What is it, Frederick?"

"She's here, my lord."

She?

"What are you going on about?"

"You have a visitor. Miss Radbourn."

He blinked as if Frederick had announced the house was on fire. The object of his contemplations. Had his imaginings conjured her up? His impulse to run would have shocked his servant. But why should Morgan give a damn? Except that he would not give the servants fodder for gossip by appearing like a lovesick jackass.

"I gather Mrs. Beasley is preparing refreshment for Miss Radbourn and her aunt?"

Frederick cleared his throat. "Miss Radbourn is alone."

Without a chaperone? What the bleeding hell is she doing here—alone?

Morgan's gaze locked on his servant. Keeping his voice calm, he asked, "Where is she?"

"In the south drawing room."

As Morgan strode through the door and down the corridor, he envisaged a disaster. What urgency had brought Katherine to Whetherford? *Alone.* His steps quickened. When he entered the drawing room, he found her pacing madly in front of the fireplace. His breath caught. The fire cast a translucent glow around the seductive form moving back and forth. Her hands betrayed the nervousness within. Her profile in shadow, yet when she spun, the flickering flames bounced off her features and her beauty excelled from the determination of her set chin.

When she saw him she came to a sudden stop. "Lord Whetherford."

"Miss Radbourn." He closed the set of doors. Folding his arms across his chest, he leaned back against them. "I thought we had settled this."

Her brows shot to her hairline. "What?"

He almost hated teasing her when she looked so apprehensive. "My given name is Morgan. I enjoy hearing you use it."

Her breath came out in a light whoosh and her gaze lowered to the floor. Cunningly, her head rose. A smile curved one side of her mouth. "Morgan."

Hearing his name uttered so sweetly, her voice a soft caress, his heart kicked against his ribs. And the gleam in her eyes could burn him to cinders. With a control he did not feel, he took his time as he advanced toward her. She dropped her arms by her sides. The noted stiffening of her body caused him to halt.

"I . . . I am sorry I arrived without notice."

"You are a long way from home. I must admit, I am curious. What has brought you to my doorstep? *Alone*." Her beautiful mouth hung open. Yet all he could think of was how much he wanted to kiss that mouth. "It is not exactly proper for you to be here without a chaperone."

"I am on my way to visit my friend, Charity."

"Forgive me for pointing this out, but isn't the Viscount's property in the opposite direction?"

"Lord—I mean, Morgan," she stammered. "I wanted you to know . . . that is . . ."

With her temperament, he would never suspect her at a loss of words. He gestured to the sofa. "Please. Won't you sit down?" Watching her primly smooth her gloved hands over her skirts, he stepped to the side-table and poured a splash of sherry into a crystal flute. Katherine was clearly nervous. What outlandish scheme was she hatching now? Or was it something else? With unwavering steps, he moved across the room and sat beside her before putting the wineglass in her hand. "Has something happened?"

She took a sip. Then her chest rose as she sucked in a deep breath.

Dread pierced his spine. "Good God. What is it?"

Her gaze flew to his. "Nothing. I know I should not have come alone. But, I wanted to thank you."

Morgan's head spun with bewilderment. "Thank me? You have undoubtedly cursed me to the devil many times. I cannot imagine why you would want to thank me."

Although . . . if you really wanted to thank me—full pouting lips.

Katherine fidgeted on her lascivious bottom. "But, you see. It was you—wasn't' it?"

Her expression, so warm and filled with gratitude, and her willingness to show her appreciation turned him inside out. He focused on her elegant neck, wondering if the pulse in her delicate vein matched the throbbing in his cock. Abruptly, he rose to his feet and tramped back to the sideboard hoping to conceal the heated quickening in his breeches. He could conceivably control his ardor as long as he put some distance between them.

Seizing the bottle by the neck, he removed the stopper and splashed brandy into a tumbler. "I'm sorry, my dear girl. You must start at the beginning."

"When I came to Whetherford with my aunt, I told you about my brother, Stephen. I asked for your help."

Morgan recalled her tear-stained face when she had asked him to find her brother. He dipped his head. "Go on."

As Katherine talked, her voice flowed over him soothing his inner beast. His gaze embraced her smooth cheeks, then wandered, caressing her delicious lips, touching her jutting chin, cuddling her perfect swanlike neck. Following the pulsing vein down to the swells above her bodice, of which he drank freely. He raised the goblet to his lips and forced the liquid down his throat.

"My uncle told me Stephen is coming home." Kat's voice grew stronger. "I know you had something to do with finding him."

Morgan gave a slight shrug. "I merely repeated your concern to some friends. They found him." No need to mention Giles—or her uncle, for that matter.

"Nevertheless, I am in your debt."

Morgan hated being the villain in her eyes. He hated her gratitude even more. "You give me too much credit. Have you forgotten the first time you came to my home, you were brought by force?" Why the hell did he mention that when he wanted to erase the horrible experience from her memory?

"That was not your doing." She took a sip of her claret and lowered her eyes. "Besides, I have put it behind me."

Had she?

She did come here to thank him. Giles finding her brother had fortuitously dropped her into Morgan's randy lap.

He strode to the door and yanked it open. Just as he suspected, his servant stood at a discreet distance. "Frederick. Prepare a chamber for Miss Radbourn. She has come with an urgent message. Since it is late, she has agreed to accept my hospitality. Miss Radbourn will spend the night at Whetherford Manor and continue on her way in the morning. Please tell Mrs. Beasley two for dinner."

"Yes, my lord." With a slight bow, Frederick pivoted on his heel and marched down the corridor.

Morgan stepped back and closed the door. One look at Kat and his heart accelerated at an arresting pace. How the hell would he survive with her under his roof all night? Katherine licked her lips and his eyes fastened on her mouth. Full-blown lava flooded his entire lower region. God, he found her intoxicating. He locked the door.

Opportunity knocked, and he'd be damned if he would look a gift horse in the mouth. He willed control over his body before he went out of his lecherous mind. This insane hunger—this craving—for her had to stop. One taste should take care of that.

His gaze returned to hers, the magnetic pull irresistible, those mesmerizing green eyes. Slanted cat-like eyes, calling to him. Cat eyes . . . Kat . . . *His Kat*.

With unhurried steps, he crossed the room. As if hypnotized, he never took his eyes from hers. Her spring water scent enveloped his senses. He reached out, palm open, and waited for her to place her hand in his. She sat her crystal down and placed her warm palm into his. Dynamic sparks shocked his inner core making him mad with longing. He pulled her to him, not once taking his eyes from hers, and lowered his head.

Her eyes fluttered, then closed. That was all the invitation he needed.

Soft lips meshed with his.

She was heaven in his arms. He deepened the kiss. Her body trembled and she readily kissed him back.

His tongue slid between her lips, searching, delving in her depths. Tasting her sweet nectar drowned his sanities, drawing him deeper into her hold. Fire spread through his chest. The heady sensation made him crush her firm against him. She clung to him while his hands roamed on a path of their own. He found the knot in her rich, vibrant hair and loosened the pins from their confinement. His lips made a trail down her neck to kiss the pulse at her throat. God's blood, she had the softest skin. He had to taste her mouth again. Sweet. So sweet.

Her breath came in quick gasps. Another bolt of desire shot to his loins making him clasp her tighter. She whimpered and trembled against his frame. Every nerve stood to attention. Her reaction encouraged him. His very essence strived for control. If she kept pressing against him his head would explode—both of them.

Christ! Before it came to that, he had to govern his randy cock. She was not one to throw up her skirts and get the deed done, even if his rod was stiff and ready to burst his breeches for freedom.

Morgan groaned and reluctantly ended the kiss. He stared down at the beauty with eyes still closed, and he almost—almost—threw caution to the wind.

"Katherine. We are in my drawing room where servants are about. Frederick would not utter a word, but I will not give the housekeepers more to gossip about. I spent a lot of time in the scullery when I was a boy. A youth can acquire a wealth of knowledge from nattering servants."

He willed himself to step back, but his feet never moved. Passion-swollen lips roused and yearning eyes beckoned him.

Morgan clasped her palm and pressed it against his chest. "Can you not feel my heart pounding?" He rubbed his thumb across her lower lip and heard her intake of breath. "I am trying to be a gentleman." He wanted more than a quick tumble. He wanted hours and hours, maybe days, making love to her. What he really needed was the strength to control his raging lust.

"This is what you do to me. Your beauty takes my breath away. Your voice sends chills down my spine." He turned her delicate wrist over to place a kiss in her palm. "Your touch makes me shiver with delight. My heart pounds, and blood races through my veins just to be near you. You are exquisite beyond words."

Her eyes flickered.

Holding her hand, he returned her palm to his chest, laying it across his heart, not daring to embrace her further. With his eyes closed, he drew in a deep, exalting breath. "Your fragrance incites my senses."

Her hand caressed his chest making his nostrils flare and his breathing constrict. Soft fingers slid around his neck and she pressed her body against him, showing him what she could not voice with words.

Young in years, young in experience, but exceedingly mature, and the loveliest mouth this side of heaven. An innocent, yet the body of a woman. How he would love to teach her all the delights in making love. His cock was stretched to the limit. There was only one way to make the ache go away.

Like a man drowning in the ocean, he succumbed to the waves overtaking him. He covered her mouth and feasted. With both hands tilting her head, he slanted his mouth to thrust his tongue more fully into her wet haven. She trembled and gave back as much as her innocence would allow. Thrilled, Morgan tightened his embrace. He could not get enough of her sweetness.

His hand moved ever so slowly to her waist, caressed her there, then circling, teased its way up pausing at her ribs. He deliberately tormented her, enticed her. Then at last he palmed her breast. Her startled gasp drove him on. His cunning tongue stroked along the line of her lips, while his fingers grazed her nipple.

In her eagerness, Kat pressed closer, working havoc with his control. He tried to restrain his passion, but her incredible response only drove him further. He could not lose control, for he would regret taking her in a hurry. A raw ache formed in his belly.

He bent down, slipping his arm under the back of her knees and lifted her. She gripped his neck as if she would never let him go, and kissed him with vigor. He gently placed her on the sofa, then stretched his length beside her. His Kat looked at him longingly, wanting whatever happened next. God, she was beautiful. Desirable. His fingers tugged her gown, inch by enticing inch. Pulling the ribbon free that held her chemise, her full breasts came into full view. His gut twisted. She was a treasure beyond words.

He had to taste.

He took one pouting bud between his lips. A mewing sound escaped her and she surged toward him.

Need gripped him in the ballocks.

While he worshiped her with his mouth, her hands tightened in his hair. Such passion stifled his restraint. He laved her bud, and then lightly sucked. She clasped his head, her hungry, awakening body twisting in his arms. She jerked as his teeth grazed her nipple, sending a delicious thrill of satisfaction through him. He made love to the other breast just as thoroughly and as leisurely, taking his time, relishing in her body language that begged him to move lower with his kisses.

His hands eased their way down her sweet, soft flesh. Their clothes a barrier, he quickly made short work of the confining material. He grazed her silken thigh, anxiously seeking her pleasure spot. When he cupped her woman's mound, Kat arched her back. His fingers parted her woman's flesh, slick with dew. Satisfaction swamped him. He brushed one finger over the center of her cleft, a shocked moan escaped from her throat. He stroked her there again. She lunged, nearly bucking him off. When he inserted his finger, she shrieked and he captured it in his mouth.

Heart pounding, he devoured her mouth in another heated kiss and let his fingers begin their love-play. His throat convulsed as this sweet blossoming woman fastened her hands about his waist and buried her face in his throat. Open mouth kisses caressed his neck, making his cock scream for intimacy. He angled and pressed, aiming to heighten her senses, intensify her pleasure. Her ferocious movements in her raging passion inflamed his fevered mind. With everything in him, he fought the urge to thrust his throbbing cock in the wet warmth awaiting him.

This moment was for her.

His fingers worked their magic on her woman's bud and she rocked wild in his arms. He inserted another finger and Kat cried out. He kissed her with fervor and all the passion raging in his body, thrusting his tongue in and out of her mouth, in the same manner as he thrust his fingers in and out of her slick folds.

She stiffened and ground her head back against the cushion. Blood pounded in his temples as she exploded from his ministrations. Guttural sounds spewed forth from her throat, the most thrilling sounds he'd ever heard.

He played with her until she calmed, and the fingers biting into his shoulders relaxed.

Chapter 22

Kat opened her eyes. And bit back the gasp at the fire blazing in Morgan's. The most wonderful sensation flowed through her body. In a sensual daze, she raised her fingers and traced his lips—the ones that had devoured her mouth and made her lose all reason.

His lower body pressed into her hip. A thrill dashed through her belly at the bulge encroaching there. After the thunder she had just experienced, how was it possible for her to want more? Somewhat embarrassed, she tucked her head, burrowing into his warmth.

She felt a finger under her chin. He lifted, bringing her gaze to meet his. His expression did not change, but she'd swear his eyes darkened.

She had no control over her thoughts or her actions. Better yet, she didn't want to. She wanted to touch him. She needed to put her hands there, where she knew she shouldn't. More determined than ever, she was ready to experience love. Morgan's love. Eager for him to do those unimaginable things to her body that would make her a woman.

She ignored the niggling voice of her conscience. This dark handsome devil that electrified her to her very core. That promised her delights beyond her wildest dreams.

Curiosity and daring had always been her weakness. Morgan made her weak with longing. She had the man of her dreams in her arms and he had just given her the most extraordinary experience of her life.

She wanted to please him. She slid her hand down his chest, making her path known before she reached her goal. Holding his gaze, she inched closer and closer. His eyes glinted as if he dared her to continue. When she grazed the hardness beneath his clothing, the breath hissed through his teeth.

She covered him the way he had palmed her *mons* and wondered if he received the same intense joy. Excitement drove her movements. She squeezed. His groan of delight exhilarated her with power.

She recalled her daring when she caressed his chest through his shirt. Then he'd jerked it over his head and tossed it to the floor. And the thrilling satisfaction she'd received when she caressed his bare chest. Dark hair generously spread across finely chiseled muscle and how good he felt.

Soft silk. Warm flesh. Rock-hard muscles. He felt so delicious, she did not want to stop touching him. She could not caress him enough. Would it be the same—

With a ragged curse, his hand jerked hers, and he opened his placket. His manhood burst free. "Like this, Kat. I beg you, like this."

Her surprise turned quickly to enthusiastic surrender. She was about to find out.

His hand covered hers as he showed her how to stroke him. Hot, so hot. Smooth as silk. Hard as steel. Good Lord, this was astounding.

Perplexing.

Spectacular.

And Morgan wanted her touch. Liked her touch. He gritted his teeth, but she knew he did not want her to stop. Sheer pleasure unlike anything she had ever known flowed through her entire body knowing she held such intoxicating power. She closed her hand around him and squeezed.

He groaned.

"Am I hurting you?"

"God, yes. The same as you, just before you found your pleasure, when I had my hand on you."

"Am I giving you pleasure?" she whispered.

"Ahhh, yes. A sweet, welcome agony. But, if you do not stop, I'm afraid my pleasure may embarrass us both." He buried his hand in her hair and kissed her as though he were a man dying of thirst. Suddenly, he broke free and stilled her hand. "We must stop."

"Please, Morgan. I do not want to stop."

"Good, God, Kat. I want you."

"You have me."

"No. You do not understand. You are still chaste."

"Make me yours."

He closed his eyes with a such a grimace, she wondered if he was in real pain. When he opened them again, his black eyes smoldered. If eyes could burn, Morgan's would have left her in a melting heap of cinders. With something between a growl and a groan, he fastened his mouth to hers. He squeezed her buttocks and pulled her fully against his erection while his hips rotated, grinding his pelvis against her belly. Her excitement grew. Then his mouth gentled, and his lips left a trail of hot scorching kisses along her neck.

Kat never knew she could be so relaxed and so tense at the same time. Her hands fisted in his hair, so soft and thick. His lips trailed lower to her breast.

"Ohhhh, Morgan." The tingling sensation was so fierce, she felt it throughout her entire body. She was caught in a fog-like trance of pure emotion. His passionate kisses had her head spinning. Morgan had swept her off her feet, but this was no white knight that carried off the princess in a fairy tale. This was a real flesh and blood man. He looked at her as though he could eat her alive. The way she felt right now, she would gladly let him.

Her anticipation knew no bounds as he held her gaze while his naked chest rubbed against her aching breasts. Remarkable sensation took her breath. His hands moved down her body, caressing every inch of her exposed flesh. Another wave of longing thumped her center.

When Morgan eased the silky gown over her hips and tossed it to the floor, she thought 'at last'. Her chemise quickly followed. He took her breast, again, into his mouth, sucking hard, while his fingers searched below. And then she was lost to an explosion of phenomenal sensations lancing through her body. So many, she could not react on one before another—as violent as the first—came pouring over her.

A bolt of pressure swelled between her legs, so severe, she knew she was going to die. Suddenly he removed his fingers. Before she knew what was happening an invasion of slick steel infiltrated where his fingers had been.

Morgan tried to go slowly since it was her first time. He knew she was a virgin, but she made him lose some of what little control he had. She was so slick and wet. Gritting his teeth, he pushed himself inside her, only a bit. Holding back was killing him. Their gazes locked for a brief eternity, then he slowly gave a slight thrust forward. The halting penetration gave a vibration of sorts creating a suction sensation so powerful, it nearly blew his head off. He could hold back no longer and plunged through the barrier of her maidenhead.

Finally. He was inside her. His cock ready to explode from the sheer sensitivity of her honeyed sheath. Tight. So tight. He closed his eyes which only made the whirling sensation consume him. He gritted his teeth hard enough to make his jaw ache. After a few heart pounding moments, he ground his hips against her, opening her, stretching her to accept his size.

When he lifted his hips, she threw her arms and legs around him in desperation, imprisoning him. If he had not been so near to bursting, he would have laughed at her reluctance to let him go. Hell. He wasn't going anywhere. He pulled out just a bit, then pushed back into her depths.

She tightened her arms around him even more. He pulled out, and pushed in again—the milking chafing crazed his brain. Her kitten-like mews drove him. Again, and again, he moved in and out of her. Damn, this felt too good. His strokes grew faster, harder, deeper. His breathing ragged. His weight heavy, but still she clung to him. She rocked with him trapped between her legs. Feeling her shudders, he plunged one last time, thrusting his cock as deep as it would go.

Blood pounded his temples, his body rigid as stone. He threw back his head as wave after wave of blinding pleasure poured through him. Teeth clenched, he groaned over the most shattering climax he'd ever known. This slip of a woman had brought him to his knees.

❦

All through dinner, Morgan could not take his eyes off her. Unable to perceive a coherent thought, for he remembered the staggering passion of this afternoon—in the drawing room, no less. Was he out of his mind?

Yes.

Out of his mind with lust. Lust for Kat. To the point that his servants could go hang. Whetherford Manor was his home. His domain.

But he would not want to shame Kat. Although the object of his desire did not appear dissuaded by any discomfort. She sat as beautiful as a fiery angel, as confident as a maiden warrior. After their bout of lovemaking this afternoon, he had worried a moment of awkwardness. But the charming beauty amazed him again. Her face—and delectable body—glowing with the aftermath of their passion, she'd gathered her clothes and dressed with quiet dignity. He swore he felt the kiss she coyly blew in his direction as she sashayed through the door.

His eyes locked on her elegant neck. His mouth salivated at the thought of tasting her sweet flesh. Of his tongue teasing the lobe of her ear. Feeling her body squirm as he blew a hot breath over her delicate shell. He resisted the urge to cross his legs. As his gaze followed the pulsing vein down to the swells above her bodice, he allowed the heated quickening in his breeches to flow through him. He raised his goblet to his lips and forced the liquid down his throat. His heightened arousal made it difficult to breath, let alone swallow the damn drink.

If only he could undo the damage he'd already done. No matter how hard he tried, he could not erase the experience of this afternoon. Never mind she'd been an innocent. Never mind she'd come to his home on her own. The facts were the facts. He had taken her virginity. He could not undo that. Yet, he franticly looked forward to having her in his arms again. Preferably in bed.

Damn his lusty hide. If he thought she would accept him, he'd swipe the plates from this table—most recklessly—and have her panting beneath him on its surface. Looking at her now, he wondered if she would protest. Maybe not. But his servants were a damned inconvenience.

From hooded lids, Morgan feasted on her comeliness. Besides being quite lovely—her lavish breasts an added boon—her inner beauty enlivened him. He could get used to having her in his life.

A clatter of silverware jolted him out of his musings. With a deep breath, Morgan rose from his seat and ambled around the table. He inhaled her fragrance as he pulled her chair back and held out his arm.

Warm rain.

A field of sunshine.

"How about a walk in the garden?"

"I would like that. Thank you, kind sir." Kat rose gracefully from her chair.

Morgan reacted with a slight wince at her formal 'kind sir'. Taking into consideration this afternoon, perhaps darling, sweetheart, or even lover would be more appropriate. She rested her fingers upon his sleeve. After knowing her taste, which hinted at what delights lay beneath her surface, his senses had sharpened. He wanted to taste her sweetness again.

He escorted her through the open doors, moving onto the garden path. He fought a battle with his conscious.

Just one taste.

One taste would never be enough.

It was all he could do not to crush her back against him and make wild, passionate love with her.

His hand lifted and he jerked it back to his side. He silently groaned.

With a catch in his voice, he spoke softly. "You are quite lovely. Please forgive me for forgetting myself earlier."

Her entire body went still.

Damn his thoughtless mouth. Had he made her uncomfortable by reminding her of their indiscretion, or had she perceived an incorrect interpretation? He had a mind to show her just how much he wanted her, by giving in to the urge to carry her up to his bed and rip her clothes off. Or, maybe, if he was too impatient, he'd leave them on. He nearly swallowed his tongue at the picture in his mind.

With a renewed force of will, he shook the image away.

One taste of her and he craved more. Days of making love to her would not be enough. What he really needed was the strength to reign in his raging lust.

He closed his eyes and drew in a deep exalting breath—which was a mistake. Her fragrance incited his senses beyond his control. Lifting his lids, he swallowed the lump lodged in his dry throat.

Bloody hell!

"I think we'd better go inside." Struggling for control, he turned and led her back up the path. When he met her gaze, her expression was one of confusion. "I am trying to be a gentleman," he explained.

Her mouth opened slightly and her expression changed. He would swear it was disappointment.

Warmth spread through his chest. No conundrum here. Her openness, her honesty, her spirit ignited emotions in him he did not know he was capable of. God what a woman. What she did to him. What she inspired in him. He leaned close to her ear and spoke softly, "You do not need to say anything. Your eyes tell me everything I need to know."

When they reached the bottom of the staircase, he released her arm and waited for her to ascend the stairs. She hesitated. Her beautiful green eyes held questions.

"Goodnight, sweet Kat. I have work I must attend to. I will see you in the morning. Mrs. Beasley will have her kitchen staff scurrying around in fervor, preparing a considerable feast before allowing you to go on your way." Losing the battle with his conscious of resisting at least a touch, he lifted her hand and dipped his head giving a brief brush of his lips across the back.

He turned and marched to his study. Had he stayed a moment longer, he would have dragged her up those stairs—if they would have made it that far.

Kat never dreamed there could be this kind of craving for a man's touch. Not just any man. No one had ever made her as much as tingle. Morgan made her quiver. He made her hot. He made her yearn.

She paced the floor in the middle of her bed chamber. His words ran rampant in her mind.

Your beauty takes my breath away. Your touch makes me shiver with delight.

She could still feel his hardness, smell his intoxicating scent. He had created a frenzy of longing that gripped her all the way to her toes.

She hugged her arms around her middle.

Merciful Heavens!

There was an ache between her legs even now. A craving, so new to her, grew beyond anything she could ever have imagined. She had no idea why her body acted with a will of its own and she did not care. She just knew that in his arms, she had been totally consumed.

She had the strength of mind to be in those arms again. The need to feel that overwhelming sensation again. A sensation that he—and only *he*—had created.

She walked over to the window and looked out at the black night. The gentle breeze blew across her face as she gazed up to search for a star in the night sky.

My heart pounds and my blood races through my veins just to be near you.

He was just down the hall.

You need someone to make your blood race and your heart sing. Byron makes my whole body sing.

A melting satisfaction spread through her. "Now I know what Charity meant." To experience a man's hardness was quite exhilarating. And, she'd clung to him like wet clothes clung on a body after a dip in the lake.

She went to the mirror and stood there, trying to see herself as Morgan would see her. The gown she now wore was far more revealing than her day gown. The sheer covering looked like it should not be worn at all—especially out of the bedroom. She'd found it buried in the back of the clothes closet.

I am trying to be a gentleman.

Well, her thoughts were not exactly those of a lady, right now.

She had never considered exposing her body in front of a man. Since meeting Morgan, she had considered quite a lot.

Like this afternoon.

In his home.

Her mind went spinning again.

In the drawing room.

Heat flushed her face.

In the daylight with servants about.

She let out a soft moan. Shivers of delight flared through her body making her stomach clench. *And she would gladly do it again.*

Good Lord, how she longed to know this man and his mysterious secrets. He was stimulating, invigorating, fascinating . . . mouth-watering. She yearned to explore the delectable things he made her feel, things she'd never imagined were possible.

Kat strode back to the window. With her arms crossed over her chest, she stared out at the starlit night. During her time in Morgan's home, she'd learned there was so much more to the man. He had shared his pain, his grief. His family values. Surely, he had feelings for her if he shared so much of himself.

He had hinted at a dark past. Dangerous jaunts and rescue missions. She hoped that they were no longer a part of his life. He explained how he needed an heir to carry on the family name. Would he consider her for the mother of his child? Could he love her?

She knew she had already lost, if not her whole heart, a very large piece of it, to him.

Leaning her head against the window pane, she longed for even a small piece of his.

Chapter 23

Morgan sat brooding in his study. His shirt unbuttoned to the waist, one hand rested on his chest, smoothing the dark fur subconsciously. His other arm flung out, an empty glass dangled by the tips of his fingers. He'd already taken off his boots. He stared moodily at the burning logs.

This overwhelming need was suffocating. There was no use in going to his room, for sleep eluded him.

He'd never met a woman like her. She should hate him. She didn't.

He had been responsible for the gratification he saw on her face. *He* had been the one to bring her undeniable pleasure. *He* had been the one to make her shatter in his arms.

His chest tightened, amazed at how much her response affected him.

He needed to keep a much tighter rein on his emotions.

Cursing under his breath, Morgan pushed from the chair and stalked to the side table. He jerked the top off of the decanter and poured, missing the glass, sloshing brandy over the wooden surface.

Hell!

He brought the bottle to his mouth. Taking a hefty swig, he spun on his heel and strode to the window. Looking into the dark night, he saw Kat's radiant face in her moment of ecstasy.

Breathtakingly beautiful.

He wanted her.

He should leave her alone.

He wanted her.

He should let her sleep.

He wanted her.

Don't make things bloody complicated.

Like they weren't already.

His heart was not involved.

He wanted her.

She had come apart in his arms, by God!

What the hell was he doing down here when he could be upstairs with her?

Hurling the glass at the fireplace, he cared not if it smashed into a thousand pieces. He threw open the door and charged into the hallway in his stocking feet. He vaulted up the steps, taking them two at a time. In a few easy strides, he stood outside her door. If he knocked and she was asleep, he'd wake her.

Damned rutting fool.

He hesitated, persuading his conscience she wanted him. Didn't he prove that this afternoon? Her tiny cries of release still rung in his head. A tantalizing response he wanted to experience again.

Damn, she was beautiful. No woman had ever affected him this way. She was definitely and very firmly planted under his skin. He wanted to spend every waking moment with her. He needed her with him. Under him.

His cock was hard and straining to be set free from its confinement. Now that he had tasted her passion—knew the excruciating pleasure to be found in her arms—he could no longer deny his craving for her. Watching her face during her climax had given him pleasure beyond his imagining. Fulfillment beyond his envisioning. Completion beyond his dreams.

Since thinking of her gave him a permanent ache in his groin, he needed to find ecstasy with her soon or become a permanent cripple. He eased the door open, allowing his eyes time to adjust to the darkness.

On the far side of the room, Kat stood in silence with her brow against the windowpane. Her hair hung about her in luxurious waves, making a halo around her form. He could not take his eyes from the lovely vision of his dreams. The breath caught in his throat, making him mute. She stood in a cloud of lavender so pale he could see the outline of her breasts, the curve of her slim waist. He blinked, hoping the enchanting creature before him was not his imagination.

Her name croaked out in a whispered hush. She turned, her eyes grew wide and held him spellbound. She floated in a cloud of pastel mist, taking the steps necessary to close the distance, but then seemed to catch herself as if she were unsure.

Sheer magnetism drew him forward, within a hair's breadth of her, not touching, just devouring her with his eyes. His struggle was at an end. No more fighting his will. No more fighting his emotions.

With the gentlest of touches, he stroked her cheek. When her eyes closed and she leaned into his caress, a sense of elation filled his soul. His hands unsteady, he gathered her, drawing her into the circle of his arms.

He had wanted to go slowly. But, one touch and he was lost. Tenderness turned to passion with lightning speed. He grasped her thick auburn tresses and splayed his fingers across the back of her head so he could better capture her mouth with his own.

His free hand slid down over the delicate covering to settle on her waist. The transparent material hid nothing. That, or maybe his urgency to possess her, caused some difficulty breathing. Gasping, he jerked his head up, searching Kat's eyes for any sign that he had been too rough or that she would reject him. Finding none, he croaked, "Heaven help me. I must have you again."

Swaying slightly, she drew his head down. He captured her breath with his kiss. She attacked his mouth with passion and fire. Feeling her urgent need created his own. Her fingers tangled in his open shirt, gripping as though she wanted to crawl into him. He welcomed her urgency, his mouth plundering while their overheated passions took control.

With a groan, he broke the kiss, and swooped her into his arms. Placing a knee on the quilted coverlet, he gently lowered them both, bracing one arm on the feather-tic, the other tight around her body. His gaze pierced hers while he trailed his hand across her hip like a whispered caress, down her thigh with tantalizing slowness, around her calf and to the hem of her gown, sliding the thin delicacy upward.

Eager in her movements, Kat helped him remove the gossamer covering. Totally naked before his eyes, he feasted on her beauty. Painful anticipation centered in his chest.

Kat.

His.

Ever so slowly, he trailed a finger from her ear down the throbbing vein in her slender neck. Unable to resist, he placed open mouth kisses on the same path his finger had taken. He tasted every inch of her sweet flesh as his kisses moved lower. He wanted to savor the moment, delight in each stroke of his tongue, absorb each sigh, every quiver, make slow sweet love to her endlessly.

This feeling of unhurried sex, of languorous lovemaking stirred an emotion he quickly denied. Encouraged a feeling that tempted him to succumb. Having Kat in his arms gave him warmth and a craving he'd never known. He wanted to lose himself in her enchantment and bask in paradise.

She tugged his hair. Her breaths came out as hard pants making him more ravenous. He kissed her with hunger, communicating his desire with every stroke of his tongue. His fingers teased her curls and he felt her heart thunder in anticipation. When she seized his arm in a death grip between her legs, he released a chuckle. His Kat had more passion than he could have imagined. He palmed her woman's mound, and pressed. One finger stroked between her nether lips causing her hips to buck, making an already raging fire burn out of control.

"Oh Heaven! Oh, dear God!" She writhed and panted. "Ohhhhh, Morgan, I need . . . I ache . . . Morgan . . . I yearn . . . please . . ."

"Come for me sweeting. That's it. Come for me."

He thrust his tongue savagely into her mouth at the same time he thrust two fingers inside of her. She moaned and wriggled closer while tangling her hands in his hair.

Desire filled his entire being. A hunger for this woman he'd never felt for another.

His Kat.

For God's sake, man. It's only lust. Yet it threatened his peace. After only one taste, he had desperately craved more. The fulfillment he found in her arms soothed his aching soul. How could one man endure this much pleasure?

But he did. Giving her ecstasy gave him immense gratification in return.

And he was not done.

"You are so responsive. So sensual. When I touch you, I am responding to you, Kat. What you do to me . . . your touch . . . your cries . . .

Her eyes clouded over. Her arms tightened. "I want you."

Her words lanced his concentration, and heightened his arousal. He never dreamed such words could be so piercingly sweet. He lowered his head, not taking his gaze from hers. He caressed her lips with sensual longing. On and on, he plundered, his chest swelling with tenderness. His hands drifted across her belly while his lips took a path of carnal bliss. One blissful inch at a time, he worked his magic. When he brushed kisses from her neck, across her collar bone to her shoulder, she shivered. Delighted, he drifted lower. And lower.

He skimmed his hands down her sides to her hips. Taunting hot, open mouth kisses followed, each a deliberate attempt to heighten her joy.

She quivered.

Delight twisted in his chest. He smiled, then he slid down to kiss the exposed flesh of one calf. Shifting, he placed both hands under her knees and urged her legs apart. Latching onto her gaze, he licked his lips, and ever so slowly and lowered his head.

Burning desire flooded Kat's entire being. Morgan stared at her with blazing eyes, a savage hunger in their depths. With that famous stray-lock of hair falling over his forehead, he looked like the devil himself.

He bent to kiss the inside of her thighs. Surely she'd fallen, for she should not want his head there. She should not want his kiss there. He spread her legs a bit further with each open mouth kiss, her blood rising higher as he drew closer to the center of her being. Her eyes closed, she pressed her head into the pillows. Closer . . . the breath constricted in her lungs and she waited—her body wound as tight as the string on a hunter's bow—she waited . . .

"I love touching you. I love kissing you. And now, I'm going to kiss you here."

His breath caressed her before a feather-soft kiss landed against her—there. Even though she expected—hoped—desperately wanted him to kiss her there—she never dreamed his lips would feel so heavenly. She wanted to scream. She was incapable of breath. It was maddening. Shock and pleasure joined to send alarming signals of unbelievable need within. It felt sinful. Delicious.

Hotter than she believed possible, Morgan's dancing tongue sent sparks of fire through her veins—from the crown of her head down through her receptive, taut toes. He kissed her and nuzzled her until her mind lost all rational thinking. She could only feel. His darting tongue shocked her into a frenzy. Already beyond reason, she had no idea how she could take anymore.

Gasping, she clutched his head and tangled her fingers in his hair, holding him prisoner. He'd stunned her. He'd thrilled her, into a maze of elated emotion. His kisses drifted upward, caressing her belly in tantalizing circles.

Go back! Go back!

She ached. Her womanhood demanded that he take her and put an end to this thrilling torture. The path of his kisses rose higher still as he placed one enflamed kiss after another on her sensitized skin. Warbled moans escaped from her throat, her hands reaching while her legs opened and clenched around him. Her mind, a helpless mass of fervor, she had no control of her body's movements.

The rough texture of his tongue laved her nipple, sending sparks of fire in her chest and longing through every cell in her body. His breath chilled her nipple, and then his electrifying hot mouth covered her again. She whimpered. The hot-cold sensation kept her unbalanced, causing an ache so intense she clawed and pulled at him, and advanced an attack of her own.

Pressing her mouth on his breast, she worked her way across his beckoning chest. Finding his male pebbles erect, she nipped at him. His reaction stirred her to do it again. Oh, it was exciting. So hot, so lost in overwhelming emotions, she wanted to flame the fire in him as he had in her. Her intent to please him, she would not be denied. She could not touch him enough. Kiss him enough.

Morgan took charge as he moved on top of her, rubbing her breasts with his body. His thick, silky chest-hair made her sensitive breasts tingle with impatience. He held her thigh, sliding his knee underneath, and lifted her leg over his own. He grasped her other leg placing it high over his hip. She felt exposed.

She closed her eyes. Yet, the burning sensation in her belly over-road any thought of self-consciousness, giving way to agonizing anticipation.

"Kat, look at me."

His words came through the fog in her brain. Her eyes fluttered. In one swift move, he thrust. White-hot heat scorched her. His breath came heavily against her ear. Their intimacy had her spiraling out of control again.

He focused his attention on her burning breasts, loving them with his tongue. Every bone in her body melted. Every nerve heightened. Consumed in her burning passion, she clenched him as he slowly drew out and thrust in again.

"Put your legs around me, sweeting."

Each stroke penetrated deeper, sweeping her higher. Her blood boiling like a volcano ready to explode, she writhed against him. A guttural cry of pure rapture escaped her lips. Molten lava poured through her veins. Fire rushed through her legs to tingle in her toes. Mind-numbing . . . blissful . . . ecstasy.

He held her in desperation. Straining against her, he flung his head back, a growl of satisfaction rumbled from his throat. He pressed into her, prolonging the long moment. His release as powerful as her own. Then he shifted, and gathered her into his arms so tenderly, she felt safe, and cherished.

Pressed together from shoulder to thigh, her heart thundered against his.

"I love you," floated from her lips.

Morgan stiffened—his body rigid as stone.

Chapter 24

Flames gone, only red embers glowed from the hearth. Shirtless, sprawled in his beloved leather chair, he crossed his bare feet at the ankles and stared at black coals, dawn mere minutes away. Desperate to clear his mind after their bout of lovemaking, he'd uncapped a bottle not bothering with a glass. Hell. He was becoming a damned drunk.

Morgan had imagined having Kat in his bed—she haunted his dreams day and night—but nothing compared to experiencing such bliss. Her uninhibited response, her gasps and cries had sent lightning bolts to his already engorged cock. He'd wanted to give her pleasure. He never envisioned that he would receive as much pleasure in return.

He took another pull and swallowed. Then rested his head on the back of his chair

I love you.

How could three little words turn his world upside-down?

Sometimes women said ridiculous things in the heat of passion. Kat may have been drowsy and gloriously flushed—every naked inch of her—but she had spoken. And she'd uttered those damning words.

With the bottle propped on his chest, he stared through the glass into the depths of the amber colored liquid. *Love. Ha.* A word that could open hearts. Give hope. Allow the notion dreams were possible. And then rip the guts right out of a man's soul.

Out of habit, he rubbed the stubble on his jaw. Kat's image flooded his mind. Her heavenly fragrance still lingered. Her breasts were made for loving. Basic need drove him to squeeze, to bury his face in their lushness, to kiss, suck, and make love to them forever. As he plunged within her body, her moans of ecstasy plunged him to unimaginable heights.

He'd lost himself.

Completely lost in her.

She was the most delectable creature he had ever known.

Passion. Yes. His Kat certainly had passion. He had found, much to his delight, that she was a sensual woman. His chest tightened, amazed at how much her response affected him.

He scratched the fur on his ribs. A man had to keep his head. Not allow a woman to take over his mind. True, he'd planned to marry. But, good God. Not for love. Never for love.

What was he supposed to do now? Since he'd been unable to keep his randy cock in his pants . . . He shoved out of the chair.

Bloody hell. He could not marry Kat. She would become essential to his life. Needing her every day. Making love to her every night. She'd worm her way under his skin making him dependent on her.

Like she hadn't already taken root.

No. He needed a wife to run his home. Give him an heir. One that would not occupy his mind all day and keep him from sleeping at night. A woman who would not demand his time and expect to hear words of endearment that were not a part of his life. A woman who did not love him would not expect him to return any sentiment. Feelings he was incapable of giving.

Emotions had not surfaced in a long time, and as far as he was concerned, they never would. Passion and sexual cravings were not emotional. They were simply a body's cravings.

Explain that to Kat.

He skewed the bottle and drew hard, then wiped his mouth with the back of his hand. In his mind, he saw her sleeping form.

Exquisite.

He had gathered her in his arms, not willing to let go of such a delicate treasure. While he'd cradled her against his body, he'd been utterly enthralled. He still marveled at how, in that shattering moment, he'd found fulfillment beyond anything he'd experienced in the bedchamber.

Peace.

Contentment.

Like he'd finally come home.

The back of his head dug into the soft leather. Emerald eyes filled with adoration. His gut twisted. Something like pain flickered in one corner of his heart.

My Beloved Kat.

Blood and the devil!

He knew what he must do.

She would be gone in the morning.

Kat woke to find Mrs. Beasley with a tray beside her bed—and hoped no evidence existed of how she had spent the night.

"I brought you some hot cocoa and coffee, not knowing which you would prefer."

"I'm afraid the hot cocoa will put me back to sleep. Better make it coffee."

She sat up and put her back to the headboard, every muscle smarting. After Mrs. Beasley left, she lazed about, dreaming of Morgan. She felt gloriously naughty. Deliriously happy.

Morgan was a magnificent man. She snuggled deeper into the feathered mattress. He had kissed her and touched her in places—her skin still tingled from his touch. She had cast fate to the winds and plunged into delicious wickedness.

Drawing in a breath, she heaved a profound sigh. She'd had no control. Her body had taken over her mind, and she'd hung on for dear life. There had been no thinking, no concept about what they were doing. Only need. For whatever was to be.

Never before had she felt so safe, so cherished, as she had the moment when Morgan pulled her head to his chest and held her. Had she imagined his loving caress, his cuddling possessiveness? Content and snug in his arms, she'd dozed off. She had not meant to, but she had been so relaxed, and downright exhausted. So blissful in the cocoon of his arms.

She threw back the covers and put her feet on the floor. Locking her fingers, she stretched her arms high above her head. What a wonderful morning. Suddenly, a cloud covered her joy. Soon she would be on her way to the Viscount's.

Could she stay at Whetherford Manor longer?

What a wonderful—dangerous—idea. She giggled. Her humor disappeared at the thought of her little detour being found out by her aunt and uncle. She headed to the bathing chamber where a bath awaited her. She trailed a finger in the water finding it still warm. A quick bath and she would go in search of Morgan.

A short while later, she left her chamber in search of Morgan. With one hand on the polished wood, she crept silently down the wide staircase. Her anticipation made her eager, her tread quickened. Excitedly, she entered the dining hall and came to a halt. Morgan was not at the table. Disappointment clouded her earlier elation. Her steps slower now, she took her seat and waited. Mrs. Beasley and her cheerful smile sailed through the doorway.

"Eat up now, miss. You have a long journey ahead."

Kat stilled. Of course, the staff expected her to be on her way. "Where is Lord Whetherford?"

"He took that horse of his out for a ride this morning at the crack of dawn. Came back a while ago and went to his study."

Kat's joy plummeted. Morgan would not be joining her? *Why?*

A sense of unease crept into her thoughts. Had she behaved badly? Had her brazen willingness appalled him?

Surely not. He enjoyed their union as much as she. But then, he was a man. The thrill of the chase and all that rot.

No. She would not believe it. His kisses were sweeter, tenderer, more meaningful than if he were a rogue.

Like she would know the difference.

He'd caressed her as though he cared.

"That man spends too much time alone."

Mrs. Beasley's voice brought her out of her deliberation. No longer hungry, she picked at the food on her plate.

"I prepared a basket of food for you to take along. You never know when you might get hungry."

Maybe her appetite would return in the carriage. *If* she left today. Hope and determination surged anew.

Kat had never been one to put off the avoidable. Placing her silver fork beside her plate, she exited the room. Her destination—Morgan's study. Would he welcome her—or send her on her way? Devil take him for putting doubts in her head.

Solid wood stood between her and answers to her misgivings. The same door she'd stood before, not that long ago, agonizing over meeting Whetherford, determined to find why she'd been abducted. Had it only been a few months? Kat raised her hand with determination.

"Enter." Morgan's rough voice attacked her nerves sending a wave of awareness down her spine.

Seeing him again brought back the cravings of the night before. Her pulses raced. Goodness, he looked simply mouth-watering. Did one look at his rugged form have to make her body betray her this way?

His eyes narrowed, yet they pierced. The blood in her veins grew hot. She had lowered her defenses toward this man and now he was controlling her body, without even touching her.

"Good morning, Katherine."

Last night he called me Kat. My beloved Kat.

"Good morning," she said.

"Did you come to say goodbye?"

The bottom fell out of her stomach. Had he dismissed her already? "Morgan. Is something wrong?"

Regret flickered in his eyes, immediately replaced with coldness.

Had she imagined his fleeting unhappiness?

"Why would you think that? You are continuing on your journey today. It is expected that you would say goodbye."

Her heart shattered. Judging from his behavior, he wanted to be well rid of her. Anger concealed her distress. "Of course. I would not be so rude as to slip away without thanking my host."

Something flashed in his eyes, again. *Surprise? Guilt?*

Reservations assailed her. She took a hesitant step forward. "Maybe . . . that is . . . I assumed last night . . ."

"And just what did you assume?" One brow raised in question as his voice hardened.

Courage fled, making her gaze drift from his eyes. Yet she forced out the words. "You came to me."

"Yes. I came to your room. *You* came to my home. *Un*-chaperoned."

Horrified, she recovered her gasp before it left her mouth. What was he saying? Why was he acting this way? This was not the man of last night. He had been tender, affectionate. Where had her amorous lover gone? The man in his place was cold, abhorring. "You throw my innocence in my face?"

"You seemed willing enough."

Seething, she fought to steady her breathing. The darkness of the study seemed to suit her mood, for her fury stemmed from a dismal place in her soul. She shoved her shoulders back and curled her fingers into fists, resisting the urge to tear into him. "I believed you were a man of honor. Tell me, Morgan. Where is that honor now?"

He laughed.

Damn his hide.

"Surely you don't expect me to marry you, now. I offered once. I will not foolishly do so again."

Pain lanced her heart. She clenched her teeth to keep her mouth from hanging open. Tears did not dare defy her will. Never would she have believed him to be so cruel. "You go too far."

"*I* go too far?" He rose from behind his desk. "*You* came to Whetherford, my dear."

The hateful man. She glared, wishing she could singe him with her eyes. "You have been turning my head with your words since we met. Now that you have claimed the prize, you no longer want me."

His bitter laugh tore her to shreds. "Far from it."

Had she been nothing more than a plaything? A tasty morsel to be devoured. A sport to be triumphed. Sick with remorse, she lashed out. "You got what you wanted."

His eyes smoldered and his jaw grew tight. His leer maddening. "Yes, I did. And so did you."

His words penetrated deeper than any arrow could. "You devil! I hate you."

A grin curved one side of his mouth. "No. You don't. And for a long time, there were those who believed I was the devil."

"Tell me again how I was a mistake. How your men kidnapped the wrong woman. I do not blame her for running away. I know I was a mistake. And I made a *mistake* in trusting you."

His eyes flared. His jaw so tight, she thought it might crack. "The mistake was in how you were brought here. *Not* in what happened between us."

Pride was a great weapon when it was all one had. Her shoulders back, her head as high as her neck could manage, she drew on every bit of strength she possessed. "Do not concern yourself. I won't expose you. After all, you did not take advantage. I gave myself freely. If it had not been you, I would have picked someone else. You see, I was ready to lose my virginity. I naïvely held on to it long enough."

His smile vanished and he took a threatening step toward her. The devil himself could not have looked as fierce.

"Don't you dare come near me," she said in a hard voice. "Your attentions are no longer welcome." She whirled around, ran out the door and blindly flew up the stairs.

Chapter 25

T he moment he took her hand, Kat realized this was not
the same footman who had assisted her when she arrived
at Whetherford Manor. Holding back burning tears, she ignored the thought and climbed into the waiting carriage. Desolation loomed. Right up until the moment she walked out the
door, she had wanted to believe in him. She wanted to believe
in herself. How could she have been so wrong?

Kat leaned her head against the squab and let the tears flow.
The one man she'd finally given all she had, and he'd used her.
Soaked the life out of her like a useless sponge. Then tossed her
away as though she meant nothing.

He had given her moments of unbelievable joy. Taken her to
un-imagined heights. Rapture she'd never known existed. She
would not let him belittle that. He had held her as gentle as a
mother held a newborn babe. His caring could not be feigned.
His affection could not be false. For his own ludicrous reason,
he had behaved horrendously. If her life depended on it, she
would bet his joining with her body had been more than mere
lust.

No matter now.

He sent her away—just like her brother. Unwanted.

Well, not so much like her brother. At least Stephen loved
her. She pulled a piece of linen from her reticule. The carriage
jerked as she tried to wipe her nose.

What the devil? The phaeton picked up speed. Kat leaned over to look out the window. The landscape flew by in a blur. True, she wanted to leave Whetherford long behind, but what was the blasted hurry?

"Feldman," she yelled.

No answer.

She yelled louder. "Feldman!"

A lurch nearly unseated her. Were they being chased?

Kat clambered to the square hole on the other side and found—to her horror—Feldman was not driving the coach. She screamed through the opening. "Who are you? Where are we going? Slow down!"

To her relief, the phaeton slowed. Then stopped. The door flew open and a large man climbed inside, barely squeezing through the small space. A man she'd never seen before. Unease crept up her spine.

"Who are you?"

The man ignored her and hefted his weight on the opposite seat. The carriage took off again. Smells of horses and dirt assaulted her. His clothes seemed clean enough. Still, his beard hid his face and his scowl gave him an unsavory appearance.

"Do you speak?"

The cold stare aimed at her made her burst of bravado sizzle.

"Just do as you're told." He crossed his arms over his chest giving her the distinct impression that he would accept no argument from her.

This man was quite different than the two ruffians who grabbed her in that London side street. She stared at his large arms and the knuckles on his fisted hands. A large brute, who no doubt won his share of fisticuffs. She glanced at the door. She may as well disregard that idea. There was nowhere to go.

Dear Lord. Not again.

The silence stretched into an eternity. "Where are you taking me?"

More silence.

So much for conversation. Although she preferred not to talk, she needed answers. The carriage raced. She held on for fear of losing her seat. The broad-shouldered man across from her rocked in an easy gait as if the bumps were no bother to him at all.

She leaned back and prepared, as much as she could, for what was to come.

A shout from outside and the carriage jolted to a stop. Kat's eyes fluttered open. She'd fallen asleep. When the door opened, the burly man gestured with his arm for her to go first. Another man helped her step down—*the mystery footman.*

A stone building stood before her. Not exactly nobility. No peasants lived here either. He pushed her forward. Realizing the futility in angering her captor, she moved without resistance. A third man waited at the entrance. Ignoring Kat, he faced the big man behind her.

"Take her in there." He pointed to a room off the corridor.

She glanced up. An unspoken threat evident in his glare.

Fear choked her. This was real. What did they want?

Do not fall apart now.

She barely had time to scan the corridor before the sham footman took her arm and hauled her through a set of doors. Her gaze landed on a lone chair in the middle of a cold room.

Pointing to the chair, he said, "You can do this the easy way or . . ." he slowly wrapped a piece of rope around one hand making his meaning clear, ". . . the hard way."

She swallowed and tried to control her shaking.

He had made his point.

She settled on the hard wood, clutching her fingers in her lap. He yanked her hands behind her and wrapped the rope around her wrists, then he jerked, confirming she could not get free. She bit her lip to keep from crying out. He stepped over to the stone hearth, lifted the poker and in a short time flames licked the logs. Without another word, he replaced the poker, and left the room.

Terrified, she remained immobile, unaware of how much time passed before she discovered she'd been holding her breath. On a small table beside her, three flames fluttered unevenly on a candelabra. She blinked, focusing on her surroundings. All shadows.

She was at their mercy. Would she see Morgan again? Would he know what happened to her? Would he care?

Her body started to shake in earnest—from cold or fear?

Tears threatened. Allowing her emotions to cloud her thinking would not help the situation. Stephen would tell her she must remain strong. Would he return only to find her gone? Despair flooded her chest. Would she ever see her brother again?

Kat flexed her shoulders and flinched as tingling pain shot through her arms.

"You may as well relax. You're going to be here for a while."

Kat inclined her head. A woman stepped from the shadows. Surprise turned to shock. Kat's breath came out in a rush. She stared at what seemed to be her own reflection. Her mind whirled.

The revelation was a jolt to her gut.

Juliana?

The famous mystery woman? The one everyone had thought was Kat? It had to be. Because she did not know what else to believe.

Walking over to a desk, Juliana gathered something. She returned with more candles. She took a lighted candle from its holder and lit another one, then one after another and placed them about the room.

Kat took in the sparsely furnished room that had seemed so empty in the dark. This must be the parlor, although it had seen better days. A sofa of gold which appeared old and faded. No pictures or other items littered the table, only the candelabras. A desk in one corner. A clock on one wall held a motionless pendulum. Another chair completed the list.

Juliana came back to face her.

The lines about her eyes were proof that the woman had seen more years than Kat. No need for the burning logs to heat the room. The fire in her blazing eyes could generate enough heat to warm the entire house.

"Well, well, well. You look almost . . . like me." Her hostile eyes took in every detail. They stared at each other for a long disturbing moment before she spoke again. "Who are you?"

Still unable to believe the woman stood in front of her, Kat knew the time had come to accept reality. With everything in her, she faced her nemesis. "My name is Katherine."

"What are you to Whetherford?"

Renewed pain lanced her chest. "Nothing."

With her arms crossed, Juliana stood there glaring. Fuming, as if Kat had done her harm. "Are you his mistress?"

"Certainly not!" Kat huffed.

"Then what were you doing at Whetherford Manor?"

A dizzy feeling went through Kat, making her ears ring. "Delivering a message. I was his guest."

"A guest," she repeated, sauntering around the room as if she were taking a stroll in the park on a Sunday afternoon. She stepped to the back of Kat's chair, then drifted around to the side, touching the wooden arm. The move clearly meant to intimidate. She slowly wandered to the side of the room, then deliberately traced her finger over the corner of a table, as if she were studying the texture. Without turning, she spoke over her shoulder. "Now I understand. The resemblance . . . yes . . ."

The woman made no sense. "What do you mean?"

She came to a stop and her calculating eyes flashed. "We had a . . . disagreement," Juliana said quietly.

A disagreement? She was a thief.

"What has that to do with me?" Kat asked.

A triumphant smile lit her face. "Don't you see? He is trying to make me jealous. Morgan could not find me so . . . he tried to replace me. Just temporarily of course. He needed someone to warm his bed."

He wouldn't. Morgan held me and kissed me like he wanted me.

But then he sent me away.

Kat wanted to wipe that evil smile off the woman's face—preferably with a rock.

"It's too funny really. He found a woman who looks like me. A woman with red hair, remarkably like my own. We are about the same size." Juliana's gown brushed the table leg as she lifted her head and refocused her direction. "I know you've been in his bed. He is a man after all. A man has needs. But, do not make the mistake of thinking he wants you." She pivoted, with a suspicious expression on her shrewd face. "Did you know we are lovers?"

Pride to the rescue, again. Add an unruly tongue and she would not give in so easily. "That is not true."

Juliana gave a throaty laugh looking like a cat that just swallowed a tasty bird. "You have no idea what we have, or what we have shared together."

Juliana's words shook Kat's confidence. It sounded like Juliana knew Morgan very well. *Could this woman be telling the truth?*

"He has a temper." Juliana slanted her nose down leveling her gaze on Kat. "*And* a dark side. That's why I left. When he gets angry . . ." Juliana gave a violent shudder.

Was it for effect? Or had she truly been reliving a terrifying experience? After all—what did Kat really know about Morgan?

"Once he calms down, he is the perfect gentleman. And eager to beg forgiveness."

She wanted to cuff that smug expression off the odious woman's face.

"He can be exceedingly generous. Most men are when they want to appease their lust. But, you poor girl. You could never replace me. "Why do you think he tried so hard to find me? I'll wager every time he took you, he pretended it was me."

Kat's blood pounded. Her head throbbed. A piercing ache went through her entire body. She squeezed her eyes closed. *No. Merciful Heavens, no!*

"Whetherford is no different. I simply needed to give him time to cool down. You happened to be available. And now, he no longer needs you." Juliana seemed entirely too sure of herself.

He no longer needs you. At least that part was true. Morgan made it very clear he did not want her. At least, not anymore.

Heaven help me. I must have you again.

She wanted to believe Morgan.

How desperate she must have seemed.

You got what you wanted.
Yes, I did. And so did you.
She was a fool. The hateful bastard. Devil take him.
If Juliana wanted him, she could have him.

❧

Giles tied his horse to the hitching post and charged up the steps to the double doors of his colossal mansion. He stepped inside and flung off his coat. Cuthbert was there to greet him.

"Glad to have you home, Your Grace."

Giles pulled off his gloves, thinking of the nasty business he'd left behind. A long and grueling journey. Thank God, with a satisfying end. He'd found his quarry. If Morgan had not already heard the news, Giles would fill him in on the details tomorrow. Luck played a big part in his search and seizure. As well as having the good sense to take along plenty of men.

Rejuvenated blood pumped vigorously in his veins.

Like the old days.

He heaved a sigh of satisfaction. He had not exactly planned to get back into the old life of murder and mayhem. But he would be open to the idea of a challenge now and again.

"Glad to be home, Bert. Does Cook have any food warming on the stove?"

"Yes, Your Grace. Cook has prepared a salver every night for the past week in the likelihood of your arrival. I believe this evening's fare was lamb."

"Good. I'm famished."

As Giles handed his gloves over, the butler held out a silver tray containing a single white envelope.

"What's this?" He recognized the crest from Whetherford Manor.

"It came two days ago. It may be urgent."
Giles hastily opened the note and read its contents.

Come immediately.
It is a matter of life and death.

Chapter 26

Stephen stood with one arm braced against the mantel above the hearth. The cracking of the fire made popping sounds as sparks flew about, scorching the stone. He breathed deep, inhaling the comforting scents of home. Even the leather of his uncle's favorite chair gave off a consoling scent of familiarity.

Home, at last, only to find Kat gone. Thank God for his uncle's connections. Kat's trail had been found. She took a slight variation from the path to Charity's. Hard to believe the girl was a Viscountess—the impudent chit. From what he gleamed from Kat's childhood accomplice, his little sister had planned to rescue him just before she got carried off. Her and her damned, hare-brained ideas. He thought she'd outgrown such tomfoolery.

His little sister had been worried about him. She'd gone looking for Danvers at the docks thinking the captain had information. "I ought to tan her hide."

"Talking to anyone special, Stephen?"

Caught mumbling, his gaze flew to Albert. "Uncle."

Stephen straightened to his full height. Albert was a tall man, but then Stephen was used to towering above the heads of most. He had lost the bulging muscles that he'd accumulated from years on a ship, but they would come back in time. He longed to get back on the seas—after he cleared up this mess with Kat. He nodded to his uncle.

Chuckling, Albert strode to a table placed beside his favorite chair. He leaned down and picked up his pipe from the marble dish. "If she had known you were coming this soon, I grant you she never would have ventured out of doors."

"I should go after her."

"My dear boy, you just got here. If you leave and get lost again, your aunt and Katherine, both would have my skin. One is bad enough. But two women . . ." He gave an exaggerated shudder.

"I did not get lost." If only that were true. His gut twisted at the thought of where he had been. Closing his eyes, he saw the darkness. Subconsciously, he rubbed his wrists. He doubted the marks would ever go away. The other scars on his body had healed. The scars in his mind would take much longer. Thank God, he had escaped. And the very man responsible for bringing him back was also responsible for his sister's abduction.

When Stephen had been told his sister planned to find him, he'd been furious. When he discovered she had been taken, he wanted to kill the man accountable and everyone else in his path. Kat had been taken by mistake? Well, someone would pay for that bloody mistake.

Yet, the man, Giles, had assured him she was safe—after he nearly choked the life out of the mate. The damned man was nearly as tall as Stephen himself. But he had been in a sorry state. Not fit to take on a pup, let alone a full-grown man. For a gent, the bloke had some crafty moves.

Stephen still thought of Kat as his *little* sister. Still a child. He had to accept Katherine was not a child anymore.

Even if the brat still acted like one.

His irritation changed to fear. Fear of what could happen to a young woman on her own. He'd known women who had experienced the hardships of life. In more than one port, he'd saved females from the cruelty and unwarranted behavior of belligerent men. A few years ago, he had saved one poor girl of rape. The bastard would never be able to do that again.

Beating a woman was beyond his tolerance. Hell, he had a temper. He'd been in more than his share of fist-cuffs and down-right brawls. He loved pounding his fist on a well deserving person. But he had never hit a woman. And he would not stand by and allow anyone else to, either. It was inexcusable.

He was not an impatient man, but the worry from his sister's absence unnerved him. He turned back to stare into the fire.

"I know, son," Albert said. "We sent news to Viscount Roxborough of your arrival. As soon as Katherine hears, she will come back straight away. You are my sister's child. I love you, boy, as if you were my own son. I'm sorry to cause you such worry."

"You?" Stephen jerked from the hearth. With a deep sigh, he braced a shoulder back against it. His stance belied the tension in his limbs. "Kat is strong willed and stubborn as an as—er—donkey's butt."

"We all suspected something was wrong. Your aunt fretted over your absence and Kat worried that some evil fate had befallen you."

That was the closest Albert had ever come to poke about his disappearance. His uncle suspected more, but he would never openly ask. Stephen would never tell them the true horrors of that particular nightmare. It was over. He was free.

And alive. Although for the longest time, he had prayed for death.

"We hoped and prayed for your safe return. We had no idea your ship was destroyed, or that you were injured."

Except Kat.

Theirs was a special bond. Maybe because they had lost their parents. Even when Kat was very young they had been close.

Stephen spoiled her even when his parents were alive. It was just like her. Kat—afraid for her brother. And, then she landed in a heap of trouble. He stopped his arm just before his fist struck the mantle.

"What proof do we have the Earl kept her safe?"

"You can trust me on this one, my boy." Albert's voice had the ring of assurance.

"You know him?"

"Take my word. Katherine came to no harm while in his care."

Stephen knew Albert had connections with important people. But he suspected there were some secret connections his uncle did not want made public. He could respect that. He'd had to trust a complete stranger with his very life?

One of those connections?

Albert loaded his pipe—one of the few vices that he had developed. "It took some doing to calm Elizabeth down. With you missing and Katherine gone . . ."

"Putting the tale to the gossips that she *did* go with the Countess was quick thinking on your part, Uncle."

"Yes. The Viscount was accepting of the tale to appease his wife."

"It boggles the mind. Charity, a Viscountess. I still remember her as a rascal. She has been by Kat's side ever since I brought her here. Instead of one imp hanging on my coat-tails, I had two." Stephen shoved from the mantel. "Where the devil is she?"

Albert smiled. "She has gone to visit Charity."

"Is that supposed to make me feel better? Two heads planning mischief instead of one?"

Chapter 27

"Thank you for coming, Your Grace." Whetherford's butler showed relief.

Giles had been wound tight as a pocket watch ever since he opened the missive stating it was life or death. Not one to panic, he'd left for Whetherford Manor with no time to waste. Bloody hell. He just got back from locating the girl's brother. No sleep—then the blasted note telling him to come at once. All sorts of imaginings burst through his brain. He'd run his horse into the damned ground to get here.

"It was Mrs. Beasley what sent the note. We were right concerned."

While Giles pulled off his gloves, Mrs. Beasley hurried across the hall wringing her hands.

"God bless you, Your Grace. His lordship is in a bad way. Been into his cups for days."

"Where is he?"

"Still upstairs in his room." She twisted her fingers in her apron and glanced above the stairway. When she turned back, worry filled her eyes. "He won't let anyone in. Must be a horrible mess up there. We heard things crashing, and he yelled at us to go away. He has not eaten for days."

"I will take care of it Mrs. Beasley."

Mind intent on his destination, Giles strode up the staircase. What in the hell happened? This wasn't like Morgan.

He pounded on the door with his fist. Nothing. He tried the latch, and to his surprise, it opened. He flung the door back, slamming it against the wall. God's Teeth! What a mess!

Morgan lay sprawled. Part of his torso off one side of the bed with both arms hanging over his head. An empty bottle dangled from one hand. If Morgan landed on his head, the deserving tippler would be fine. Giles could just imagine the drunken fool, trying to get up with a string of curse words slurring out of his mouth.

He smiled at the thought. With a roar, Giles yelled, "Get up, man!"

Morgan made a pathetic attempt to rise from his position on the bed—instead he nearly fell off. He tried to pull himself up, but the drink made him slow. By the way he held his head, it must be pounding like the very devil. Giles had no sympathy.

He slammed the door creating a booming sound loud enough to resemble the shot of a cannon, making Morgan curse. "Bloody hell! Go away!"

"I've been told you have been in this mode for days." Giles took a step forward.

"Good God, man. Quit your yelling. And get the hell out of here."

Giles advanced another step. "I'm not going anywhere. Now get out of that bleedin' bed."

Groaning, Morgan tried to sit up. "Are you deaf? Get out." He clutched his head again, grunted, and turned over.

"Do you think you can put me out? I'm ready for a good mill." Giles pushed back his sleeves in preparation.

"Go to the devil, Giles." Morgan grumbled.

"What happened to you?" Giles studied the disgusting form tangled in the bed covers, moaning on the huge bed. The idiot had his pants on, but his shirt lay somewhere in the massive heap.

"Mind your own damned business." Morgan muttered.

Giles marched over to the wash stand. He grabbed the pitcher, marched back to Morgan and threw the water in his face. Morgan came up sputtering and swinging.

"Damn you, Giles!" Morgan looked ready to kill him. "You were once my friend. But, I am telling you now. Go away and leave me alone."

"And I'm telling you, friend or not, I will drag your sorry hide down to the river and throw you in if I have to!"

"You and who else?"

"Damn it, Morgan! The way you look right now, I won't need any help. Look at you!"

Morgan's face screwed up as he studied Giles. "What the hell are you doing here?"

"Apparently, your butler cares about you. And Mrs. Beasley is worried."

"No need. Go away."

"How bloody long has this been going on? I would have believed it of anyone. Anyone! But *you*! What in God's name happened?"

Morgan ran his fingers through his wet hair. "Thought I'd be embalmed for a while." He flopped back on the bed.

"Embalmed?"

"Numb. No thought. No feelings."

"I know what it means." Giles scanned the room taking in every detail. Bottles strewn across the floor. "I would say you were well on your way to pickled permanence."

"No need to worry. I planned to rejoin the living . . . eventually." Morgan turned his head to Giles. "Maybe. In my own time."

"*Maybe*, I will speed things up a bit." Giles took a threatening step toward the bed.

Morgan clenched his jaw. "Do you value your life?"

"Evidently more than you do yours." One of the chairs in front of the hearth was turned over. Giles wondered if Morgan had been in it when it fell. Broken glass speckled the carpet. No wonder the household was concerned. "How long *have* you been like this?"

"Hell if I know."

"God's teeth. You don't know!" Giles was shouting again.

Morgan scrubbed his hand over his face and shoved his fingers through his mop of hair. "Giles. Now that I have decided—with your help of course—to come out of my stupor . . . do you suppose we could carry on this conversation downstairs?"

Giles crossed his arms and glared with a look meant to intimidate him into obedience.

"Uh, after . . . I clean up a bit."

Gauging his diligence, Giles accepted Morgan's word and strode to the door. "I will send up more water."

"How about hot water this time?"

Giles turned around with a smug look. "Would you like me to serve it in the same fashion?"

Morgan's mouth curved into a smile. "I think I can manage it myself."

Morgan dressed and met his friend downstairs in his study. When he walked in, Giles sat in one of the high back chairs, a glass of brandy in his hand. Heading to the side table, Morgan opened the cabinet door and pulled out a bottle. He worked the cap free and took a hefty swallow. After releasing a deep breath, he took another. He swiped his mouth with the back of his hand and scuffed over to drop his frame in his favorite leather chair.

"All of this over a woman?" Giles flung at him.

"You've been talking to the servants?" Morgan slouched with a bottle in one hand and a cold towel in the other. He nursed his head feeling like all the drums in South America had taken up residence there.

"Would *you* care to tell me," Giles asked.

Morgan lifted the towel and glanced up. "I do not need your lecture."

Giles cocked a brow. "I doubt one would do any good."

Morgan took another pull from the bottle and replaced the cold cloth over his head. "Women. They just keep chipping away. Until you let a woman into your heart and what happens? She stomps on it. Then throws it away."

"Did I hear you correctly? A man who claims to have no heart?"

Morgan glared at his friend. *Former* friend, if he kept goading him.

Giles nodded to the bottle in Morgan's hand. "You will have another big head tomorrow, my man."

"Leave me alone. It is what I deserve." Morgan tipped the bottle and took a long draught. "I deserve it for letting a fool woman . . . I am the fool. Capital F-O-O-L.

"I cannot believe that I am sitting here watching you do this to yourself."

"It helps me to cope."

With an ambiguous expression, Giles asked. "*This* is what you call coping?"

Morgan ignored him. "I chase after one red-headed schemer and get waylaid by another."

"Schemer? Are we speaking of Katherine?"

"Do not mention her name. A curse on the wench." Another bout of dejection welled and shook him.

"Just what did she do?"

Morgan gulped more brandy, then swallowed the burning mouthful. Too bad it didn't burn her memory from his mind. "She wormed her way into my . . . head."

"Don't you mean heart?"

"Hell no. The damned bottle's empty. I need another one." He lifted his unsteady frame and clumped to the wooden cabinet. After retrieving another, he flopped back into the comfort of his chair. "To hell with women."

"Um, hmm. Now you have an aversion to women." Giles shook his head.

"I never want to see another redhead." Morgan tossed his head back and turned up the bottle. A bit dribbled onto his chin. He swiped it with the back of his hand. "God, her hair was so beautiful. The most resplendent, rich color I have ever seen." Morgan stared at his hand while he rubbed his thumb and fingers together. "It was like silk between my fingers."

"Good God, he is blubbering like an idiot."

"It hung down in curls covering those luscious mounds." Morgan groaned in frustration. "I can feel them in my hands . . . and with my mouth . . ."

"Better drink up, my boy. Randy Rod is bound to be hard as steel by now. You will not get the satisfaction you expect from that bottle."

Did Giles need to remind him?

"Are you going to tell me why she left?"

"No." Morgan gave him a glare that dared him to ask again.

Giles spoke quietly. "You lost your heart to her."

"I have no heart. Remember?" Morgan tried to convince himself.

Giles took a deep breath. "You sealed your heart when you lost your family. I can relate, as you well know, not wanting to open your heart to pain. Katherine embedded a crack. It is called living."

"I never thought a woman could get under my skin like that. Hell, even when I plan to marry, it would not be for love."

"Ahh. Now we're getting somewhere."

If Giles were anyone else, Morgan would have told him to sod off. But he would just pick and prod until Morgan professed all. With a shrug of his shoulders, he replied, "You read me too well."

"Yet here you sulk. Does she know you love her?"

Love?

He could deny it.

"No. I pushed her away." When the silence lengthened, he looked at his longtime friend. Giles' gaze delved deeper. "Are we having a damned staring match? Oh, all right. She told me."

"Told you what?"

Frustrated, he cursed under his breath. "I love you. At a most appropriate time."

Giles whistled through his teeth. "I see. And, what did you do?"

Reflection cast a nasty glow. Morgan held the brandy bottle in the air.

"You left her for drink?" Giles brow disappeared under straight black hair.

Morgan hated being put on the defensive. He hated even more the picture he'd painted of himself. "I waited until she was asleep. Hell, Giles. I am not a complete bastard."

"Women are romantic creatures. They need to hear the words." Giles pointed out. "What did you say to her?"

"She left." His friend's expression convinced him he sounded absurd.

"Did you try to stop her?"

Morgan put the bottle down and stood, running his hands through his already disheveled hair. What could he say? That he deliberately drove Kat from his home? That he shamed her, accused her, lay the blame at her feet, and then cast her out?

"Look at it from her point of view," Giles said. "Consider how she was brought here. By force. Under false pretenses. She was the wrong woman." He paused. "Then you pursued her. Followed her to London. When she surrendered and confessed her feelings, you took to the bottle. Didn't you want her?"

Morgan whirled around and growled, "Of course, I wanted her."

"Wanted her body? Or wanted the woman for herself?"

Blood and the devil!

Giles couldn't make him feel any lower that he already did. And he loathed being the dung on the bottom of a man's boot. He scowled.

Giles glowered back.

His jaw tight, Morgan trudged over to stare out the window. His grandfather's flower garden—the one he'd created for the love of his life—his wife. Kat loved that garden. She had instilled her presence in Morgan's home. Everywhere he looked, he expected to see her. Her gentle smile. Her emerald loving eyes. She had left her mark in every corner of his house. Sometimes he thought he could smell her fragrance. His house was so damned empty without his beloved Kat.

Empty like it was when his parents . . . He'd turned off his feelings. He killed his heart long ago. But, Kat made him feel again—rejoin the human race.

God, how he missed her.

He put his hand behind his head and rubbed his neck. When he spoke, his voice came out a notch above a croak. "I decided long ago I would never open my heart to love. You know what I was like when you met me. I never want to go through that pain again."

"I remember."

He turned to his friend. "I pushed her away. I let her believe she was just another woman in my bed."

"After she told you she loved you?" Giles' mouth turned down in disgust. "You destroyed her."

The twinge in his chest grew bigger. "You should have seen her, Giles. She bucked up and snarled at me. I thought I had a tiger caught by the tail." Morgan frowned and blankly stared out the window. "I was so damned proud of her."

If it had not been you, I would have picked someone else.

I was ready to lose my virginity.

He closed his eyes at renewed anguish.

"The only thing the girl could do was leave," Giles said. "Pride is a damned annoyance, but we all have our pride."

Morgan released a frustrated breath. True. Look where his pride had gotten him. He took another deep breath and released it. "I cannot marry her."

"Why the hell not?"

"How could I spend every day with her—every aching moment—and not fall more in love with her? My heart would not survive losing her."

"What?!" Giles roared as he came out of the chair. "For Christ's sake, Morgan. You're the bravest man I've had the fortune to come across. Daring, courageous, reckless, risking too many treacherous missions to mention. I never thought it possible for you to be a coward. You are afraid, by God. Afraid of a woman. Tell me. How does your heart feel now?"

Pain. Anguish. Torment.

"By the looks of you, there's no need to answer. Life goes on. *This,*" Giles gestured with his hand, "is not living. You have taken risks, my friend. Those that were life threatening. But this is the most important venture you will ever take. And the reward . . . Is it not worth the gamble?"

The flame of hope flickered within his soul. He had to admit, he already loved her. He had no life without her.

"The woman is proud, Morgan. If you sit here and do nothing, mark my words, you will have cause to regret it."

Would she give him another chance after the hateful things he said to her? He must find her. Where? Would she be with her uncle? Would she have gone elsewhere? He would search to the ends of hell, but he would find her.

He glanced to the man who was more than a friend to him. "You are good at this."

Giles frowned. "At what?"

"Making me realize not only what I have done, but what I must do."

"Noticed that, did you?"

"You were worried I wasn't going to crawl out of the bottle."

"Beg to differ." Giles refilled his glass with brandy. "Do I look worried?"

"You bloody ass."

"Well, that's rather unfair of you," Giles said.

"Thank you. Is that more to your liking?"

"Thank me when I tell you about Katherine's brother."

Morgan froze. "Good God! You could have mentioned him sooner. Where is he? How is he?"

"You will be happy to know he is in one piece, and ensconced at Thornton's."

Chapter 28

"**B**ut, I didn't know," Charity argued. "Kat asked me to send an invitation and I did. She said she was coming to see me. I swear it."

"Do not say anymore." Viscount Roxborough's deep voice penetrated the room. He squeezed his wife's shoulder. "Mr. Radbourn. I suggest you direct your questions to me."

Stephen had a habit of shouting. It was his nature. Even though he stood in his uncle's drawing room and not on the deck of his ship, he never thought to lower his voice. And Charity was Kat's friend. He'd known the mischievous scamp since she was in pigtails. True, she was a married woman, now. A viscount no less. Her husband's thunderous look convinced Stephen to lighten his tone and take a much calmer approach.

"Forgive me, Viscount Roxborough. I have known your wife since she . . . uh . . . for a number of years. I mean no disrespect."

Charity covered her husband's hand with her own. "It's alright."

Lord Roxborough gentled his features. "I will not have you upset."

"Stephen would not hurt me. He is distressed."

"With good reason," Stephen bellowed. At Lord Roxborough's glare, he apologized. "I beg your pardon. But I know these two. She and my sister have schemed plenty of times in the past. Some which had us all pulling our hair."

"And what a bushy lot of it you have," Charity said with a beaming smile.

How could the little imp tease at a time like this? Bloody hell. Where was Kat?

"I apologize for my nephew's forgotten manners, and I appreciate you coming to my home so quickly. The fact remains my niece is missing," Albert said to the viscount.

Stephen grimaced from the scolding. He glanced to his aunt. Elizabeth mutilated the handkerchief she held, her eyes red from crying. Albert had stayed beside her, murmuring words of reassurance since the viscount had entered their door.

Where the hell had Kat gone? He felt the need to pound something.

Preferably Whetherford.

Stephen's growl came from the bottom of his stomach causing all heads to turn. "Whetherford. She is with Whetherford."

"Now, Stephen. Hold on." Albert moved from the hearth.

"Uncle. You know that's where she is."

"I don't know any such thing. But if she is with Whetherford, she's in no danger."

"No danger," Stephen bellowed. "She's alone."

Viscount Roxborough spoke. "Whetherford may have been gone for years, but he is an honorable man."

Stephen swung around. "How the bloody hell would you know?"

"Stephen," Elizabeth gasped.

There he was, shouting again. Damn Kat. "Sorry, Aunt."

"Lord Whetherford is an honorable man. He would let no harm come to our girl." Albert declared.

"I will find that out for myself." Even if he were one of Uncle's chosen few, Whetherford was still a man. With a man's needs. He would kill Whetherford. Even if the bloody devil *had* provided men to search and aid in his rescue.

Stephen spun around and headed for the doorway.

"Wait," Albert called. "Do not go charging off half-cocked, my boy."

Stephen halted. He slowly turned and braced his fisted hands on his hips. "Don't worry, Uncle. I am fully loaded and primed for bear."

"I propose to go with you." The Viscount stepped forward.

Stephen looked to Charity's worried face and back to her husband. "Suit yourself."

"The Earl of Whetherford," the butler announced.

Raised voices came hurtling from the double set of doors where Morgan waited. One boomed above the others. He winced thinking of the poor soul on the receiving end of that one. The butler proceeded to the doors without any sign of trepidation, and with the assurance he'd done this many times. Morgan wondered if the turmoil within was a common occurrence. Without hesitation, the butler knocked and opened both doors. Shouting continued as the butler made his presence known. But when the butler announced him, the room became silent. Every head turned in his direction.

A burly man with eyes of iron and a body rigid as stone faced him. Before he could take two steps into the drawing room, the hulking man charged toward him. With years of trained reflexes, Morgan's arm flew up. A blurred face in the middle of a red cloud went out of focus just before his head flew back from a fist to his jaw.

"Stephen!" Albert shouted. "Stop this at once."

Stephen? This is Kat's brother?

Sitting on his backside on the floor, Morgan tussled with his dignity. The red-haired giant's threatening manner could make a man think he was facing the very devil. The hands fisted at his sides were sure signs of his self-restraint.

"Stephen, old friend." Wesley stepped forward.

Now he speaks.

Morgan had hoped some comradeship between the two men remained. That's why he brought Wesley along.

"Well, well, well." Stephen braced his hands on his hips. "*Old friend*. You are with this bit of muck? You helped abduct my sister?"

Wesley cast his hands up as if that would protect him from the fuming man. "Stephen, wait! You must listen."

"Listen to who? You?" Stephen challenged.

Morgan could see where men would be intimidated by this man's fierce temper alone, and his height stood above most. Wesley already knew he was dangerous—which must have been the reason his tongue wagged in explanations that Stephen, perceptibly, did not want to hear.

"We did not abduct your sister. Whetherford saved the girl." Wesley spread his arms wide. "For old times' sake?"

"For old times' sake, you are still standing." Stephen raised a bushy brow and glared at Wesley. "You should already know how I deal with anyone that goes against me. The tale that my russet hair matches my temper is a true one."

"It was a mistake." Wesley offered Morgan his hand and helped him up.

Morgan tested his chin to be sure his jaw was still attached. Kat's brother packed one hell of a wallop. "Couldn't you have said something sooner," he mumbled to Wesley.

Bringing fisted hands forward, Stephen took an aggressive step. "Where is she?"

Morgan's head jerked to Stephen. "What are you saying?"

A thirst for blood manifested in Stephen's eyes. "You're the bloke responsible. Where is she?"

"This time I am ready for you," Morgan warned, arms up and locked.

"Stop. Both of you. I will remind you, Stephen, you are in my home." Albert stepped between the two men. "Lord Whetherford. Surely you understand our concern. Just tell us if Katherine is with you."

Dread centered in Morgan's chest. "I came here to see her. Are you telling me you do not know where she is?"

"What blooming nonsense," Stephen thundered.

"Stephen." Albert's harsh reprimand silenced Stephen, but his distrustful look remained.

A shout came from the entry way.

"I've got to see his lordship! It's urgent!"

"You cannot go in there."

"Get out of my way!"

"What the blue blazes is going on out there?" Stephen glanced at Morgan. "One of yours'?"

Ready to bark *No*, Morgan halted. He recognized that voice. *Bloody hell. Jeremy.*

Stephen marched into the vestibule, Morgan right behind him. "What's all the ruckus?" Stephen asked.

Breathing hard, Jeremy spotted Morgan and pushed past the servant. "This came right after you left. It's Juliana."

Stephen looked down his nose. "You have your doxy sending you notes here?"

He would put his fist down Kat's brother's throat, yet.

Morgan tore at the slip of paper. "My God." The blood drained out of his veins. His heart kicked and dived to his throat. Kat—in the clutches of madmen. Startling fear turned into blind fury. He crumpled the paper in his fist.

"The man who delivered it said it was urgent, so Mrs. Beasley sent me to the duke." Jeremy quickly inhaled another breath. "He's gathering men as we speak."

Morgan moved to step around Stephen, but he crossed his arms in front of his chest and blocked Morgan's path.

"Just where do you think you're going?"

Morgan was nearly blind with rage and in no mood to be civilized. His eyes clashed with Stephen's. "To get Kat."

Chapter 29

"This waiting could kill a man. When I was held captive—" Stephen's gruff voice caught and his lips tightened into a grim line. He swallowed. "When I was in captivity, minutes had seemed like hours. Hours like days. Days of waiting to see what horrific torture they would use next." He hesitated and raised his gaze to the sky.

When Kat's brother insisted on coming along, Morgan did not refuse—he would never have made it out of that house without a fight. Together, they had come up with a plan to rescue Kat, and now they waited, hidden from sight. He stared at the building where his informants said she was being held. Listening to her brother, Morgan understood the man's anguish too well.

A muscle ticked in Morgan's jaw. He'd had his share of daring missions. Undertakings where the danger outweighed common sense. Risk more imperative than considering his own safety. The prize, the rescue, was the goal. But the thrill of danger, playing with fire, mocking death—that's how he earned the name *dark devil*.

"I was captured once," he said. "Didn't stay long. Giles saw to that."

Stephen shot him a disturbed glance. "I never thanked you . . ."

"No thanks necessary." Morgan said off-handedly, showing that words were not needed.

"I've been through hell—lived in hell . . ." Stephen's voice sounded discouraged, "yet the torture of waiting until I see Kat with my own eyes is worse than anything that blood-thirsty bunch could have done to me. Damn." He thrust his fingers through his thick hair and pivoted on his heel. "My little sister. This standing around has my brain ready to explode."

Morgan's heart had stopped when he'd read Juliana's note. His mind hurtled into complete turmoil, suspecting any manner of injustice done to her. Knowing Juliana had Kat tormented every breath he took.

He never panicked. But, what he felt now came damned close. In his youth, he'd handled missions better. Excitement had pumped his blood. He charged in without a care. Killed without a second thought. But now? He wanted to scream and rant like the very devil. Yelling his frustration like a soulless warrior would do Kat no good, and could very well end him in Bedlam.

"Waiting is always the hardest part." Morgan spoke to calm himself as well as Kat's brother.

"That is why I'm the one in command of this rescue."

Both men turned to the voice of Giles, slipping up behind them.

"You both are too close. Juliana would expect you to come alone," he said to Morgan. "We've both been on too many missions to go blindly charging in without a plan."

"What did you find out?" Morgan asked.

"Jeremy and Piers took care of the guards in back. Two more in the house with Juliana."

"What about Kat?" he ground out.

"She's there. Juliana's got Katherine tied to a chair in the middle of a front room, off to the side. We can't get to her without being seen."

"I'll kill them with my bare hands." Stephen shoved his gun in the band of his pants and pushed forward.

"Wait." Giles grabbed his arm. "Juliana is unpredictable. Who knows what she might do if you go storming in there. Let's stick to the plan. Morgan, you go in the front door. Give us enough time to get in position. While you talk to Juliana, the other two guards will be distracted. Then, Stephen and I will make our move."

With his cool head, Giles had always been the one to formulate the plans. He analyzed every mission, thoroughly assessed every step before proceeding with any operation. His blood would churn, but his composure and strategies gave them success.

Morgan dipped his head in acquiesce.

Stephen faced Morgan with troubled eyes. "Whetherford. Get my sister."

"I plan to do just that." Morgan held Kat's brother's gaze as an understanding was met between them. Then Stephen and Giles disappeared.

Morgan had never been in this position. One where the outcome involved him emotionally. Where the end result could shatter his entire being. And he did not like it one bit. His fear for Kat terrified him. If she were hurt . . .

Before Kat, he'd only been existing, without feeling. He'd suppressed all sentiment the day he lost his family. *She* made him come alive. Now that he was ready to live again, he only hoped it was not too late.

More than anyone, he knew the importance, the need to clear his mind before action. More than ever, he needed to focus.

Emotions could lead to disaster. A missed sign. The wrong timing. Every sense had to be on alert. His love depended on him. He would not fail her.

Glancing around, he found no one in sight. Even the wind stilled. No rustle in the trees, no leaves stirred. His heart in his throat, he climbed the steps to the front door, his boots echoing on each rung.

He hesitated, trying to make up his mind whether to knock or just open the damned door. His hands fisted. Taking a deep breath, he slowly turned the knob.

The door creaked open. He shoved it a bit farther, his eyes combing the interior. Not a sound. No one about. He stepped inside.

To the right, a light glowed from a doorway. He searched down the corridor, up the stairway and to the left—nothing. He forced his pulse to slow. Keeping his ears tuned for any sound, he closed the door. At this moment, he felt like a rabbit ensnared in a trap. Juliana and her henchmen waited for him. But he would turn out the victor.

He scanned the stairway again. With determined steps, he silently strode to the entrance of the manifesting light, his shoulder even with the doorway so not to be seen. A fire cast shadows throughout the room. Kat sat on a chair with her arms pulled behind her back. Her head hung down as if in despair. Blood pounded his temples. He needed to blink, but his lids refused to close. His lips pulled back with malicious intent while his jaw locked so tight it threatened to crack.

Falling back on instincts skilled into his bones, he willed the blood in his veins to slow, the beat of his heart to quit pounding like rolling thunder. He could not fall victim to rage. No matter how much he wanted to kill the shrew who held his love, he had to remain calm and follow the plan. His palms prickled in want.

Be strong, my sweet.

From this position, his view was limited. He took one step forward.

"I see you decided to join us." A woman's voice came from the blackened corner. She stepped into the light.

Juliana.

If he could have incinerated her with his eyes, she would already be in flames. A blur of Kat jerking her head, moved at the side of his vision—he dare not look.

Vibrant red hair piled on top of Juliana's head with a few stray curls dangling around her ears. Adorned in gems, she wore a silk gown that skimmed her curves. The bodice cut low to show off the swells of her full breasts. Once, he'd thought her beautiful.

"Come now, Whetherford. Do not fret."

"I'm here," he growled.

Juliana gave a triumphant smile. "It would be rude of me not to invite you, since I already have a certain guest." She gestured to Kat.

Only by sheer will, he kept his gaze forward. "You have me. Let Miss Radbourn go."

"Miss Radbourn is it?" Juliana tilted her head as if she focused on the ceiling while one finger lightly tapped her chin. "I had the impression you two were . . . shall we say *closer* than that." Then her eyes locked with his. "Your mistress, perhaps?"

Morgan took a fortifying breath. "I am in no mood for games."

Her lips lifted at the corners, a smile that did not reach her malicious eyes. "A man of your reputation surely has a weapon. Please remove it."

When Morgan did not immediately comply, a form moved from the shadows. At first he thought it was Stephen, until his eyes locked on gray steel. *Blood and the devil!* Another brute the same size, holding a gun.

"You do not want my man to have his pistol go off by accident." Others may have been taken in by her smile and winsome ways, but Juliana's sweet voice sickened him.

Seeing the gun aimed toward Kat filled him with dread. He lifted his jacket and removed his gun from his belt. With a cold stare at the other man, Morgan lowered his pistol to the floor. "Harm a hair on her head, I *will* kill you."

"There's no need to be dramatic," Juliana said as she gave a slight wave of her hand.

He saw her hand shake. So, Juliana was not so sure of herself, after all. "What do you want?"

"Is that any way to speak to me after everything we have shared?" She glanced at Kat, her meaning clear.

His gut ached at the thoughts going through Kat's mind. "That was over long ago."

"Not that long ago." She gave a slight chuckle. "Seems like yesterday. Your breath on my neck sent tingles down my spine. But your touch—"

"Enough!" Morgan had to stop her before she could expand on their sexual meaning.

"Does my speaking of our intimacy cause you unease? Does the memory of our heated kisses make you burn?"

Dammit. He could not stand here and allow Juliana to spew such rubbish. Her intention clear, every word aimed with precision. Stab Kat's mind, shoot daggers into her heart. It was bad enough the things Juliana said were true. But she would twist everything to her satisfaction, making it seem the two were star-crossed lovers.

Kat would not understand.

Juliana swayed with each step as if she were dancing at a ball instead of holding a hostage at gunpoint. The closer she got to Kat, the more he feared the woman's unpredictability. She lifted a strand of Kat's hair. "I thought I was the only woman with hair this particular shade. Obviously, you still want me. You took a woman who resembles me. How is that?"

"She is nothing like you."

"Yes. I can see that. She is a child. What was your plan, Morgan? To train her? If you could not have me, use her as a temporary replacement?" Kat's gasp was one of surprised recognition which emboldened Juliana. "Now that I am here, you have no need of a substitute."

Kat's eyes pierced him and he knew Juliana's words had hit their mark. Pain, rejection, agony, defeat—all the signs that Kat believed Juliana's hateful slurs. Fire burned his chest. If he denied her accusations, he risked endangering Kat.

Blood and the devil!

"What do you want?"

Juliana ran her fingers across the back of the chair as she ambled to the side. "You are the Earl of Whetherford now. The title you told me you did not want."

Morgan wanted this business over with and Kat out of here. "I will ask you again. What do you want?"

"Simply to share a bit of your wealth." She straightened her back as if gaining courage. The smile on her face cold and cunning. "You have so much. Surely you would not begrudge me. You shared more than that with me, once. You owe me."

"Owe you?" Morgan asked incredulously.

"I am family."

"The relations of my mother's great-great-grandfather are but a listing on the pages of family records. I owe you nothing."

He aimed for a heated stare that had on many occasions reduced men to ashes.

The composed self-assured woman suddenly became a mean-spirited shrew. "If you had stayed dead, I would not have had to flee Whetherford Manor."

From the corner of his eye, Morgan saw her bodyguard slump and Stephen quickly take his place. Both men being the same size—and Juliana on her harangue—she did not notice.

"Now the truth comes out," he said.

"You were gone so long, we thought you dead. Of course, I planted the idea. But once my father and I moved to Whetherford Manor, he thrived. He became the man he used to be. Full of life. Full of power. I actually think the title meant more to him than the wealth."

"But not to you. What happened? Did he not spoil you enough? Did he not give you your every whim?"

"The titled lord decided his daughter needed a husband," she gritted through her teeth.

"That does not seem too much to ask." Now that one of her miscreants had been replaced, Morgan relaxed his shoulders and placated her. Appeasing her into a false perception of sureness.

"He didn't ask. He demanded."

"And you object to his taking the upper hand."

"He watched me closer."

"A father's right." Morgan shrugged.

She bristled. "He was determined to make me a proper lady with a proper match."

"Surely you could not object to that." Morgan spread his hands in supplication. "Was there no duke or king available?" Then his voice lowered. "Or did he find the task of evolving his daughter a proper lady nigh impossible?"

"Careful Whetherford." Juliana pulled a dagger from her skirts. "I was good enough for you."

Air constricted in his lungs while his body temperature rose ten degrees. "I profusely apologize."

By her smile, she knew she had Morgan just where she wanted him. By the ballocks.

"Oh, yes. I heard you were alive." Her evil smile grew wider. "I'd also heard of your mother's jewels, and once I saw what was in that safe, I could not resist."

A movement to the right caught his eye. This time it was Giles. *Thank God.* Now, if Morgan could just keep her busy. Give Giles enough time to sneak up on Juliana without detection.

"Why didn't you just take the blasted jewels and keep on going," Morgan asked. "Why did you come back?"

Juliana gave a brittle laugh. "I knew you, with your sense of righteous honor, would follow me without end."

"You have the necklace. What do you think you will gain by taking Miss Radbourn?"

"Miss Radbourn, again," she echoed in a sing-song voice. She made to turn and he knew he had to keep her attention on him.

"You mentioned a trade."

Juliana faced him and crossed her arms.

Now, Giles. Now.

"I find it interesting *Miss Radbourn* is a replica of me."

"Pure coincidence," Giles stated close to her ear.

Juliana's eyes flew open in shock. She whirled to the voice behind her, but Giles had anticipated her movements. He grabbed both her arms and slammed them by her side. Then, he jerked her around and smashed her against his chest, knocking the breath from her.

"Sorry to spoil your plans, my dear." His arms tightened, imprisoning her resisting body.

Juliana screamed. "Let me go, damn you."

Giles glared down his nose. "You best shut your lovely mouth, or I will shut it for you."

Morgan's eyes darted to Kat, but Stephen was already there, pulling the ropes free. Kat hurled herself into her brother's arms, tears flowing freely down her cheeks.

"Kitten," Stephen whispered.

"Stephen. Oh, Stephen. Thank God you're alive," Kat cried. She buried her face in his chest while his chin rested on top of her head. His hands stroked her back, assuring her she was safe.

Leaning back, Kat placed a palm on her brother's cheek. "Oh, Stephen. You're here. You are really here."

Just like his Kat. They rescue her, but she's worried about her damned brother. And, he's getting all the attention.

Stephen's eyes snapped fire. "Are you hurt? Has anyone harmed you in any way?"

"I'm fine, now that you're here." She hugged him tighter. Stephen grabbed her and held her in a bear hug while she laughed and cried at the same time. Then her cries turned into whaling sobs.

A sting smarted in the middle of Morgan's chest. God's Teeth! He wanted to hold her. He turned back to the struggling Juliana with hatred. He grabbed her arm jerking her to him. She yelped in alarm. The fingers of one hand bit into her arm while the other hand closed around her throat. Her breathing surged, then grew shallow and labored.

"I could snap your pretty little neck like the wing of a delicate bird," Morgan grated through his teeth. "Or I suppose I could lock you in a room in the East-wing where no one would ever find you." His fingers caressed, and then tightened with purpose.

Her eyes bulged. Soft choking sounds escaped her throat. A power struggle ensued—*squeeze, squeeze,* his mind kept saying. In the old days, he would not have used restraint. In the old days, he would not have cared. He would have broken her like a twig and felt no guilt about it. The days when his dark soul commanded his movements were gone. He was no longer the *dark devil.*

Knowing Kat watched, Morgan flung Juliana aside. The spiteful bitch was not worth it.

"Damn you! And damn her!" Juliana croaked.

"I'll take care of this," Giles said. "Why don't you two go on?"

Morgan glanced at Kat and her brother. "In case you haven't noticed, there are three of us. You know what they say." He shrugged his shoulders as if he had not a care. But the pain in his heart confirmed otherwise.

"Are you going to play the sacrificial lamb," Giles asked. "You and I have already been round the bend."

"For God's sake, Giles. Look at her. That's the first time she has seen her brother in two years."

Giles glanced at the couple embracing, then back to Morgan. "As long as I do not get another note to pull your sorry arse out of a damned bottle."

Morgan's lip inclined at the corner. "Learned my lesson the last time."

"I'm taking her home." Stephen's voice penetrated Morgan's brain.

When he looked at Kat, her head was buried against her brother's chest. Her cheeks were flushed, her nose red from crying. She clung to her brother like a child would cling to its mother after a terrible fright. "Kat?"

"She has been through enough," Stephen continued.

Morgan silently agreed. Why wouldn't she look at him? "Kat?"

Her fingers tightened on Stephen's coat. "Please, Stephen. Take me home."

Her rebuff struck Morgan harder than any blow. Stephen caught his gaze above her head. In silence, he gave a negative shake as he mouthed the words, *Not now.*

With everything in him, Morgan controlled his actions. He wanted to yank her away. He wanted to pull her against him and hold her in his arms until the end of time. He wanted to kiss her senseless and hear her cries of pleasure.

Fear of rejection made him powerless to do any of those things.

I may have to let you go, for now.

But, I will get you back.

Chapter 30

Twilight had fallen and rain pelted against the window-pane. It was difficult to make out if the bleary droplets were water running down the glass, or tears that were a constant in Kat's eyes. The dismal weather outside reflected the gloomy atmosphere inside the room as well as inside her soul. Her body numb with cold, the flames of the crackling fire in the hearth were the only source of warmth in her bedchamber.

"Will there be anything else, Miss?" Alice sniffed and rubbed the back of her hand across her red nose.

Kat turned to the young girl. "No. Thank you. Go get some rest."

She wished Charity were here. She ached and needed her friend. She wanted to unburden her soul, pour her heart out. Instead, Kat relied on the strength of spirit she had left. That and her pride would get her through this.

Turning back to the pouring rain, she let the pinging sound of raindrops against her windowpane soothe her. It had not taken much convincing for Stephen to spirit her away. Kat barely remembered those last moments of that dreaded scene. When Morgan walked into Juliana's trap, she feared losing him forever. She thought Juliana meant to kill them both.

She hated to admit how her heart soared at just the sight of him. How her breathing had constricted when his eyes met hers. How tingling awareness returned with remembered passion.

She hated the devil. He'd used her.

During the short time Kat had become familiar with Morgan, she knew enough not to believe the balderdash Juliana spouted. Declaring the two of them were lovers and he wanted to pick up right where they left off. But, then she repeated the lie in his presence. Pain knifed Kat again, as fresh as when Morgan made no denial, and she realized the damning words were true.

Juliana offered a *trade*—Kat. She must have mistakenly thought Kat of some importance to Morgan. Then again, he must have some feeling for her if he allowed Juliana that leverage. Guilt? Him and his blasted guilt.

Merciful Heavens, she loved him.

The days were bad enough, but then the nights came, bringing such misery Kat thought she would die. She lost count of the days. Had it been weeks? For her family, she must continue to go on while she mourned her love for Morgan.

With a sigh, she released the curtain and walked over to the bed. The click of the latch bought her from her feverish thoughts. She turned to the voice that softly spoke her name. Aunt Liz held her arms open wide and Kat ran into them.

"Now, now child," crooned Elizabeth.

Aunt Liz held Kat tight against her ample bosom, while the grief in Kat's heart poured out through her tears.

"Child, you cannot go on this way." Heartbreaking sobs slowed as Aunt Liz soothingly stroked her hair. "Dear, you must not aggrieve yourself so."

After a few more moments, Aunt Liz turned Kat, leading her to the four-posted bed. "Come sit, my dear."

Kat held her aunt's hand, blindly following as she swiped her other hand across her eyes. Aunt Liz studied Kat's face, raised her kerchief and dabbed at the moisture on her cheeks.

"Darling, you know Albert and I love you very much. I have not pressed you since your return. We were so thankful to have you back unharmed."

"I'm sorry, Aunt Liz."

She grasped her niece's hands and breathed a heavy sigh as her aging eyes searched Kat's green ones. "It has been weeks. Now, it is time you told me *everything*."

"Oh, Aunt Liz." How she wanted to pour her heart out. The pain was so great. How could she speak of the pain in her heart? Morgan's betrayal. And how, after everything, she still loved him.

"You have gone around long enough in mourning. It's the same look you had when you first came to us as a haunted young girl. You've lost your spirit. The vibrant girl you were before this incident."

I am no longer a girl.

Kat straightened, dabbed her tears, and stared into the kindest eyes she'd ever seen. The gentlest woman she'd ever known. The woman who had given her unconditional love. "I'm so sorry I have worried you so."

"We love you, dear. Allow me to help. I will not judge. Just listen."

Kat looked down at their joined hands and felt renewed strength flow from her aunt. She knew in that moment she had to share her burden, and Aunt Liz would understand. Getting her tears under control, she slowly disentangled her fingers and rose from the bed. She put a finger to her lips as if to chew on her fingernail, then walked over to the dreary window where she'd been standing earlier, before her aunt came in.

She took several breaths to steady her already shattered nerves.

"I am in love." Kat waited a moment. Not hearing any kind of response from her aunt, she went on. "You see, when Lord Whetherford found me . . . you know he was looking for someone else. A certain woman. They shared a past."

Kat took a moment to glance at her aunt. The gentile woman sat quietly and communicated with her eyes that she would remain so. Kat faced the window again, seeing nothing outside. Her mind was on her decision—to divulge everything. She turned back to her aunt in misery. "Which is precisely how I ended up being abducted by her."

Aunt Liz's face grew puzzled. How could Kat put into words everything that had happened? How could she explain the demons that were hiding within her soul? Her heart and her mind were crying out to release her heavy burden.

"Whatever it is dear, we will weather it together," her aunt said lovingly.

Kat approached the bed gathering her much needed courage. With trembling lips, she blurted, "Oh, Aunt Liz." She dropped down to the bed, tears clogged her throat. "I love you. And yes, it's time to tell you what happened." Kat began her story. Once the words started, they flowed freely. She poured out everything that was in her heart and her very soul. Yet she could not reveal the most intimate moments with Morgan. She must keep those to herself.

———ele———

Again, his sister had not come downstairs to dine with the family. A concerned Stephen had watched his aunt go upstairs in search of Kat.

"You know, Stephen, I'm not hungry either. But there is a feast at this table. I do not remember seeing you so thin."

"I'm not thin, Uncle. I'm not as large and robust as I was the last time you saw me, but I am a far cry from being thin."

"True, you are gaining back some weight. It's just that you normally have the appearance of the trunk of an oak tree. With arms the size of the oldest branches."

Stephen inwardly cringed, for he did not want to visit the reason of his lost muscle. He stabbed a piece of meat with his fork. "I hope you don't mind, uncle. I'd rather not discuss that issue. Soon, I will return to sailing the seas. Once I'm back on my ship, I'm sure hard work will put the bulk back into my body."

He was saved from any further comment when the downstairs maid asked if she should take a tray upstairs to Miss Katherine.

"No. Aunt Elizabeth is with her. The women are not to be disturbed."

His jaw tightened as he remembered the missive announcing Kat had been taken. His heart did not start beating again until Giles had that vicious hellcat snarled in his grip. He'd wanted to kill the shanghaiing bastards that were with her. But even that impulse had lessened once he held Kat in his arms. His little sister. Although, she was not just his little sister anymore. Stephen had to admit she had grown into a beautiful woman.

After that harrowing ordeal, he noted the strain of getting through each day was making Kat much too thin. Something was dreadfully wrong. He couldn't stand to see the haunted look in her eyes. What he would give to see her eyes sparkle, and a smile that would be as full of mischief as her younger years.

His sister showed all the signs of a young girl's first love. But, she was so damned miserable. On the sea, he did exactly as he pleased. Right now, murdering the scoundrel responsible for his sister's pain would please him greatly. The idea of being in shackles again killed that bloody thought. That, and his little sister wouldn't be too thrilled with him, either.

Right now, Kat needed him more. He would honor her wishes. But, if Whetherford had harmed his Kitten in any way, the man would pay with his very life.

"Looks like we've finished here. Shall we retire to the study?"

Stephen glanced up to see Albert gesture toward the doorway. After dinner, his uncle went for his usual cigar and a glass of brandy. Stephen rose and followed him out of the room.

Love and concern blazed in the depth of his uncle's age old eyes. "You know, son. Elizabeth and I could not love you more if you were from my own loins."

Sudden warmth washed over him. Stephen dwelled in his own private hell, afraid of what secrets might be revealed in Kat's room. Now he had to congest the sentiment his uncle cast at him. Of course, Albert, in his own way, tried to lessen the worry.

Kitten, the way she always followed him around. Kitten, the way she clung to him, curled up with her little arms around his neck, purring in her little girl's voice. That was how she earned the pet name he had given her.

"What in the hell happened to her?" Stephen growled

"Your aunt is strong enough to cope with whatever Katherine may divulge. I pray she will not suffer from this unfortunate experience."

"Can you not see it, uncle? She is suffering already. It tears me up, not knowing what she went through. She was kidnapped, for God's sake. She may be home now, but she still suffers."

"Together, we will give her all the love and support she needs to get her through this crisis."

"This bloody business of waiting and worrying is twisting my insides. Bloody hell!" Seeing his uncle pause in lighting his pipe, Stephen winced. "Sorry uncle. I am used to saying what I feel."

With the match still in his hand, Albert waved away his comment. "Women are sensitive creatures. It may not be as bad as what we think." Shadows obscured his uncle's face. Stephen suspected suspicions haunted him as well.

Stephen crossed to the window that had no light. Dark had descended. Another night. This waiting and not knowing exactly what happened to Kat, was pushing his patience to the limit. What he'd endured on his last voyage seemed insignificant compared to Kat's welfare.

Damn, and double damn. The women had been alone for hours. He couldn't stay inside any longer.

"I've got to get out of here," he growled. He marched over to the set of doors, throwing them wide, and came to a dead stop. Two women—arm in arm—were smiling as they descended the stairs. *What the hell?*

I have been imagining lascivious things and here she appears. Stephen stepped through the door with his uncle following close behind.

"Stephen," Kat called. "Aunt Liz and I have had the most wonderful chat, and now we find we are late for dinner."

Stephen was dumb-founded. Chat, she called it. Late? Hours late. Who cared? He had not seen her smile—really smile—since she had returned home. He could not help but return her grin with one of his own.

"Late," he teased. "I'm afraid Albert and I could not wait. If you want me to leave *you* any food, you must be on time. After all, I am still a growing boy, don't you know."

"Good Lord, Stephen," Kat returned playfully. "You tower over everyone, now."

Seeing his sister behave this way after the days of desolation was balm to his troubled soul. "That's to show I am a cut above the rest."

Kat lightly cuffed him on the arm.

"You are not too big for me to take a warmer to the seat of your breeches," Elizabeth scolded. "Growing boy, indeed."

Albert looked to his wife, his brows raised in wonder. It seemed both women were cheerful. And Stephen and his uncle, both, were relieved.

"Katherine and I are going to have a snack, dear. Would you like to join us?" his aunt asked.

The smile Albert gave her was full of warmth. Extending his arm, he replied, "I would love to, my dear."

Even though Stephen had basically lived his life on a ship, he never forgot the manners of his rearing. He held out his arm in a gentlemanly custom to his sister. "Would you do me the honor, Kitten?"

Kat smiled. "Of course, kind sir."

From over his shoulder, Stephen heard his uncle whisper, "I have never loved you more than I do at this moment."

Stephen could not keep from smiling. Aunt Liz had pulled a miracle out of her hat. He leaned down to Kat and spoke softly in her ear. "All I want is your happiness."

She looked up at him with imploring eyes. "I'm fine, Stephen. I really am. Let's not dwell on the painful past."

He covered the small hand on his arm. "I love you, Kitten."

"I know. And, I love you. Tomorrow we will talk. You will tell me where you have been and why we did not hear from you."

"I was on a ship." Stephen hoped to put her off.

"There is more."

He should have known his little sister would not give up. "You do not need to know everything," he said teasingly.

Kat stopped in her tracks. "Stephen. I will tell you my story. It is only fair that you tell me yours."

He raised a brow meaning to intimidate, as was his norm. But, this was Kat. "Men's things are men's things, Kitten. You have been sheltered, only exposed to certain ideas."

"You have no idea what I have been exposed to."

Fury at the unknown flooded his senses making his body stiff and his jaw tight.

Kat hurried to calm him. "Not anything bad! Nothing, really!"

"Kat, you'd best tell me everything," he growled.

"Stephen, I am fine. Nothing bad happened to me."

Stephen studied his sister until he was satisfied she was telling the truth.

"But, I fear what happened to you. You are much too thin."

Stephen gave a bark of laughter. "The pot, my dear. You have gone to bones these last few weeks."

Her eyes squinted with intensity. "Stephen. I know you. And, I know something dreadful must have happened."

His eyes seared hers. He did not want to think about the hell he lived through, let alone talk about it. He spoke in a tone that indicated he would tolerate no argument. "I will not tell you. Do not ask. I will never speak of it."

He led her into the kitchens, where Albert and Elizabeth were sampling some sweet meats. All was well in the household. Stephen savored the fact that Kat was home safe, back in the arms of her family. The calming relief that flooded his body was most welcoming.

"Aunt Elizabeth." Stephen wrapped his arms around her and gave her a big bear hug. "You have brought a sparkle to my sister's eyes. You have been mother and friend to her. You were just what she needed when we lost our parents. Solace to a lost and fearful child. And now you have done it again." Stephen took a step back to look into her eyes, "I love you."

Elizabeth's eyes misted and she sniffed back tears.

Damn. He'd made her cry. "I don't know what happened, but . . ."

She put her fingers to his lips to silence him. "Stephen, I will not tell you. It is Katherine's story to tell. Not mine. I will not betray her confidence."

"I would not want you to. I only need to know that Kat is all right, and no harm came to her."

Elizabeth released a heavy sigh. "Her first love."

Stephen sighed in recognition. "So, my little sister fell in love. I thought as much." He glanced at Kat, then back to Elizabeth. "I take it, it did not work out."

"I think she was deeply in love. Katherine is young, but you know as well as I that her feelings run deep." Elizabeth turned her gaze across the room. "It may have been the real thing."

"Well, ah . . ." Stephen pushed a hand through his thick, wavy red hair. He did not need details, but his concern made his voice gruff. "She's home with her family now. She will be all right. Won't she?"

"It will take time."

Stephen draped his arm across her shoulders. "I understand, Aunt. I will do all that I can to help her."

"I am glad you realize Katherine is a woman now. You cannot treat her like a little girl anymore."

With bewilderment, Stephen shook his head. His gaze settled on Kat. His heart warmed as he saw her laughing with their uncle. He had to admit, she had grown up. "It will take some getting used to. When I left, she was still my little kid sister. I must admit it is a shock to find her so grown up. But, does she have to be so beautiful?"

Chapter 31

Morgan slapped his leather gloves on the side of his leg as he stomped toward the house. Slamming the door behind him, he took the stairs two at a time. As he turned to walk down the corridor to his suite of rooms he heard voices.

"Oh, dear. Oh, good Lord! The sparks are gonna fly!"

Mrs. Beasley? What had her in such a tither?

"There's trouble, that one. You're right. Sparks are gonna fly."

Morgan rounded the corner to find his servant and Mrs. Beasley. "Am I right to assume you are not speaking about me?"

Mrs. Beasley nearly jumped out of her skin. Morgan felt guilty for scaring the poor woman. Frederick did not fare any better. The man looked white as a ghost.

"Well? Care to tell me what is going on?"

"Oh, dear. Oh, dear, Lord!" Mrs. Beasley twisted her hands.

"I believe you already said that." Morgan looked from one servant to the other. "Anything to add, Frederick?"

Once again, his servant seemed caught by the seat of his pants. *What the bloody hell?*

Frederick stiffened and stood as tall as his thin frame would allow. He seemed to gather six feet of courage all at once. "My Lord. You have a caller."

Morgan had little patience these days. With much of his time spent missing Kat, his tolerance for everything had a very short fuse. "Out with it."

Frederick cleared his throat. "The gentleman . . ."

"Oh dear," Mrs. Beasley began fluttering again.

Morgan glared at the woman and immediately regretted his action when she lifted her apron, and with tears in her eyes, scurried away.

"Confound it. Spit it out!"

Frederick blurted, "He appears to be Miss Radbourn's brother."

Blood and the devil! What the hell is he doing here?

"Where is he?"

"In the front drawing room."

Bloody, bloody hell. This could not be good.

"Is he alone?"

"Yes, my lord."

So, she didn't come with him. No. Not good at all.

"Tell him I'll be right there." He smelled of horse manure. He needed a bath. And keep Kat's brother waiting? Better to get this over with. "Never mind. I will see him as I am." At his servant's elevated brows, Morgan added, "Do you think I should keep my guest waiting?"

"No . . . no, my lord." Frederick quickly said and stepped back to let Morgan pass.

"Didn't think so."

He headed down the front stairway, each step taking him closer to his possible doom. Stephen was a large man. He must have been an ox before he'd been captured. A few less pounds were in Morgan's favor. The furniture was old and heavy. It could withstand some pounding. He only hoped his face would survive those massive paws.

Blood and the devil.

He *would* have to be Kat's brother. Morgan had never run from a fight. Hell, if truth be known, he'd instigated most of his skirmishes. Probably due to his hell-for-leather attitude. He'd taken down men more powerful than this one.

That was then.

Now his emotions were involved. A certain redhead chipped at his heart until it opened and yes, tender feelings developed. How in the hell was he supposed to fight her brother?

The red-bearded giant stood in the middle of the room. And he looked every bit the domineering captain as if he were standing on the deck of his ship. Good God. He'd put more than a few pounds back on.

What the hell was I thinking?

Morgan swallowed with difficulty. "Mr. Radbourn. To what do I owe this honor?"

Stephen glowered. "No need to go all noble on me. Let's dispense with formality. I'm here 'cause of Kitten."

Morgan frowned, and then remembered he'd heard Stephen call Kat by that nickname. The air went out of his sails. His own troubled voice was unrecognizable. "Has something happened? Is she alright?"

"Hell, no, she's not alright. She is miserable, you bastard."

Morgan's jaw clenched so tight, he could hear his own teeth grinding. "Did you come here to take a piece of my hide?" He deserved anything Stephen threw at him, and more.

"Any man worth his salt would stand up to an insufferable brother to protect the woman he cares for. Got anything to drink around here?"

Not much surprised Morgan, but damn if he could keep up with the brute's change of topic.

Stephen stood with his hands braced on his hips. "Not much of a host, are ya? Can't you offer a gent a drink? We have a heap of talking to do."

"Talking?"

"Are you a bloody parrot? I'd like to take a piece of your hide, but Kat would probably have my head if I did. I've got to face it. My willful little sister has grown up."

The damned man wanted to talk?

"Follow me." Morgan turned and strode down the hall to his study. He went to the side table and opened the cabinet door. He pulled out two bottles of his best cognac.

"That's more like it." Stephen seemed pleased enough, but the expression on his face never changed.

Morgan picked up two glasses, handed one and a bottle to his *guest*. He gestured to the two leather chairs.

Stephen splashed a good amount into his glass and turned it up, downing it in one gulp. "Mighty fine." At least he enjoyed the spirits. Suddenly, he dropped his frame into one of the chairs. "I cannot stand any more. She cries all the time."

The bottom fell out of Morgan's stomach. Kat? Did he dare believe she cried for him?

"She'd have my hide if she knew I was here, mind ya. You will not tell her." Stephen gave a threatening glare.

"She will not hear of your visit from me." His size was one thing, but the scowl on his face could make a normal man's heart stop from sheer terror.

Stephen poured more brandy, raised his glass in a salute, and then downed the contents. "She says she's fine. But I know she is not. She don't eat. She's too thin. What are you gonna do about it?"

Morgan choked. The cognac stuck somewhere between his throat and his nose.

"Take matters in hand like a man. Or you will have to deal with me—Kat or no."

When Morgan got his voice back, he croaked like a frog. "What can I do about it? She will not have anything to do with me."

"Come now, Whetherford." Stephen swirled the glass around as he spoke. "Don't you know how a woman works? She says one thing and most times means another. You just have to know which is which."

"This is one time I definitely think your sister hates me."

Stephen's eyes narrowed as he leaned forward in his chair. "Why is that, I wonder? Something happen I should know about?"

Good God. He can't know.

Morgan searched his mind for something that would send Stephen's mind in another direction. "It was my fault Kat was kidnapped."

"Oh, that weren't your fault." He settled back into the leather. "A greedy woman wanted what's yours. A foolish woman for taking my sister. Lucky your man got to her before I did."

Morgan wanted to do some throttling of his own. But his love for Kat outweighed his retaliation toward Juliana. Still, if not for him, Kat would never have been in Juliana's clutches.

"Of course, it's my fault. Juliana thought to use Kat against me."

"That's over and done." He threw back his head and upended the glass.

"Look, Stephen. I just do not think she will have me."

"Then why is she crying her eyes out over you?"

That stunned him. *Had she gone to Stephen?*

"I had hoped to speak with her, return her to her family and plan a life for the two of us, together. You were there. She would not talk to me."

"And then there's Aunt Elizabeth. I do not like the worry in her eyes, neither." Stephen held up the empty bottle and wiggled it back and forth.

Damn, the man could drink. Morgan got up to get more. After handing a full bottle over, he lowered his frame in the leather seat, and picked up his own glass which was still two thirds full.

"Do you care for my sister or not?"

He didn't hold back, did he? "Yes. I care a great deal for your sister. I have the most honorable intentions."

"Then do something about it." Stephen rested the bottle on his knee and set the empty glass on the table. "I know you have a reputation. Yes, I heard you were the *dark devil*. But I am here to tell you, you needn't worry about that with me. And it don't have nothing to do with you sending men to find me. I can take a man's measure, and I accepted what I saw."

Morgan forced himself not to react. He concentrated on his breathing wondering how in the hell he was supposed to respond to that.

Stephen leaned on the chair's arm, his gaze pierced Morgan through to the inside. "And if my sister wants you, she will have ya. If you plan to make an honest woman of her, that is."

Had he heard right?

Was it Stephen's plan to hand him over? Just like that?

God, how he missed her.

"You love your sister enough to give her a man you do not like?"

"Never said I didn't like you. Never said I didn't respect you." Stephen settled back in the leather. "From what I hear from my uncle, you are a man to be trusted."

So that's how—

Morgan's ears tightened and he sharpened his gaze.

"Don't worry. My uncle is very careful with his secrets. I know he has what I call *special* friends. I do not ask questions. But he did say you could be trusted. That's enough for me."

Never give up, never surrender. For years, he'd lived by those words. Those words had kept him going. Directed his every thought, every move.

And now . . . admit defeat? Or fight.

Fight for what? She had made her intentions quite clear. His precious Kat had turned her lovely back on him. Him and his damnable pride.

Kat had wormed her way under his skin. Without consciously knowing, he had opened his heart to love. He loved her. From the very center of his soul, he loved her. He wished to God he could make her love him. And Stephen had just offered him a chance.

No one knew the future—he only knew he did not have one without her.

Stephen picked up his glass and poured a generous amount of liquid. He tossed it back and wiped his mouth with the back of his sleeve.

"Like I said. She cannot know. Here's what we'll do."

Chapter 32

K at closed the door to her uncle's country house and pulled off her gloves. She still missed Morgan, but she was stronger now and her exhilarating morning rides helped. She had accepted a life without Morgan. Aunt Liz convinced her it was time to go on living and not throw her life away. To cherish the love she had for Morgan, put it in its proper place—her memories. Her loving family was all she needed!

She headed for the stairs. She reached the third step when she heard Stephen's angry voice.

"So. You're back are you? What are you doing here?"

"I came to see Katherine."

Her heart jumped to her throat.

Morgan?

"Why?" Her brother asked in a tone that brooked no argument.

"That is our business."

Good Lord. What is he doing here?

"I am making it *my* business."

She could just imagine Stephen standing with his arms crossed in front of his chest, the well-known deportment that he used when on the deck of his ship. His already harsh voice grew louder.

Oh, no.

She hurried down the few stairs she had climbed and ran to the drawing room only to come to a dead halt at the door.

Morgan. The one man she thought she would never see again.

Her eyes devoured his tall form. Black curls brushed the collar of his dark coat. Her fingers tingled at the remembered softness, like silk against her fingers. Broad shoulders, her hands had spanned and caressed with loving tenderness. She closed her eyes. Immediately, longed-for visions of lovemaking flooded her mind.

He is here.

Her chest squeezed the breath in her lungs.

"I want to put things right." Morgan's voice rocked her to her toes. Then his words registered.

Blast his guilt.

Her eyes flew to Stephen when he shouted again. "Don't you think it's a little late for that?" Stephen's fierce expression warned her. He was ready to use his fists.

This could only get worse. Knowing her brother's fierce temper, she should know better than to attempt to defuse an already volatile situation. But she had to try. She ran to her brother.

"What are you doing?"

"What does it look like I'm doing?" Stephen fired back.

"Stephen . . . Stop!"

"Stay out of this, Katherine!" Stephen shouted with a little less volume.

"No!"

"Damn it, Kat. Stay out of this," Morgan echoed.

Before she could chastise Morgan for his rebuke, he and Stephen were at it again.

"Do not speak so to my sister. I will split your gullet." Stephen's arms were elevated and his hands were curled as though he prepared to strangle his opponent.

"Try it." Morgan retorted in a deadly undertone.

Stephen had barely taken a step when Kat jumped and threw her arms around him, as much as she could reach. "I won't let you. I love you. Please don't." Tears streamed down her face. When she looked up, Stephen glared at Morgan over her head.

"Now see what you've done. Her tears are your doing."

"Stephen, please."

"Aww, Kitten." He held her so tight she thought her ribs would crack.

"Stephen, not so tight." He loosened his grip.

"But, you said you did not want him."

She could not lie. She wanted Morgan with everything in her.

After a long, tension-filled moment, he took her shoulders and eased her away. The love in his eyes made her want to weep all over again.

"You look so much like our mother." With a firm finger curled under her chin, Stephen lifted her face and studied her eyes. His thumb wiped the lingering tears from her lashes. "Does he mean so much to you then?"

With a trembling lip, Kat nodded.

Stephen glanced up and scowled, his words directed to Morgan. "I would speak with you alone." At Kat's indrawn breath, he met her gaze and his gruff voice softened. "It will be all right, Kitten."

She loved her brother and trusted him. Even so, she hesitated.

"Go on, now. It will be alright." His eyes conveyed his love and assured his trust.

She had avoided looking at Morgan since she entered. She did not dare do so now. One look and she would fall madly into his arms. Her fear of being rejected again kept her eyes aimed to the floor. Why was he here anyway? With a deep breath, she carefully placed one foot in front of the other until she was safely out of the room.

She paced the carpet in the upstairs sitting room. She had accepted that any future for them had been merely a fantasy in her mind, a hope in her heart. She never expected to see him again and certainly not in her uncle's home.

The mental upheaval she had suffered returned to her in full force. Her heart torn asunder, she'd had to accept one little detail—Morgan did not love her. But, God help her, she would forever love him.

Her fierce, over-protective brother. He cared so much for her, he was willing to be civil to a man she knew he wanted to tear apart. He thought Morgan unworthy of a decent hearing, let alone his precious little sister's attention. Yet, Stephen's gesture, that he would tolerate and even accept Morgan, for her. His loving, caring nature brought Kat to tears.

If only she could have that kind of love, that kind of loyalty, that kind of trust with Morgan.

Kat stopped in the middle of the floor, she pounded one fist to the open palm of her other hand. What was Morgan doing here? Had he come for her? Nonsense. She knew they could never be. He only *wanted* her.

Lust.

Morgan would never love her, no matter how much she wished it would happen.

What was going on behind those closed doors? She did not hear any more yelling. No loud noises like furniture being over-turned.

The sound of Morgan clearing his throat sent alarming signals down Kat's spine. She tensed, knowing he had entered without her being aware of his presence. She tried to hide how much seeing him again affected her. Kat wished she had never laid eyes on him. Taking a deep breath for composure, she turned to look in his direction.

Her body swayed at the sight of her love standing there. How she missed seeing that unruly curl hanging over his brow. She fought to control her fingers as she yearned to touch. Hunger sizzled in his eyes and a wave of heat instantly consumed her with a force as powerful and as strong as the last time he'd held her in those familiar, robust arms. She still craved him with every fiber of her being. Yet, she had to hide her sorrow at unrequited love.

She willed her mind to be strong. To get through this torment. "Morgan, I have done a lot of thinking."

"I've done a lot of thinking, too."

Hearing his deep voice weakened her resolve. His whiskey hum vibrated from her chest, through her stomach and on down to curl her toes. She faltered. Hating the weakness that claimed her body, she forced her mind to remember what happened the last time they were together. Gathering her courage, she met his gaze. "We have no power over love. It just happens, and you have no control." Like she could not kill the love she had for him, he could not offer love that did not exist.

"I am glad you see that."

Did he have to agree with her? She wished him to the devil. "I am not mad at you. I do not hate you."

"I certainly hope not." The corner of his mouth lifted in a grin.

Ignoring the ache in her heart, she continued, "I understand."

"And what is it you understand? Kat, I—"

"I really do." She cut off what he was about to say. The smirk on his face made her more determined.

"I'm not sure you do," he replied.

"But, I do."

"Kat." Morgan frowned. "Will you at least let me tell you why I'm here?"

"I know why." The fingers of one hand clutched the other as she tried to sound care free. "You do not need to feel guilty."

"I don't feel guilty," he said.

"Oh." And here she was trying to make him feel better? The confident poop. How could she let him break her heart again?

Morgan took a step forward. "Let me explain."

"There's no need to explain. I told you. I'm not mad at you." She scooted around the floral-patterned chair to have something between them.

"Mad at me? I expected you to be furious with me." He took another step in her direction.

Kat gasped at his advance. "No, Morgan. I . . ."

She had been determined to be strong and now she was about to fall apart. She still could not believe that he stood here in this very room. The trembling started, and she feared her lip would quiver and he would see. *Don't you dare cry.* She moved a few steps away.

"Let me explain."

"No!" Her self-control slipping, her voice came out stronger and sharper than she had intended. "I told you. You don't owe me . . ."

"Bloody hell! Will you listen to me?"

How dare he yell at her? Gathering her anger around her like a cloak, she arched her back, and faced him like a warrior preparing for battle. "Of course."

"Damn it, Kat! This is not going the way I planned." Morgan ran his fingers through his hair.

"And just what was it you planned?"

"Well, I came here thinking maybe you . . . well . . . you would be glad to see me."

His stare probed her—as if waiting for an encouraging reaction. She did not give him one.

"I had hoped you still cared for me, as I do you."

If only he did.

She loved him with all her heart to the very depth and breadth of her being.

He *cared* for her.

She chose her words carefully. "I do care for you."

Morgan let out a relieved breath. "That's good." He reached for her hands. "I intend to make you my bride."

She tore her hands away. "That is not necessary."

"Will you stop?" Morgan shouted. "You just admitted your feelings to your brother!"

Kat raised her brow in anger and gave her best cutting look without saying a word.

He stood there brooding. After a long maddening moment, his stormy expression softened. He released a heavy sigh as though he were surrendering. His mouth formed a pained line as he said, "Kat. I love you."

Her heart cramped with regret. How long she had waited to hear those words. She had dreamed of this very moment, of him expressing his love. It made her heart break even more to know he did not mean them. If she held any doubts they were clearly extinguished when she had seen him grind his jaw as he spoke the words. His disgruntled expression revealed the truth. She tried to erase the memory of his kisses and the sensations he had caused within her.

Somehow, she found the strength to utter the words she hoped would set her free from the turmoil in her soul. "You do not love me. And I wish you would not pretend that you do."

Morgan's head flew back in shock. He recovered and prowled forward. "You must believe me."

She held up a hand to hold him off. If he touched her, she would crumble. She had to put an end to this once and for all. She did not want to be a substitute. She did not want his love out of guilt. She wanted him heart, body and soul. If she could not have that, she did not want him at all. "I do not love you."

"The hell you say!" If the situation had not been so serious and the pain not so intense, the look on his outraged face could have been laughable. His narrowed eyes studied her. "I don't believe you."

"Please, do not make this more difficult." She stood taller. Back straighter. Taking a deep breath, she kept her face a cold mask. For she had to convince him—and herself—it was over.

"I know there is no one else. I did not imagine your feelings for me. I took your virginity!"

Humiliation seeped through her core. "Don't you think I know that? I do not need your damned guilt. Get out!" Unable to stand there another moment, she gathered her skirts, and ran.

Chapter 33

What he'd just seen scared the hell out of him. His beloved Kat. His spirited Kat. The cold portraying woman before him had a crack in her make-believe rigid shell. He was not fooled by her pretense. Sparks still flew between the two of them, which proved it could not be his imagination. She did love him.

Morgan knew he'd handled it badly. He told her he loved her, and in the next breath he yelled that he'd taken her maidenhead. Good God, he mucked that up. What was she supposed to think?

He deserved her scorn. She thought he was here out of obligation and guilt. But, he had to make her see he was lost without her. He had to prove that he had no life without her in it. She owned his heart . . . his very breath . . . his very soul.

Morgan knew she didn't believe him, but he also knew she cared deeply or she would not have reacted so strongly, or tried so hard to send him away. He had never accepted defeat before, and he would not start now. She spun around and darted past him.

His arm shot out. "Not so fast."

He pulled her across the room and into the hallway. Ignoring her shouts, he bent down, and with one arm under her knees, hoisted her into his arms.

"What do you think you are doing? Put me down this instant." She pummeled his chest. "How dare you. You brute." When he came to a halt at the top of the stairs, she glanced at him, then followed his gaze.

Stephen waited at the bottom.

"Oh, God, no. Stephen will kill you." Kat pushed at Morgan's shoulders and kicked her legs in earnest. "Please. You must let me go."

He was not about to do that—today or any other. He cocked a brow. "It warms my heart that you are worried about my welfare. You see, my sweet. I have every intention of abducting you again."

"Oh, no."

Morgan started down the stairway.

Realizing that her pleas were not working on him, she targeted her brother. "Stephen. Wait—Don't—Stop—" She held her arms out as if her attempt would hold him off.

Braced in a stance, with feet apart and hands on his hips, her brother smiled.

Kat's brow creased in confusion. "What are you smiling about?"

"You got your hands full." When Stephen spoke to Morgan, Kat's face crumpled up even more.

His chest swelled with satisfaction. Their plan had worked. Kat admitted her feelings and he was taking full advantage. Morgan grinned with happiness. And a hell of a lot of smugness. "Looks like I do, Stephen. What are you going to do about it?"

"Why, I thought I would open the door." Stephen gave a hearty laugh and did exactly that.

Kat's confusion turned to utter bewilderment. Smart man that he was, he kept his mouth shut.

Kat glared at one man and then the other. "Stephen. Aren't you going to do something?"

"I am." He gave her a wink.

"You cannot let him take me! Aunt Elizabeth. Uncle Albert. Do something."

The couple appeared from the side of the stairs. Elizabeth dabbed at her eyes while her uncle smiled, one arm draped around his wife's shoulders.

Kat crossed her arms beneath her bosom and huffed. "Traitors. All of you."

"You are welcome, Kitten."

Kat had not said one solitary word to Morgan since he carried her from her uncle's home. But she planned to give him a tongue-lashing the minute they got some privacy. To believe her family just stood there and allowed—no encouraged him—to take her. And if he thought for one minute . . . ooohh.

She bit her tongue and seethed with anger. When the carriage stopped, Morgan jumped out, and then reached inside, not giving her a chance to alight on her own. The salty air and shouts of men warned her they were at the docks. Yanking her in his arms, he marched up the boarded plank to a ship. The swaying motion had her clinging to his neck. She had no desire to fall into the murky water. The devil smiled. He tightened his hold and carried her to a large cabin. Once inside, he kicked the door closed.

Finally, he set her free. Kat tugged at her clothes, trying to get them in some kind of order. Her twisted bodice exposed more of her bosom than she liked. Her gown was wrinkled beyond repair, so she gave up trying to smooth her skirts. Ready to lose her temper, she whirled around and ... gasped.

"What are you doing?" Her breathing became irregular.

"Doing?" he repeated. "Why, I am removing my shirt." He smiled at her like the cat that smiled at the canary just before he ate it. Searching his eyes, she found them filled with wicked mischief and . . . yearning desire.

She chewed her bottom lip.

And watched him, taking his time as his adept fingers slowly worked each button free before moving on to the next.

And another.

When he got to the last one, she sucked in a breath.

"Morgan." And then she was in his arms.

He gathered her to his chest. "You feel like heaven. Let me savor the fact that you are really in my arms."

For long moments, he just held her. He felt so good. How could she have ever let him go? She had been so foolish.

"I know it was unorthodox the way you came to me, but fate stepped in and took over. I am very glad it happened, because I met you. Thank God, my men had the good sense to take you to Whetherford Manor."

"They abducted me."

"Had they not, we would not have met."

Yes, in that case, thank God.

"When I first saw your face, you took my breath away. I told you then, there had been a mistake. It was no mistake that you came into my life. I also said you were the wrong one. You proved otherwise."

She stared at his face, into his eyes. She was not a mistake.

"Kat, I love you. You left before I had the chance to show you." He cradled her head against his chest. "This is where you belong."

Oh yes. Most definitely. Morgan loved her. Hearing his heart-felt words, she wanted to cry.

He curved his hand along her jaw, tilting her face, bringing her eyes even with his. "When you came into my life, you turned it completely around and made me whole. You gave me light, peace, love. So much love I don't even recognize myself."

Her hand curved around his face. Oh, how she loved this man. His words brought pure balm to her soul. She kissed him with all the pent-up longing she'd kept inside since she left Whetherford Manor. And Morgan kissed her as though he would never let her go.

Groaning, he bent down, and in one smooth move, he lifted her, and swung around toward the bed. His arms never left her as he lowered her down onto the feathered softness and crawled beside her.

Morgan tipped her chin up and stared down into her eyes as if he were communicating his love through his powerful gaze alone. With calloused fingers, he smoothed the tears from her cheek, then his thumb drifted to her lips.

"Kat. I love you with every breath I take. You complete my soul." He lifted her hand and kissed her fingers, then placed her palm over the center of his chest. "My heart is yours. I will spend the rest of my life proving you are *the right one for me*."

THE END

Thank You

Thank you for reading my story. I hope you enjoyed reading it as much as I loved writing it.
And, if you did, would you consider leaving a review online? It really would mean the world to me.

Thank you!
Samanthya

**One and Only
Collection Book 2 –
My Angel, The True
One**

*F*ind out what happened to Kat's brother in the thrilling sequel to *The Right One For Me!*

His ship in splinters and his men captured, Stephen is a broken man. Yet the torture he received by his enemies is nothing compared to the torment he bears from an angel with lavender eyes.

Jennifer left England full of a young girl's fantasies of romance and adventure. When she cares for a near death captain, memories emerge of the family she left behind. Will the passion they share be enough? He must choose—her or revenge.

Turn the page for a SNEAK PEEK of *My Angel, The True One.*

My Angel, The True One

Cape Verde Islands
1824

The noise from the taproom flowed through the open door. Jedediah stood to the side while one man staggered out. When the way was clear, he slid through the door into the dimly lit room. His eyes searched through the smoke and barrier of bodies until he found a large man with a red beard. His informant had not exaggerated when he said the man had arms the size of tree limbs, and a chest as wide as the trunks in England's glens.

Finally, his search was at an end. In the ten months it took to find the captain, Jedediah had apparently been one port behind him at every stop. Now, his quarry was in sight. Soon he could return to London.

The bearded man threw back his head and roared with laughter. His arm snaked out and grabbed a barmaid landing her firmly in his lap. Mayhap this man was not as fierce as Jedediah had been led to believe. But then, appearances could be deceiving. After all, his employer certainly kept his clandestine dealings separate from his noble status. Especially when he ventured to the London docks.

Disreputable men lurked everywhere.

Jedediah stared at the captain of *Serpent's Ghost*. If tales were to be believed, his particular ship sailed in and out of ports as slick as a mate's whistle. Disappearing into thin air. Named appropriately, he supposed. And its commander was a man to be feared—yet awed.

Some said he was ruthless.

Dangerous.

Deadly.

Diverse few said his haughtiness was more confidence than conceit. His temper flared as fierce as his red hair suggested—seemingly rooted from passion. Everything Jedediah had learned painted the man ruthless, devoid of mercy. Yet from more than one man's lips, the words trust and loyalty were added to the intense captain's qualities.

Those redeeming traits had convinced Jedediah's employer that Captain Stephen Radbourn was the right man for this task. Being a staffer, Jedediah had been sent to find the notorious captain.

Without drawing attention to himself, he stayed in the shadows of the island's tavern. He had come here for a reason. He could not back out now. Slowly, he stepped forward, making his way around the raucous room to the table of the man with hair so thick, green eyes blazed in the middle of a red cloud.

"Go on with ya," the barmaid cooed.

"Give me a taste, wench." The captain pulled at the scanty top barely covering the girl's bosom and lowered his head. She giggled and pretended to push away while giving him a generous view of her globes. The captain playfully drove a hand down the front of her blouse. The claim of his fondness for women was unquestionably true.

Clearly enjoying his advances, the girl wiggled closer. Her slender fingers grasped a lock of red hair and she whispered in his ear. The captain growled, removed his hand and squeezed her hip. He tilted his head and laughed again. The girl jumped from his lap with a siren's grin and a promise in her eyes.

The captain lifted his mug, giving a salute. Another sailor, obviously in his cups, bumped into the raised arm spilling the ale. The red-haired giant growled and lunged out of his chair, swinging his arms like a ship's sails dithering in the raging sea wind. After a good blasting, the poor sod trembled in fright and scurried away.

Indeed. Jedediah had found the right man.

Inching closer, he stood beside the colossal man's table. "Excuse me. Would you be the captain of *Serpent's Ghost*?"

The huge man spun around, amazingly swift for a man his size. He lifted his brows in a gesture that very effectively managed to convey his displeasure. Jedediah swallowed. Maybe this was not the best way to approach the man, especially in a place like this.

With eyes as green as the palms on the island, the giant's gaze held a calculating chill, dissecting every pore of Jedediah's skin. The bushy beard covered a good bit of the captain's face, but not enough to hide his scowl, which made his scrunched brows look about as malleable as granite.

"And who are you?" Captain Radbourn said with such a booming voice, surely the rafters shook.

Jedediah ignored his quaking knees and put on his best business face. "My name is Jedediah, but I am not important. If you are the captain of *Serpent's Ghost,* I have a proposition for you."

The hulking captain crossed his massive arms over his chest. "Go on."

"You will be rewarded handsomely." Jedediah gestured toward the table where the man had been sitting. "If you will allow me to buy you a drink, I will explain everything."

The captain's eyes narrowed with skepticism while he contemplated his decision. With a jerk of his head, he pulled back his chair and lowered his bulk. Thank goodness. Jedediah had a stiff neck from looking up. The man stood over six feet and a half foot more. The muscles on his frame looked like he'd pilfered the butcher's shop and tied hams around his arms and thighs.

Jedidiah pulled out a chair and motioned a barmaid to their table, while trying to maintain his composure. Knowing this large man could break his thin frame like a twig did not embolden him. Nevertheless, he had a job to do. "My employer is a very wealthy man." He wished his voice sounded stronger.

The captain propped his forearm on the wooden table, and leaned in close. "And just who is your *employer*?"

"A gentleman in England who prefers his name be kept private. However, he has instructed me to make you an offer."

"Me," the captain repeated.

"The captain of the *Serpent's Ghost*," Jedediah said and then held his breath.

The big man leaned back in his chair making the wooden legs creak under his weight. "Why would *your employer* be wanting the *Serpent's Ghost*?"

"Your reputation, of course. It is told that your ship can go places none other can. There are stories about its captain. I have heard he is ruthless and fears no one. It is said that his men—*your men*—are steadfast and loyal. Your ship has been known to slip in and out of ports of interest without notice."

"And you would want my ship not to be noticed?" Lines creased the captain's forehead.

"Undetected, yes." Jedediah gave a sharp nod.

"The destination?"

Jedediah's mouth was suddenly dry. He swallowed, then answered, "India."

No movement. The captain, still as stone, gave no clue to his thoughts. Then his jaw tightened, and his eyes narrowed. Jedediah's stomach coiled from the heated glare.

A mug of ale landed on the table, right in front of him. He nearly jumped out of his chair. Deeply involved in his purpose, he had not noticed the girl's arrival. But the interruption gave him a moment of reprieve. With a saucy smile, the bar maid placed another mug in front of the captain. His eyes remained on Jedediah. Unable to coax a response from her previous admirer, she swung around to the next table.

"Why?"

Only one word. But the abrasive tone insisted Jedediah answer. "My employer has an interest in the Indian states."

Captain Radbourn braced one arm on the table, leaning forward in the same position as before. "If you have learned anything about me, you should know I am a man who is informed about things happening on the other side of the world. I am familiar with the skirmishes among the Indian princes with the British military taking away the rulers' independence. I assume your employer is aware there are warlike Rajputs who fight against being ruled by the British."

"There are those who fight for good, and there are those who fight purely because they are evil. Should you run into such a group, they would be relentless."

The captain's eyes bore into him. "I have no intention of running into, as you say, such a group."

As the captain—thankfully—relaxed back on his chair, Jedidiah sighed in relief. The captain lifted his mug, and Jedidiah took the moment to do the same. He took a quick sip, the cool, wet ale assuaging his thirst.

"I suppose you did your research before you singled me out for this undertaking."

"Yes," he replied, sitting his mug down. "We delved into your background."

A devious smile lifted one corner of the giant's mouth. "So, what were my credentials for this particular job?"

"Your brash manner captured my employer's attention. You strike fear in the hearts of men. A more ruthless character would not be found."

"Ruthless?"

"And fair," he added quickly, not wanting to offend the captain. "Those two . . . qualities do not usually go hand in hand. Your men are loyal, to the point they would lay down their lives for you."

"And you learned all this? You have been asking around more than a few places. And how do you know the loyalty of my men?"

"Such allegiance speaks exceedingly well for a man. Word gets around." Every port Jedidiah had visited knew the red-bearded captain.

When the captain's eyes blazed, Jedediah hoped he had complimented the man and not mistakenly insulted him in some way. He took another approach. "This undertaking would make you a fortune."

Captain Radbourn leaned back once again, crossing his arms over his massive chest. "I will not trade in opium."

"No . . . no one expects you to." Jedediah hated the catch in his voice. He shifted his weight, suddenly aware of the wood beneath his seat. Hard, unyielding. Like the man in front of him.

Jedediah took a steadying breath. "There are Indian spinners and weavers who do not want to fight. These men believe in fair trade but are being forced by some armies to follow certain rulers, to give up their independence. Those are the ones my employer wants to help." He waited a moment for his words to sink in. "I must have your answer before I give you more information."

The giant seemed to be considering. Then he asked, "Would I be carrying guns?"

Jedidiah hoped his answer was the right one. His employer wanted this captain, but he would not lie to get him. "Yes. You would travel as a merchant transporting goods manufactured in Britain." He reached to his inside pocket and carefully removed a dark cloth. He watched the captain as the man realized an object hid inside the folds. Making sure no one could see, Jedidiah pulled back one corner exposing a ruby the size of an egg.

The captain's eyes darkened, but no other expression appeared on his face.

Jedediah waited breathlessly for a response. The man was maddeningly composed. He stared at the ruby, not with greed, but as if he were trying to discover the reason behind this meeting. Lives depended on their secrecy. Jedidiah would not let his master down.

"As I said, my employer would pay you well."

He grew uncomfortable under the captain's stare. Sweat broke out on the back of his neck. He willed his hands to remain still. Even though he desperately wanted to loosen his neck cloth, he dare not move a muscle. Trying not to blink, he prayed the giant would not plant a fist in his face. Or worse, choke the life out of him.

The master had assured Jedidiah that this was the one. The captain they could trust. He had based his decision on Jedidiah's findings, of course, and he had been thorough. He needed to trust his employer's instincts.

And pray.

"The money does not play a part in my decision," the captain finally replied. "I own three other ships. And make a tidy profit. However, I feel a bit restless and suddenly find myself in need of a distraction." The captain slammed both hands on the table with a bang. "I accept."

After Jedediah nearly jumped out of his skin, relief unlike anything he'd ever known poured through his limbs. He had taken a risk, not knowing if he would be permitted to walk away. He quickly covered the gem, and put it out of sight. Men had killed for less than the priceless stone he housed in his pocket. "Are you certain? Once I disclose the details of this voyage, you must follow through. I need your word."

Anger flared in large green eyes, and Jedediah feared his life had come to its end.

"Let me assure you of something, *little man*. Once I give my word, it will suffice."

The captain's harsh tone unsettled Jedediah to his bones. "Our matter is of a timely nature. It has taken me months to find you. My employer hopes you will set sail right away."

"Is that so? Your employer must be an impatient man."

"Quite the contrary. As I said, it has taken me months to find you. I will meet you tomorrow morning, at your ship, with more instructions." Jedidiah collected himself and waited, hoping the captain would accept.

"I will speak to my men."

"I bid you, do not say anything of our plans to your crew. At least until after you sail. I trust no one." If anyone got wind of the reason behind this voyage, it would spell disaster—for everyone involved.

Stephen watched the squirrelly man slip away, wondering what he had just agreed to? He lifted his mug and doused his apprehension as quickly as he slaked his thirst. He'd been in sticky situations before.

"What was that all about?" Stephen's first mate, Abe, plopped his ale on the table and lowered his frame into the chair the wiry man had just vacated.

"Our next voyage." Stephen's gaze remained on the little man until the crowd swallowed his form. "I just received an intriguing proposal."

"Who was that?" Abe gave a jerk of his head.

"A man of a man." Stephen shifted in his chair. "Who just offered me a fortune."

"Another boasting of treasure?"

"Something a mite different."

"You have the look of mystery. If there is secrecy, there must be a threat."

"There is always an element of danger." Stephen regarded his first mate. "What would you do if you had a fortune, Abe?"

"Same as you. Get my own ship and sail for the rest of me life." He lifted his mug and took a hefty swallow.

Stephen absentmindedly rubbed the handle on his mug of ale. "With one large score, I could go home for Katherine."

"And be right back on a ship in a matter of months. Your sister is fine with relatives in London. You love the sea."

Stephen gave a knowing smile. "That's why I still captain *Serpent's Ghost*." His eyes darted to the tavern door. Who was the little man? More important, who was his employer?

It mattered not at the moment. He had made a bargain. He would follow through.

"So, what's it to be?" Abe asked after some moments.

Stephen looked to his mate. "The men have tonight. I'll not disappoint them." He lifted his mug and drained it. "Tomorrow, round up the crew."

"Rounding them up will be a chore. May require a day or two. Most of them scattered the instant we docked."

Stephen swiped the foam from his beard. "We leave as soon as the ship is stocked with supplies."

"The little man in a hurry? Where are we headed?"

Stephen elevated one brow. "India."

"India?" Abe stared, hesitating. Finally, he said what they both already knew. "We have not sailed in those waters before."

"Aye." Stephen frowned.

Again silence. Abe was trustworthy, and close as a brother could be. But he would not ask his captain to explain his decision. When Abe did speak, his voice was raspy. "Are you expecting trouble?"

"Hopefully, we will avoid it. We will not discuss it here. And not now." He would learn the details in the morning. Tonight was for ale and women. He called out, with a wink. "I'm off to find me a willing woman."

Abe laughed and turned to the barmaid heading in their direction. "I have a hunch you won't need to go far."

**Order your copy of *My Angel, The True One,*
Scan the QR code below!**

About the Author

Samanthya Wyatt writes sizzling hot romance with suspense. Intensely emotional characters with a deep passionate love for friends, family, and most importantly—between the hero and heroine. Although her first love is historical romance, this award-winning author also writes contemporary romance under the pen name S. R. Wyatt. Additionally, she has written a book of one family's struggle based on true life events.

Samanthya left her accounting career and married a military man traveling and making her home in the United States and abroad. She now lives in the Shenandoah Valley. On a sunny day, you can find her and her husband driving on the Blue Ridge Parkway or going to car shows in their 1969 Mustang convertible. She loves long walks, and a book to read on a sandy beach. Starbucks is her favorite drink and she likes hearing from her fans.

She invites you to lay the worries of the world off your shoulders and get lost in the pages of a romance, where you embark on a journey with the hero and heroine, become involved in a dream, plunge into a world of fantasy, and live an adventure your heart can share.

To find out more about Samanthya Wyatt and her books, please visit her website: https://samanthyawyattauthor.com/